SUCH PRETTY CONFUSION

NIGHTMARES FROM A DAMAGED MIND

PETER N. DUDAR

TREPIDATIO
PUBLISHING

ISBN: 978-1-68510-108-4 (trade paper)
ISBN: 978-1-68510-109-1 (ebook)
Library of Congress Catalog Number: 2023943900

First printing edition August 18, 2023
Published by Trepidatio Publishing in the United States of America.
Cover Artwork and Design: Don Noble
Edited by Sean Leonard
Proofreading and Cover/Interior Layout by Scarlett R. Algee

Trepidatio Publishing, an imprint of JournalStone
3205 Sassafras Trail
Carbondale, Illinois 62901

Trepidatio books may be ordered through booksellers or by contacting:
JournalStone | www.journalstone.com

Contents

Dedication

Acknowledgments

Introduction by L. L. Soares
9

The Thing with No Face
15

Last Supper at the Miss Hollywood Diner
26

The Pressboard Factory
36

Mr. Expendable
50

Portrait of an Old Woman with Crows
58

The Ghost of John Lennon
69

The Perfect Parent
76

The Old Guide's Tale
88

The Diary of Mary
101

The Strange Medicines of Dr. Ling
102

The Three Billy Goats Sothoth
114

A Taste of Green Voodoo Healing
120

Two Slugs in the Belly
135

Sunset at Devil's Gulch
150

And So Shall the Gods Feast
155

The Church of Thunder and Lightning
163

Cattle Cars
173

Peripheral Vision
185

Trailertrash Annie
195

Rest in Peace
204

Publication History

About the Author

Dedication

In Loving Memory of James C. Harriger II
(a.k.a. Jim, Jim, Clever Bastard)

Acknowledgments

The book which you are about to read represents two decades of my best collected short fiction, from my very first professional sale to three new unpublished titles that I'm absolutely delighted to share with you. It's strange to revisit those earlier works, and while compiling this collection I got to reacquaint myself with the younger version of me; the aspiring writer living in a studio apartment in Portland's Old Port district. As the years go by you tend to lose focus on the past and just keep moving forward, never subliminally wanting to relive those days of apprenticeship and rejection letters. The seasoned veterans almost always feel awkward about those years. They remember all too well those days of trying to emulate their literary heroes as they churn out subpar pastiches of those who came before. I'm certainly no exception, and there are more than a few stories that will not be included here, for myriad reasons. The good news is that I eventually found my voice as a writer, and that I've found my inner circle of comrades and confidants who have helped me along the way. Nobody succeeds in this business alone. That's a fact.

Having said that, I wish to thank all those folks who've helped me along the way. In no particular order, thank you P.D. Cacek, Scott Goudsward, Dan Keohane, David Price, Trish Wooldridge, Robert and Jennifer Wilson, Mark Scioneaux, Michael Evans, Malina Roos, Tony Tremblay, Stacey Longo, Kristi Schoonover, Tracy Carbone, Greg Dearborn, my sisters from The Tuesday Mayhem Society Morgan Sylvia, April Hawks, and Emma Gibbon, my newest publisher Scarlett R. Algee and her team at Trepidatio Publishing, everyone who has helped me with editing, publishing, and promoting my fiction, everyone who has taken the time to post a positive review of my work or recommend my fiction to other people, and most important, thank you to my mentor and bestie L.L. Soares, for the decades of great advice and friendship. The angel in my corner is a devil, and I love him to death!

Lastly, thank YOU, dear reader. You're the reason I keep on keeping on. I suspect you'll recognize a lot of these stories already. I do hope this collection keeps you satisfied and has you sleeping with the lights on. Horror writers are not monsters, they are guardians. They're the ones holding a candle in the darkness, taking your hand and guiding you safely through those moments of primal fear and terror. You have nothing to fear, my friend. I've spent so much time in the darkness (over two decades now) and I know my way around quite well. Take my hand and join me, and I will keep you safe!

Introduction

A big, glowing, disembodied eyeball hovers near the ceiling, watching all. The past. The present. It even gets glimpses of the future in its peripheral vision.

What it sees...

***

The first time we met was at a horror writers' convention in Rhode Island. It was 2001, I think. We were introduced by another writer and mutual friend, Dan Keohane. Pete is carrying his bags up to his room in the college dorms we stayed at, and one bag is a guitar case. Late at night, some convention-goers gather and have big sing-alongs to acoustic guitars, but I've never attended any of them. This guy was obviously really into it. He seemed nice enough, but at the time I had no idea that a year or two later we would become best friends.

***

Dudar gives me his manuscript for REQUIEM FOR DEAD FLIES (it had a different title then). I have no idea what to expect, but when I read it, I am very impressed. It has fleshed-out characters and the book has a strong tone of melancholy. It's a very effective ghost story. After I give him my edits, he drops by with a bottle of Chivas Regal, which I often drank back then. Unfortunately, I was going through a period where I was cutting down on drinking, and had (at least temporarily) lost my taste for scotch. But the gesture was incredibly nice.

After years of friendship, it was cool to be exposed to the full light of Pete Dudar the writer. In those days we went to conventions a lot, but we hadn't really proven ourselves as writers, not the way we wanted to. When you're around successful writers, you want to prove

PETER N. DUDAR

that you deserve to be in their company, and Pete proved that with this book.

***

My first novel, LIFE RAGE, just came out from Nightscape Press at Killercon in Las Vegas. Pete's first novel, the previously mentioned A REQUIEM FOR DEAD FLIES, had just come out a few months before from the same publisher. In fact, Pete is the one who suggested I send my book to them. We sit at a table in the dealer's room in a Vegas hotel, signing our books for people side by side, with big grins on our faces, feeling that after years of obscurity, maybe we'll finally get noticed in the horror community for our writing.

***

Jump to a table at the convention StokerCon — it was in New Orleans that year — and both of our novels are on the final ballot for "Achievement for First Novel" category. Lots of people we know are coming up to the table saying they think Pete's going to win the Bram Stoker award. In fact, so many people that I have resigned myself to agreeing with them, and sort of let go of the feeling that I might win. When they announce the award — somehow, it's me — I look over at Pete at the same table, and see that he's happy for me, even though I know he really wanted it. I feel light-headed as I stand up and head toward the stage.

***

I grab a flyswatter and chase the glowing orb out of the room — so I can finish writing this damned introduction! Enough with the memories!

***

These moments play out like a series of images. I'm an "imagery guy" and I love seeing strange or powerful imagery in art, in movies. And here are some of the images that stayed with me after reading SUCH PRETTY CONFUSION:

- That weathered, red doghouse behind Old Man Grady's house.
- Abandoned tracks and railroad cars in the middle of a forest
- The cluttered and filthy interior of an abandoned factory, the air thick with the stench of old glue
- That "Portrait of an Old Woman with Crows"
- The Mardi Gras parade in New Orleans, with an aftertaste of Absinthe
- "The Church of Thunder and Lightning" on a dark, stormy night
- An old woman crocheting outside her trailer, surrounded by cats
- A coffin opening to show an eerily preserved dead man inside

There are images in these stories that will stay with you, as they've stayed with me.

And the emotions. Dudar's characters are nothing if not emotional, whether those emotions are positive or not. Just like life. And he's not afraid to show us some characters who aren't always sympathetic, just like in real life, and I appreciated that.

He definitely remembers what it was like to be a kid, sometimes cocky and sometimes scared of things you don't quite understand yet. And he remembers the pangs of first love, and that first break-up. He shows us people who are in pain and who would give anything for some relief, and others who would do anything to hide the secrets they're most ashamed of.

The collection begins with a good one, "The Thing With No Face." I'd read it before, but it worked even better the second time. It's a story about regret and guilt. We all have regrets — it's what makes us human. A regret means that at some point in our lives, we fucked up. We made a mistake; we failed to do, or not do, something. Failure is one of the ways we learn as human beings, and the protagonist in this particular story is dealing with one helluva failure, and the guilt is so strong it's almost crippling.

Another story I like a lot is "Mr. Expendable," because it's a little different from the others, the tale of an actor who has spent his whole life getting killed off in movies and TV shows, who is reaching the end of his career. But will he let other people decide his end, or will he finally sit in the director's chair? You'll see.

"Two Slugs in the Belly" is the sole science fiction story here, set it a world where abortion is not only legal, but acutely necessary. I thought it was a clever idea.

And then there's the last story, "Rest In Peace," where an artist uses wild (bordering on illegal) publicity stunts to promote his gallery shows and make sure it's always a full house. I thought this was a brilliant concept. And I think I need to buy a shovel...

But my favorite story here is probably "A Taste of Green Voodoo Healing." It takes place in one of my favorite cities, New Orleans, and involves mortality and voodoo, and has an aftertaste of Absinthe. For some reason I hadn't read it before, and it surprised me. I love that title, and I liked the story. It's a very visual story — that use of imagery again.

But I don't want to keep you here too long. You need to move on. You need to follow that treasure map to the last resting place of Adolphus Stone. There might just be some gold under the cemetery soil.

As you enter the world of Peter N. Dudar, you're in for a treat. And some moments that will make you uncomfortable. But this is horror fiction, after all (except for that one story that takes place in the future) and we in the world of horror gladly take the uncomfortable along with the grandiose, the good with the bad, the highest highs and the dirtiest lows. We enjoy *all* the flavors at the feast.

Enjoy!

L.L. Soares

May 2023

SUCH
PRETTY
CONFUSION

NIGHTMARES FROM A DAMAGED MIND

The Thing with No Face

I don't want to remember... Please don't make me remember!

    Kevin Ellis woke up just after three a.m., his heart jackhammering in his chest, his skin cold and clammy from the skein of midsummer sweat. He'd only been home (his childhood home in Latham) for two days, and the nightmares had returned. Kevin's bedroom had remained unchanged for the last three decades; a shrine to the life of an introverted teenager of the eighties that Kevin had, over the years, sloughed off like the dead scales of a snake. Faye Ellis had sworn as far back as Kevin's wedding day that she was going to box up all his belongings and either he could take them home with him or she would have them hauled off to the town landfill. His mother had intended to turn the bedroom into a guestroom, with enough space for a crib for when he and Carrie finally presented her with a grandchild. The divorce two years later put the final nail in that fantasy. There, in the darkness, Kevin found himself wishing things might have been different.

    In the dark, the sameness of his childhood bedroom made it feel like no time had passed. In his heart and mind he was twelve again, and the sameness meant the past still existed.

    Kevin pushed the switch on the bedside lamp and shielded his eyes as the light singed away the image still lingering from the dream. He sat up and let his legs slip off the mattress until his feet touched the floor. The air conditioner in his window kept the humidity at bay, but the air in the room still felt warm and uncomfortable. He found himself wishing he'd just checked into the Econo Lodge over on Route 7. He'd have had his privacy and would probably have been able to escape the nightmares that invariably returned every time he came home to visit his mother. But after his father's passing seven years ago, there was no way to escape Faye Ellis's guilt trips about how his visits were growing less in frequency and duration.

The room felt warmer than usual. Kevin stood, scratched himself for a moment, and then wandered over to the air conditioner to see if it might be dialed down to a lower setting. The green digital number read 66 degrees (the temperature his mom had pre-programmed before he arrived and would complain about if he forgot to set it back when he started his day), but he was sure it could go down to at least 62. He smiled as he pressed the button, and just like in his childhood he felt the supreme joy of secretly going against his mother's wishes. The green digits dropped to 62, and the extra blast of cold air made his sweaty skin prickle with goosebumps. Kevin crossed his arms against his chest and turned to climb back into bed when he heard the dog barking from the yard behind the fence. Kevin froze in place as the yelps pierced the darkness and echoed off the windowpane. His heartbeat pounded in his chest and temples as his mind slipped back to childhood again.

Old man Grady's dog.

Of course, that was impossible. They put Butch down over two decades ago, back when...

He crept up to the window and peeked out from the slits in the blinds.

The thing outside was watching him.

He froze in place, and let his eyes penetrate the darkness of the backyard. Seeing it now under the hazy summer starlight, the land beneath his window looked like a long-forgotten realm of sinister shadows and unnatural contours. In the darkness, lawn furniture resembled hunched dwarves offering dreadful devotions to the night. The tool shed was an ancient castle, with dragon eyes peering out whenever the headlights of the neighbor's car threw reflections on the glass. The flowerbed along the back fence was a row of tombstones whenever the full moon rose above them. These things Kevin knew by heart from childhood and he'd long since learned to see them for what they really were. But the thing standing directly in the center of the lawn was loathsome; a silhouette of spindly white arms and legs that fluttered in the hot pre-dawn breeze like a frayed flag. The apparition floated in defiance of the tangible things surrounding it, as if it somehow wanted to find the same permanence but could not. Kevin struggled to make his eyes focus harder, trying to see what was looking up into his bedroom, but the thing seemed to have no face—no eyes or nose or jawline to give it the missing touch of humanity. Whatever it was simply *was*, an ethereal reflection of something long dead.

He leaned closer to the glass and cupped his hands around his eyes to lower the glare from the lamp. Holding his breath to keep the window from fogging, he glared at the phantasm. The thing with no face tried to glare back, to make eye contact, and when it decided it could not, its head split apart where the mouth should have been and the screech from lifeless vocal cords pierced the darkness. Kevin fell away from the window just as the electricity went out and the noise of the air conditioner died away.

It was when he realized the dog had stopped barking and the night was deathly silent again, and that his nightmare had passed from the dreamtime into reality.

**

"You've hardly touched your breakfast," his mother commented as she sat down at the table and unfolded the morning newspaper. Faye Ellis had already eaten her slice of toast with cottage cheese and diced peaches, and had already cleaned her dishes. Judging by how little coffee was left in the urn, she'd also finished at least two cups, although he couldn't be sure she'd actually made a full pot. At least she was still in her pajamas and bathrobe, and to his estimation Kevin couldn't understand how she didn't melt under all those layers. The morning was already pushing 80 degrees.

"I didn't sleep well, Ma."

"Well, I can't say I'm surprised. The neighborhood must have had a blackout last night. Too many air conditioners draining all that electricity away. It happens every now and then when the summer gets too hot."

"Mom, did you hear something outside this morning? Just after three a.m.?"

Faye picked up her coffee mug and took a long sip, then flipped through the newspaper to find the obituary page. Kevin couldn't help but flinch as she spread the paper out on the table, revealing rows of names and photographs of those once living the day before. From where he was sitting, the newspaper could have been the map to a graveyard. This was her daily routine, one that hadn't changed since he moved out of the house to start his own life.

"Like what?" she said. "Maybe you heard one of the transformers shorting out. That's usually what happens when we lose power. Sometimes they even sound like a small explosion."

"No, Ma, not like that. I just... I don't know." Kevin pushed his fork into the fried egg on his plate and cut it apart. Seeing the slit he'd made oozing yellow yolk made him think of the thing outside his window again, just before it screamed. He placed the fork on the plate and pushed it away from him. "Never mind, Mom. I'm sorry, but I'm just not very hungry right now."

Faye looked up from the paper. "Honey, you get this way every single time you come here. Why won't you just talk to me about what happened? You'll feel a lot better if you'd just talk to me. I want for you to not carry things around inside anymore. It's not healthy for you, sweetheart."

Kevin glanced at the rows of obituaries in the paper and sighed. It was painfully obvious that *she* was still carrying things inside as well, that she was just as obsessed as he was with the past but in her own quiet, accusatory way. Perhaps this was her way of trying to get him to surrender and say something first, but that would require making himself remember, and that was the last thing he wanted to do.

"I said *never mind.*"

"Okay, fine. I'm not going to press it." Faye leaned over and resumed ogling the names of the departed. "If you aren't going to eat your breakfast, please scrape your plate into the trash and wash it. Maybe you'll feel hungry enough to eat later."

Kevin stood up and walked his plate over to the trashcan. He was just beginning to scrape when his mother broke the awkward silence that had risen between them.

"Oh, my! Charles Grady passed away yesterday."

Goosebumps prickled up Kevin's arms and neck. He glanced out the kitchen window at the fence behind the house, toward the house sitting on the opposite side. The Grady house was a derelict gambrel with brown clapboard siding and filthy white shutters weather-worn and rusted until they resembled scabs. From his bedroom window Kevin could see most of the backside of the Grady house, but preferred not to.

"I didn't think that guy was even still alive," he said as he turned on the faucet and squirted detergent on the plate. "I'd just assumed he died ages ago. God, he was an old man even when I was in high school."

"Charles wasn't *that* old back then. But the column said he was 81, so he lived a full life. I suppose it's been ages since I've seen him at the grocery store or walking into town. It doesn't say in the newspaper how they found him or what he died from."

Kevin walked to the window, the wet plate in his hands spattering droplets onto the floor, and looked at the house behind the fence. From the angle he was looking, he couldn't see the doghouse that he knew was in old man Grady's back yard. He'd have been able to if he looked from his bedroom window, but he...

"Mom, how long has Butch been dead?" The question escaped before he even had time to consider what roads the discussion might lead down once asked. Butch had been one of those things he was fighting to not remember. But now that his mind was rolling, the image of the mangy, always-vicious pit bull was at the forefront. He could see the leather collar that looked as if it was too tight, always gouging into the dog's neck until the fur beneath rubbed clean off. And the hate in its eyes, the way its fangs protruded like white daggers when it snarled.

Faye pushed the newspaper aside and looked at him, sizing him up with those judgmental hazel eyes.

"Oh, gosh... Well, you know they put him down after what happened. Does this mean you're finally ready to talk about it?"

Kevin felt his cheeks flush.

"No. No, I was only wondering. Did old man Grady ever get a new dog? After Butch died?"

Faye frowned. "Yes, he bought another dog long after you moved away. That one was a Rottweiler named Champ. That thing was a lot more timid than Butch was. Charles was not a good pet owner. He used to put the fear of God into them until they did whatever he commanded."

"Does he have a dog now? Because I heard it barking last night, and if they took his body away without knowing there's a dog in the back yard, someone needs to call the police and tell them."

"No, it's been a few years since Champ died. He never got a new one after that. Sweetheart, you know there are no bad dogs, only bad owners. And Charles Grady was a terrible owner. Whatever happened to Reggie that day..."

"Mom, I *don't* want to talk about it."

He turned to storm out of the room but realized he was still holding his plate. He tossed it onto the counter where it clanged and vibrated for a moment before falling still. He was already out of the room by the time it finished its vibrato dance on the countertop.

***

The bedroom had cooled considerably, and Kevin found himself glad he hadn't raised the temperature back up to the Faye Ellis setting. Sunlight streamed in from the slats in the blinds, but even with the windows partially obstructed he could detect the storm clouds moving in over town. A thunderstorm was definitely on the horizon, probably hitting sometime before sundown but destined to linger throughout the night. *The angels are bowling,* his father used to tell him when he was young and the crash of thunderclaps shook the house until he couldn't sleep. *They'll tire out eventually and go to bed, just like you need to do.*

Parents say a lot of things to their children to pacify them.

What would Dad have said about hearing the dog this morning?

Kevin moved over to the window, turned the rod until the slits on the Venetian blinds were fully open, and looked over the fence into old man Grady's yard.

The old, red doghouse was still there, only there was no dog in sight.

"It looks like Snoopy's doghouse," Reggie Acton used to say. "You know the one he flies around on like an airplane when he's chasing the Red Baron?"

The voice was in his head, but it sounded so real that Kevin gasped and stepped back away from the window. He was almost certain the voice came from somewhere behind him, but that would have been as impossible as hearing a dog barking that wasn't there— or seeing a faceless ghost standing in the backyard.

Please... I don't want to remember any of this!

Kevin gritted his eyes tight, turned around, and then opened them slowly.

There was nothing in the room with him.

He released the breath he'd been holding (he hadn't even been aware his breathing stopped) and turned back to the window. The sky was growing dark rapidly as the clouds passed like a razor's edge across the last vestiges of blue sky. He was certain the temperature outside was going to fall fast, he could feel the change in the air and on his skin...

Just like Carrie...she turned cold fast and without warning as well. How much time has passed since she demanded the divorce?

...and switched off the air conditioner. Kevin glanced down into the back yard one last time to see if the faceless thing had returned, and when he was satisfied that it hadn't, he twisted the rod until the slits were closed tight. Coming home felt like an enormous mistake, just like it had with every previous trip. The only thing left to do was start inventing a new excuse to pack up and hit the road early. Kevin lay down on the bed, closed his eyes, and tried to concoct some new fabrication to spring on Faye Ellis. In his mind, guilt was a thing with no face—only an incessant weight that tried to squeeze his heart until it stopped beating. Maybe then he would finally find peace.

***

He'd fallen asleep.

The nightmare resumed, just as he'd been certain it would. In the dream he was twelve years old again and Reginald Acton was still eleven and still living in the house next door. All the houses on Sparrow Drive were identical Cape Cods, as if the contractors responsible for developing the cul-de-sac followed the same blueprints and merely changed paints to create any sense of individuality. Kevin's home was green. Reggie's was canary yellow. But dreams never follow rules, and in the movie in his head—the memory he was trying so desperately to not remember—Reggie's house was the same red as Butch's doghouse. When Kevin squinted his eyes to look at it, the red bled into a deep crimson that clung to the back of his eyelids. In the dream, they were playing in Kevin's backyard.

"It looks just like Snoopy's doghouse," Reggie said as they peered through the slats in the fence at the sleeping dog. "You know the one he flies around on like an airplane when he's chasing the Red Baron?"

Butch's left ear twitched, almost as if the beast was eavesdropping rather than snoozing in the shade of the maple tree. Kevin could see the leather collar curling tight into the dog's neck, and the ratty piece of clothesline rope that cinched from the collar to the big iron spike in the middle of the lawn. The rope was long enough to chase intruders to the fence and nab them down before they could get away. It occurred to him even back then that the only way to escape that damn dog was to get it to chase you around his doghouse a lap or two before trying to jump the fence again, and even that was a snowball's chance in hell. The years of having Grady for a neighbor meant any Frisbees or softballs or toys that accidentally sailed over the fence were lost treasures...unless old man Grady felt generous enough to toss them back over again while out feeding Butch and cleaning up the festering piles of dog turds.

"You never did get your glider plane back, did you?" Reggie suddenly asks—a question that has haunted him for more than three decades. The plane was a Styrofoam jet nearly two feet long, with wings and tailfins you could adjust to suit your flight plan. The glider had been a birthday gift from Kevin's father, one which accidentally passed over the Bermuda Triangle of their creepy neighbor's back yard. "Grady never threw it over the fence so you could have it back?"

"Nope." He nodded to the dying hydrangea bush, with the foam jet's tailfins protruding toward the rear.

In the dream the thunderclouds roll in, and in the dying daylight Kevin turns to Reggie and says, "But I think I know how we can get it back."

"How?"

Kevin smiles as he espies the sleeping dog through the slats in the fence. He's amazed at himself for never realizing just how simple it would be. "I'll go over the fence and get Butch to chase me. If I can get a lap or two around the doghouse, that will take up enough slack on his line to keep him tied up. Then *you* jump the fence, grab the glider plane, and jump back over. Once you're safe, I'll come back over too."

In the dream, Reggie flashes a grin that is both innocent and mischievous at the same time. It makes his freckled nose crinkle and his eyebrows float up his forehead until they almost touch the bushy locks of his bright red hair. It's the same Reggie Acton that haunts Kevin every day of his life: the image of the boy while he still has his face. The sleeping Kevin Ellis is already turning and struggling in the twin-size bed, desperately wishing he could stop the dream from progressing until both children are in old man Grady's backyard and Butch's clothesline rope leash snaps, and...

***

The roar of thunder echoed off the walls around him, and Kevin opened his eyes. The ghost was hovering above him, its face still marred where the pit bull mauled away the flesh and cartilage. The freckles and the bright red hair were now thin white vapors of cold eternity. The ghost lifted a wavering hand into the air and placed it in front of its mouth as if to say, "Shhhhh." Before Kevin could protest, the thing with no face waved its arm slowly, as if beckoning for him to follow.

"Go away," Kevin whispered. "Please, just go away!"

The ghost peered silently for a moment, lowered its head as if in defeat, and floated out the bedroom door.

Kevin gripped his blankets tight around his body and cried himself back to sleep. Outside the window, raindrops pelted the aluminum siding and lightning flashes turned his bedroom into unbearable moments of daylight until the thunderclaps snuffed them back out again.

**

When he awoke, the room was freezing. He'd left the air conditioner shut off before falling asleep but now it was on again, thrumming strong at sixty degrees. Kevin sat up slowly, pulled the comforter tight around his body, and walked across the room to turn it off again. He lifted his finger to press the off switch, but before he could touch it he heard the dog barking from old man Grady's yard. He jabbed the switch, and then twisted the rod and opened the slits in the blinds.

It was just before dawn, and the air was saturated with a wall of fog that made it nearly impossible to see. The dog continued barking, agitated at first and then falling into a slow, steady howl that resembled fear or injury. Kevin leaned closer to the glass, held his breath, and gazed harder into old man Grady's backyard. The doghouse came into focus, like a blood-red heart just off-center of the decrepit lawn. And just outside its front was the ghost of a little boy that had once been his next-door neighbor. Reggie Acton was hunched over, gazing into the open front of Butch's doorway, as if trying to call to whatever was inside. Whatever *was* inside whimpered and yelped in despair. Watching the scene from his window made Kevin's blood run colder than the temperature in his bedroom.

"There *is* a goddamn dog in there," he said to himself.

He picked up his jeans off the floor and threw them on, then slipped his feet into his sneakers. The world around him felt like a dream. He crept down the stairs and slipped through the house quietly, hoping that his mother was still asleep, dreaming her own dreams in her guilt-free world where husbands didn't suffer heart attacks from too much fatty foods and where there were no bad dogs, only bad dog-owners. The world of Faye Ellis meant making justifications and excuses while neighbors moved away after losing their child to an angry pit bull. Even after Reggie's body was recovered and taken away, and after the police questioned Kevin over and over again about what happened, his mother never once insinuated that what happened was her son's fault. But it was.

It was *his fault.* Guilt *did* have a face if he was brave enough to look in the mirror and accept that what happened was because he'd convinced Reggie to jump the fence and help him get his glider plane back.

Kevin wrapped his hand around the door handle and threw it open. The cool morning fog draped his flesh, wetting it to the touch with glistening beads. He steeled himself and marched across the back lawn until he reached the white picket fence that separated the two yards. It was time to tell Reggie Acton that he was sorry, time to finally accept responsibility for what happened. He gazed over the fence at the doghouse.

The thing with no face was gone.

He could feel the tears welling in the corners of his eyes. His heart pounded in his chest, and butterflies flitted and scratched at the pit of his belly.

"I'm going crazy," he whispered.

From somewhere inside the doghouse, an unearthly howl responded as if to confirm the sentiment. Hearing it filled him with a dread deeper than he'd ever felt, deeper even than the day Reginald Acton was buried in Shady Acres Cemetery. For one brutal moment he felt absolutely paralyzed, and he could almost see the puddle of blood that had collected where Butch had knocked his eleven-year-old friend over and ravaged his face completely off. He could almost see the weathered clothesline leash, could picture where the rope had broken away from the stake and how it slithered in the mud like a snake as Butch attacked and shook his head back and forth with Reggie's cheeks and nose planted in its maw.

The moment passed, and then Kevin jumped over the fence and crept up to the door of the doghouse. He drew a deep breath, held it in, and then swung around so that his face could look in to see what was hiding inside.

The doghouse was empty, except for his Styrofoam glider plane leaning toward the back wall. The fuselage wings were bent into a crooked angle, but for the most part the toy looked unharmed.

Kevin exhaled slowly and waited for his heart rate to slow down before falling onto all fours and pushing his way inside the doghouse. He crawled to the back, sat with his legs crossed beneath him, picked up the airplane, and wept. He clutched it tight against his chest and sobbed as all the years of guilt overtook him at once. Kevin hitched and gasped for breath as he thought of his friend's lifeless body on the ground, and the way he'd jumped the fence and ran back to his own house screaming for help, waiting to feel Butch's fangs sink into the back of his legs and then rip him apart as well. He remembered the penetrating anger in old man Grady's face when they removed Reggie's body from his back yard, and the absolute hatred in his eyes when they took Butch away to put him down. Kevin remembered everything.

"I'm sorry, Reggie," he whispered, gazing down at the foam glider through tear-blurred eyes. "It was all *my* fault. I didn't know the rope was going to break. I don't care about the goddamn plane. I wish I could have you back again. I'm sorry I let this happen."

He wrapped his left arm tighter around the plane, and with his right arm he tried to scoot back to the entrance of the doghouse, then stopped when he saw the ghost blocking the doorway. The thing with no face had trapped him, and beside it was the ghost of Butch, who had planted his haunches hard onto the ground as if ready to attack. Reggie's face was missing, but the expression on the mauled and mottled specter still managed to exude terrible satisfaction. The slit where its mouth had once been spread open and the thing with no face shrieked in vengeance.

Kevin closed his eyes and waited for Butch to unite them forever.

Last Supper at the Miss Hollywood Diner

It was a one-star day for the Aquarius in the coffee-stained apron and high-heeled shoes.

Rosalita heard the bell on the glass door jingle sometime after three a.m. She turned from the horoscope column to watch one of her favorite regulars saunter in and grab the empty booth under the painting of "Miss Hollywood, 1973." There were only two other customers in the diner, and they'd already paid their bill and were sitting quietly at the far table. Most likely, the Latino dude was trying to convince the girl across from him to go back to his place, but the girl seemed young and coy and happy to be getting attention. There were still chores to do, napkin dispensers needed to be filled and tables needed to be wiped down, but these things could wait until just before the breakfast crowd arrived. She closed the paper, picked up her order pad, and hustled over to the table, already knowing what the lanky white guy in the Hawaiian shirt, khaki cargo shorts, and straw cowboy hat was going to order. Winston Crane never deviated from his standard fare of breakfast burrito and buttered toast. There's a reason they're called "regulars."

"*Buenos noches*, honey. You're a bit early today. *Qué pasa?*"

Crane sighed and waved off the menu she tried to hand him.

"The usual, Rosie. And make sure the coffee's good and strong."

"You look upset. You okay?"

Rosalita already knew the answer. The author was half-in-the-bag, as white Americans always referred to it. She could smell the whiskey on his breath and was fairly certain the bulge in his pocket was his hip flask. Winston Crane shifted uncomfortably in his seat. He took the straw hat off and placed it on the bench next to him. His thinning gray hair was wild, kinky, making his long whiskers look almost tame in comparison. "I've got writer's block. Worst bout I've ever had. I've spent almost a week now trying to get back into the zone but nothing's coming. I'm getting to the point where I think the well has run dry. I don't know if that makes any sense, but whenever I try to sit down and write lately, I spend half my day staring at a blank computer screen. It's driving me mad. I don't know what to do anymore."

Rosalita smiled politely and placed her hand on his shoulder.

"Just relax, honey. Your *mamacita* here is going to take good care of you." And then to the Latino chef behind the heat chute at the pickup area, "Carlos... Special B *con* buttered toast, *pronto!*"

There was a noncommittal grunt from the kitchen, and then Rosalita was off to grab the coffee pot and a clean mug. She moved quickly, relinquishing glimpses of her long, dark legs beneath the miniskirt and apron. Rosalita knew how to work the customers. Even in her late thirties her looks hadn't faltered, and that was long after the birth of Tomas and Consuela. Her long, curly hair was done up neatly in a bun, and her ample bosom was barely contained in the D-cups of her Victoria's Secret bra, exposing cleavage deeper than Silicon Valley. The Miss Hollywood Diner had seen its share of waitresses come and go over the years, but Rosie was a mainstay, hustling for every dime after midnight when the Latino boys finished their shifts around Universal City and came in for *huevos y salchichas*. The Caucasian customers always stood out; tourists on a bender after the local bars closed or the movie extras that were still hungry after the rolling catering carts at MGM and Paramount closed and moved on for the night. Winston Crane was neither of these. He was an author/screenwriter living in a bungalow off Hollywood Boulevard. The man was a success, at least as far as writers went. Crane had a string of novels and a few feature film screenplays that kept the rent paid and food in his belly. Now, glancing him over, Rosalita noticed that his stomach wasn't quite as rotund as it had previously been, and that the lines on his face had grown deeper.

It occurred to her that she hadn't seen him for maybe a few weeks.

Crane was staring up at Miss Hollywood as Rosie placed the mug in front of him and filled it nearly to the brim. She reached into her apron and produced a few plastic containers of creamer, which she dropped unceremoniously next to the mug.

"How long have I been coming here, Rosie?" he asked, his face still staring up at the painting of Miss Hollywood. It was a cinch that the woman in the painting was at least five feet tall, blonde, and buxom in her white one-piece swimsuit. She had a beauty crown parked jauntily on her scalp, with her lips painted a lascivious shade of red that made her blonde hair that much more striking in comparison. The woman had a pink satin ribbon running from shoulder to waist declaring her "Miss Hollywood, 1973." She had that smile, that Marilyn Monroe smile where her perfect white teeth were visible just below those crimson promises of a kiss. The woman's identity was a complete mystery. Perhaps she'd found fame as a Hollywood starlet, or maybe caught a Greyhound bus back to wherever she came from when Tinsel Town swept all her dreams away and left her an empty shell. That was the way of Hollywood: false promises and fleeting fame.

Rosie smiled politely and shrugged. "*Yo no sé.* You've been coming here for years now. Long enough for me to know all the titles of your books and the movies you've been a part of. You came in here long before you had a beard, and your hair was still short and brown." Rosalita offered a wink. "You were young and attractive when you first came in here. That's all I know."

"And now? Am I still attractive?"

Behind them, the tinkle of the bell on the door broke the silence as another figure entered the diner.

"I'm not going to answer that," Rosalita whispered politely. "I'm going to get this guy seated and take his order. Perhaps you'd be better off dreaming up ideas for your next story, no?"

She was gone in a flash, and Crane found himself digging a tiny spiral-bound notebook out of his cargo shorts. He produced a black gel pen from another pocket and began scribbling notes onto the blank paper. He was still staring up at Miss Hollywood, admiring the beautiful woman from the past as if she were still alive. Crane sat in the booth creating secrets and scandals about her on the lines of the paper when he heard Rosie gasp and drop the coffee pot onto the cold green linoleum floor. It smashed in fractals of wet glass that made him jump in his seat.

"Oh my God...you're bleeding! Are you okay?"

Crane turned and looked at the man that had just passed through the door. He was middle-aged, possibly in his late forties, in a navy-blue Brooks Brothers suit and wing-tipped shoes. The man's face and hands were indeed coated in blood, but in the dim light of the diner Crane couldn't be sure if the blood was fresh or old and tacky. It had caked onto the bare spot on the bridge of his nose and across his forehead, as if something long and blunt had struck him. The man had begun making his way to a table nearby, but when Rosalita hollered to Carlos in the back kitchen to call 911, the man turned on her and shouted, "No! Don't even bother. They're gonna come find me anyway."

Before he even knew what he was doing, Crane was on his feet and guiding the beaten man over to his booth. He eased the man down gently onto the green vinyl bench and then sat down across from him.

"What happened to you? Were you mugged? Did somebody jump you and take your wallet?"

The man slowly reached into his pants pocket and produced a pack of nearly crushed cigarettes. Lucky Strikes, a brand that Crane hadn't thought of in years. Back in his smoking days, Winston (the irony of his name never escaped him) had only smoked Chesterfields, and that was when he wasn't rolling spliffs of that Mexican shit that kept creeping its way over the border despite the constant patrolling by both ICE and the DEA. The man shook a cigarette loose from the pack, placed it between his lips, and then through bloody, mangled teeth asked Rosalita politely, "Is it okay if I light this up in here?"

Rosie nodded politely. "It's against regulations, but I ain't gonna say nothing. Are you okay, mister?"

The man lit the cigarette, dropped his pack of matches on the table next to Crane's coffee mug and open notebook, and then took a deep drag.

"They're coming to kill me," he said. His face was full of both fear and acceptance. "I crossed the wrong people. They'll find me long before the sun comes up and I'll be dead."

An explosion rocked the night air as if to acknowledge the man's statement. The concussive blast roared down Hollywood Boulevard, sending the other cars parked along the star-scattered sidewalks into a caterwaul of security alarms that howled like wounded animals. The plate-glass windows of the Miss Hollywood Diner shook in their frames but managed to hold fast. Cups and glasses on the shelves inside the diner, however, did not fare as well, shaking and tumbling to the floor where they shattered into more tiny fractals. Normally Rosalita would have cursed both in English and Spanish about having to clean it up, but for the moment she was too terrified to even breathe.

The stranger looked up mournfully at the mural of Miss Hollywood. He reached slowly into the side pocket of his coat and pulled out a revolver, which he set on the table. The gun smelled of warm sulfur and oil, as if it had been discharged recently. It looked like an angry animal on the cold glass tabletop, ready to strike at a moment's notice. Seeing the weapon made both Rosie and Winston gasp. The waitress wasn't the least bit surprised to see the Latino dude and his date slip out of their booth and hurry out the door. She found herself jealous now that she was trapped in this unfolding nightmare.

"My mother once told me that palm trees can't be trusted," the stranger said. He took another long drag off his cigarette and blew the smoke high into the air. "She came to California because she wanted to be surrounded by palm trees. She thought they were somehow the secret to happiness. But they're not. She told me when I was a little boy that they lured her in with promises of paradise. But palm trees... Have you ever looked at them *after* sunset? When the sun goes down over the Pacific and their silhouettes stand there alone against the evening sky? Palm trees are the truth *and* the lie of paradise all at the same time. Can I get a plate of steak and eggs, please?" The man turned away from the mural on the wall to Rosalita, who had been standing slack-jawed and hanging on his every word.

"*Muy bien*, of course." Rosie turned toward Carlos, who was now peeking through the space between the heat chutes and the pickup area at the bloodied stranger. "You heard the man...*huevos con carne!*"

Crane stared at the man opposite him, taking in the bruises that were neatly spreading out around the lacerations on his forehead ("Contusions," Crane noted to himself. That's three more letters than "bruises." When editors are paying you by the word, you need to choose wisely.). The guy couldn't have been much older than he was. Younger, possibly, had his cheeks not grown sallow with fright. The guy lifted the cigarette to his lips again and took another drag, this one long and slow, causing the tobacco and paper to burn all the way down to the filter. He exhaled again and began to cough. That was when Crane noticed the blood oozing out of a hole in the man's chest.

The guy had been shot once already.

"Jesus Christ... We need an ambulance. This guy is wounded."

"No!" The stranger slapped his free hand palm-down onto the table. The slap against the glass-covered tabletop caused both his pistol and Crane's coffee mug to jump. Crane hadn't noticed before, and was shocked to discover that his skin was covered in goose flesh, and that his knees were now trembling. Dread was trickling into the pit of his belly. "Nobody's calling the cops. They already know. They ain't going to arrive until I'm good and dead. The cops are on the payroll, don't you get it? They all work for *him*! I'm already dead." The stranger sighed. "All I want is my last supper."

Crane couldn't take his eyes off him. "What happened to you tonight?"

The man looked up again at Miss Hollywood. The painted lady on the wall seemed to gaze back, her eyes ablaze with youth and defiance and understanding. It struck Crane funny to realize the stark contrast of the perfectly figured white model watching over a restaurant that was inhabited primarily by poor, beaten down Latinos: a luminous beacon of what Hollywood actually represented in the 21st Century, as well as the century before. She stood for privilege and promise. She stood for white normalcy in a world where wetbacks still crawled and slithered their way across the border like brown-skinned snakes looking for freedom, and fought to make some kind of living for themselves once they arrived. Somewhere in 1973, this blonde Venus just showed up and smiled and shook her tits and Hollywood turned her into a princess. At least for that year. God only knew what happened to her afterward. How many before and after her had arrived in Tinsel Town seeking fame and fortune and success, only to have their dreams dashed?

From somewhere far down Hollywood Boulevard, a scream of sirens announced the oncoming fire trucks and police cars to answer the explosion.

"That was my Lexus," the stranger said, stubbing his cigarette out directly onto the glass tabletop. "I got the tipoff that it was wired to blow earlier this evening." The man lifted his arm and wiped the sleeve of his Brooks Brothers suit against his forehead, disrupting the clotting scabs and setting his face to bleeding again. A rivulet of crimson trickled down the left side of his nose and bled across the top of his lip. "Jesus Christ, Lefty really did a number on me."

"Who's Lefty?" Rosie whispered. She was clearly slipping into shock. Her soft brown eyes had gone wide, making her look like a deer in headlights. Crane noticed this and a trace of sympathy for her filled his chest. She was beautiful—always had been. How many mornings had he wandered into the Miss Hollywood Diner just to see her, only to have his heart broken as she regaled him with stories of her boyfriend José, who filled her womb with two children but was never man enough to put a ring on her finger and make her his wife? Fucking *machismo*!

"Lefty Cummings. Sylvia Moran's bodyguard. You know who Sylvia Moran is, don'tcha?"

Crane and Rosie both nodded. Hollywood's latest starlet. Curly brown locks and perfect rack. Another winning smile up on the silver screen. She'd just released her second picture, a romantic comedy from TriStar Pictures opposite Bruno DeAngelo, who in reality was old enough to be her father. Crane had already seen the movie and disliked it intensely. He found himself wondering if Rosie had seen it, perhaps on a date with José, but was almost certain she hadn't. If he had to hazard a guess, Rosie probably hadn't been to a movie theater in years. The best she could hope for was a cable television replay, with all the sex scenes and swear words blocked out, making it safe and sanitized if her children were around to watch.

"I'm her agent," the stranger announced, almost apologetically. "I'm the one that arranges her casting calls and auditions. I knew Sylvia wasn't married, so I made a pass at her just after she returned from her latest shoot. She'd always given me that vibe that she was kind of interested, but I was never really sure. I've banged dozens of broads over the years, all of them thinking I was their key to stardom. I helped build a lot of careers. And I've screwed a few over, knowing their careers weren't going anywhere. Sylvia was different. I knew she had a future. What I didn't know was that she has a boyfriend in the mafia out in Las Vegas. Max Sterling." The stranger sighed and shook his head sadly. "He runs half a dozen casinos, from what I understand. Lefty works for Max. At least he did before I killed him."

Carlos pushed the kitchen door open and sauntered out with a plate of steak and eggs. He placed the plate in front of the stranger and said, "Here you go, man. This is the best beef in the house." And then he was back in the kitchen again, peeking out from behind the heat chute before the guy could even unwrap the napkin from his silverware and dig in.

"Oh, this is delicious," the stranger moaned as he ground his teeth into the meat. As if to respond, the night air was filled with a series of rifle blasts. The inhabitants of the Miss Hollywood Diner all jumped for cover as the morning sky filled with the sound of tiny explosions and plate-glass windows shattering outside. Hollywood Boulevard was lined with nail salons and bodegas and astrology shacks and adult bookstores, and somewhere up the street bullets shattered their exteriors as if to alert all of Hollywood that Hell just broke loose. More car alarms blared into the morning sky. Through the plate-glass window of the Miss Hollywood Diner, Crane noticed the flames lighting up the night as the stranger's car burned and smoldered just up the block. Crane was sure he could now smell smoke wafting in off the street. His heart was pounding.

It was as if Rosie had been slapped in the face. She rounded on the stranger as he stuffed his mouth with food and chewed and swallowed.

"Why the fuck did you come *here*?" she screamed. "If somebody's after you, why did you choose *this* place to find shelter? There's nothing we can do to help you!"

The stranger picked up Crane's cup of coffee and took a sip. He set the mug back down in front of Crane, wiped his mouth with his bloodied sleeve, and apologized. "You shoulda brought me a glass of ice water, miss." he admonished the waitress. And then to Crane, "That was very rude of me to take your coffee." The man slowly reached down and unbuttoned his Brooks Brothers jacket. He pushed his jacket open slowly, exposing the row of explosives strapped across his belly. Six red sticks of dynamite nestled gently across his stomach, along with a small digital cartridge flashing green LED numbers. The numbers were ticking off backward, with a flashing colon pulsing between the numerals. The timer was down to seven minutes and forty-one seconds.

"I gotta hurry if I'm going to finish all this," the man said, glancing down at his plate. The beef was half-eaten, with yellow egg yolks running down either side. He picked up another forkful and wolfed it down. Then he glanced up at the painting of Miss Hollywood.

"That woman is my mother," he said as he chewed. "Her name was Maria Logan. She was banging the guy who built this place, so he named it after her." The stranger swallowed. "Sort of, anyway. I always suspected that the owner was my father, but never knew for sure. I paid a private dick about a decade ago to find out more about her, but most he could come up with was that she was born in Sanford, Maine, and left home after graduating high school. I guess she got tired of bussing tables during the summers at some diner in Old Orchard Beach, so she just up and left home. Mom died of an overdose when I was six. She wanted to be an actress, I suppose, but she never made it onto the big screen. She got hooked on heroin instead. I got sent off to some foster home in San Bernardino, but I eventually made my way back to Hollywood. We never stray too far from home in the end, do we?"

Crane and Rosie both stared at the flashing LED clock ticking away on his belly. It was now down to five minutes. Rosie was already backing away toward the kitchen. Crane was sure there was an exit in the back, where Carlos and the other Latino cooks and waitresses slipped out for a cigarette (or for a shot of tequila on those hot summer evenings). The smoke from out front of the restaurant was already beginning to envelop the doorway and windows. Crane was certain he could hear the sound of footsteps coming closer; hard rubber soles clicking and clacking against the celebrity stars on the sidewalk. Somewhere out front, henchmen were stomping over Mickey Rooney and Greta Garbo and Bela Lugosi. He felt his gorge rising in his throat.

"They'll be here soon," the man sputtered around another mouthful of beef. "Max Sterling and his boys. You folks probably ought to be leaving now."

Crane stood and stared at the man, noticing how the stranger's face was now smeared red with blood from the reopened wound on his forehead. The guy chewed slowly, deliberately, and the look on his face was one of stoic determination. He had the same look that actors like Brando had at the end of that war movie, where he knew Martin Sheen was coming to kill him. It was a look that said, "This will all be over soon, and I'm okay with it."

The guy took one more baleful glance up at the painting on the wall. "I'm sorry, Mom. I'm sorry it's come to this. At least you had permanence here in the diner. Even if people didn't know your name, at least they got to see how beautiful you were."

A tear ran down his face, smearing with the sticky trails of blood. The clock on his belly was now down to less than a minute.

Crane grabbed Rosalita by the elbow and shoved her through the kitchen door. Carlos was already long gone, and that was no big surprise. What was a surprise was the sound of the bell on the diner's door tinkling open (*Not just tinkling*, Crane thought. *It's ringing loud and clear. That guy at the table is a goner.*), and a cadre of dark men in heavy shoes clip-clopping over toward the stranger's table. There was enough time to hear the sound of bullets being cocked into chambers and then firing with loud reports in rapid succession as the stranger tried to gulp down his last bite of *huevos y carne*. Crane heard someone shouting out, "Holy shit, he's fucking wired to blow!" just as he pushed Rosie out the back door and into the cool California morning air. And then the diner blew sky-high, the blast ripping the front of the building apart like it was nothing more than a paper bag. Huge, rolling flames blasted upward and outward, throwing what seemed like the world's biggest fireball up into the heavens above.

The blast concussion threw the two across the alleyway, filling their ears with a resounding roar that made both of Crane's eardrums rupture. The world screamed around him, and then it was raining bricks. One large chunk sailed down from the heavens and caught him right between the eyes, smashing his skull to pieces. As consciousness began to fade, he could see the silhouette of palm trees off in the distance. They stood alone in the firelight, quiet and emotionless, like a row of forgotten promises.

I need to write this all down, he thought as his eyes closed. *I can't wait to get home and write this all down. This is my next best seller!*

California went black behind his eyes, and then Winston Crane was gone. Rosalita ran to his side and wrapped her arms around him. She clutched him tight against her shaking body and wept, for she had secretly loved him back; loved him in that painful, forbidden way that neither José nor the starlets on the Silver Screen could ever really understand. It was a one-star day, after all, and as the tears fell and consciousness began to fly away, the last thing she saw was the palm trees. They stood lonely and alone, silhouetted against the California sunrise, quietly waving Miss Hollywood goodbye.

The Pressboard Factory

I can't stand the smell of glue anymore. It makes me sick to my stomach.

I don't like talking about these things. The truth is that I never got over what happened to my friend Ryan after he ran away from home. It's easy to fall into that vortex of blame because humans are conceited enough to believe that their actions and decisions are greater than the cold manipulation of fate. I could have told somebody where he went—I'd known all along—but that wouldn't have changed the fact Ryan was who he was. Nor would it have changed the fact that the beatings and the humiliation his old man heaped on him would have continued if he'd chosen to stay. Nowadays I spend my time pondering what friendship means, and if I'm going to tell you the truth at all, I was not a good friend to him. And that's the part that kicks me in the ass. Ryan and I were only friends of convenient proximity. His family lived two houses down from our own back on Goddard Street, which made companionship easily accessible even before we were kindergarteners. In reality we had very little in common. But he was funny, and he kept me amused, and so I never complained about his company.

Ryan Alton was a waifish kid. All gangly and effeminate, as if his body was in rebellion with his gender. Young boys don't pick up on these things, at least not in the first few years of elementary school, and so I prided myself in being the bigger of us. But as the years went by and I grew taller and went through the raging hormones and drama of puberty, Ryan didn't. At least not outwardly. He remained waifish and wimpy, and I can still close my eyes and see his jarhead father towering over him, with his massive, tattooed biceps spilling out of the *Semper Fi* t-shirt and his fists curled tight against his hips, telling the poor kid to "toughen up, 'cuz I'm gonna make a fucking man out of you if it kills me."

I was his friend, and I felt bad for him, but I could never plumb the depths of his misery, could never fathom empathy, because deep down I agreed with his old man. Ryan was funny, and making people laugh got him out of a lot of tough scrapes in school, but it never ended the shadow of bullying that eclipsed him. Eventually, *his* tough scrapes became *my* tough scrapes because I couldn't stand idly by and let those asshole jocks give him wedgies out behind the gymnasium or push him around in the hallways. By our junior year of high school, I was growing to resent him, and if I couldn't have empathy I could at least show sympathy. But by that spring even sympathy had fizzled out. Even then I was questioning just why we'd remained friends for so long. I grew tired of Ryan's problems being my problems. And after that asshole Mick Munroe jumped us on our way home from school, I told him so.

"Look at these two faggots," Mick said as he walked out of the Kennebec Fruit Company with a can of Moxie in his hand and a lecherous grin spindling across his oily face. Mick was already out of high school by at least three years, and spent his free time between pillaging the local junkyard to soup up his Mustang and terrorizing his hometown. That was as far as he was ever going to go in life, and he knew it and didn't care. "Are you two off to suck each other's dicks? Billy, you must be the pitcher in your little homo relationship, 'cuz lil' Ryan here couldn't satisfy a mosquito. Look at ya! Why don't you do Billy a favor and grow some tits? Or at least put on some makeup so you're a bit more attractive. Prom is coming up soon, ya know."

Mick laughed at his own remark like he was the funniest thing on the planet. His body hitched enough to spill Moxie down the front of the sleeveless denim jacket he wore, the one with all the punk rock band logos stitched all over it, and I can still remember how Ryan recoiled in shame, his cheeks burning red as Ladder One in the Lisbon Falls Fire Department's garage just a few buildings up Main Street.

"Fuck off, Mick," I replied for Ryan. "Nobody asked your opinion anyway." My heart was jackhammering in my chest. Mick was outnumbered two-to-one, but Ryan didn't really count. I knew that and so did Mick, who wasn't about to stand down. In a lot of ways, Mick Munroe was just like Ryan's dad: all muscular bravado, in the kind of way that insisted you respect it or suffer the consequences. People in town stood aside when Marcus Alton strode past. At 6'4" and sculpted out of something more like iron and granite rather than flesh and bone, the ex-Marine had no enemies in our little town. And the whole reason the Mick Munroes of the world got away with tormenting his only son was because his daddy wanted him to learn toughness on his own.

"Yeah, fuck off, Mick!" Ryan repeated. Only, his retort rang hollow, like an echo off the brick storefronts around us. The look in his eyes said it all, a dismal acceptance that this type of thing was never going to end for him. There would always be judgment and harassment and exploitation. For Ryan, humiliation was perpetual and scraped like a knife on dry skin.

Mick's smile widened.

"Or what? What are you gonna do, ya little pansy? Are you gonna throw a hissy fit? I should make both of you my bitches." Mick's free hand slipped down inside the pocket of his jeans and fished out a switchblade. The hand holding the can of Moxie never even twitched as he flicked the knife open and held it out first at me, and then at Ryan. "Starting with pretty boy here. You wanna taste my dick, pretty boy?"

My foot flew before my brain even told it to, and then Mick Munroe was writhing on the sidewalk with his hands cupping his damaged testicles, the switchblade lying on the sidewalk with its metal blade glinting in the early June sunshine. Beyond that was a blur of me grabbing Ryan by the collar of his shirt and sprinting up Main Street toward our houses around the corner on Goddard.

Our parents got phone calls that evening, first from old lady Stevenson, who had witnessed the whole thing across the street as she came out of the post office, and then from the town's police department (who old lady Stevenson called directly after calling our parents to rat us out). Mrs. Stevenson is friends with Mick's mom, and in her haste to be Mrs. Good Samaritan, she failed to mention how that asshole had pulled the knife on us. My parents asked for an explanation, and when I explained what really happened, the issue was dropped. Ryan's parents, on the other hand...

When I got on the bus the next morning and made my way to the back where he was sitting, his left eye was blackened. It was the kind of shiner you see on professional boxers when they let their guard down long enough to get their bell rung by the opponent. When I saw it, I thought of the 6'4" Marine, who had served in the original Gulf War in the burning deserts of Iraq, just punching the stuffing out of the timid little kid I'd been sticking up for ever since we went to kindergarten. Seeing him made my heart break. And it made me resent him. I hated hurting because there was nothing I could do to help him. Even now I suspect that was why I started distancing myself.

"Jesus, what the hell is wrong with your old man? Did you tell him I was the one who kicked that asshole Munroe in the nuts?" I dropped my backpack on the floor and sat down beside him. He lowered his face into his hands and sobbed, and immediately I felt embarrassed for asking. In the back of my mind I pictured him climbing onto the bus before me and quietly passing down the aisle between all the other high school kids, his head hung in shame as he tried to wish them all away so they wouldn't stare.

"No," he whimpered into his hands. "No, it wasn't that at all. Brian, I have something I need to tell you. It's what I told my mom last night. She told Dad, and that's what caused all of this."

"Well, I've got something I need to tell you," I said, steeling myself for what I knew was going to be another blow for him. I couldn't help it. I'd thought about it all night, once I got through explaining to my parents that my New Balance sneaker introduced itself to Mick Munroe's testicles in self-defense. "I can't keep fighting your battles for you. We're not little kids anymore. Ryan, you're going to have to man-up and start protecting yourself. We're graduating next year and once we start college, we're going to be heading our own separate ways."

Ryan dropped his hands and looked at me. Tears streaked down his cheeks and snot runners were forming around his nostrils.

"I'm running away."

"Bullshit," I said. "Where the hell do you think you're going to go? You've got one more year of high school and then you can apply to college and get away from that asshole dad of yours forever. And even if you *did* run away, you'd still be little Ryan Alton from Goddard Street. It's not like you're going to become a man overnight."

He sighed, and it was as if his soul blew right out of him. It was the sound of perfect desperation, and it blew as cold as the north wind.

"That's what I'm trying to tell you... Last night I told my mom that I think I was supposed to be born a girl."

***

A few years before all this happened, I asked my dad about the pressboard factory. We were out fishing the Androscoggin River, across from the factory's riverside facade. The heat of the afternoon and the lack of nibbles was sending my mind into boredom, and I found myself staring at the rear side of the Fiber-Tech plant. The building itself rested upon a stone wall that dropped directly down into the riverside. One corner had succumbed to the elements, leaving a brick-and-mortar portal directly into the darkened confines of the building's workroom floor. The derelict building had been abandoned for at least a dozen years. In my earliest recollection I can remember standing outside on Main Street waiting for the school bus and smelling that awful glue smell that permeated the air. It was sour and oppressive, and if I breathed it in through my nose too long, I would eventually find myself dry heaving against the stop sign on the corner of Main and Goddard. And then one day, as if by magic, the scent disappeared. I can't remember the exact time and place I was when I noticed it, but it seemed like all of a sudden, I smelled Mrs. Dailey's lilac bushes and the rows of tulips planted outside Crossman's Funeral Home. It was as if the town had suddenly come back to life.

"Nobody knows what happened," my dad told me, hauling his line back in to ascertain the bait was still on his hook. "There were eight men who worked in the factory. Stanley Ripkin owned the plant, and he had seven other guys working for him, all of them from right here in town. And then one day in July, not a one of them came home after the whistle blew quitting time." My father leaned forward and whispered in a voice that was both conspiratorial and admonishing. "It was as if they all just disappeared without a trace."

"That's impossible," I replied, my mind reeling in fascination. This was an urban legend that was literally less than a mile away from our house. I could have walked down Main Street, turned left onto Route 196, and climbed over the cyclone fence into the Fiber-Tech factory's outdoor paddock where the wood pulp was dumped by local lumber companies, and then scooped up by a big yellow Caterpillar bulldozer and dropped into the hopper that led to the underground factory. Beyond the paddock was the storage yard, where dozens of pallets of particle board lay abandoned in an enormous maze and left to rot in the elements. Most of the pressboard had turned into big piles of mush, and on hot summer days you could still smell the glue that used to hold the wood pulp together. "People don't just disappear. Something had to happen to them. What did the police find when they went to investigate?"

My father shook his head slowly, the look in his eyes confirming that all of this was true.

"They found blood. Lots of it. So much blood that the crows from the woods broke through the glass windows trying to get inside and scavenge for food. But no bodies were ever recovered. No skeletons or corpses or anything to remotely identify the crew of the Fiber-Tech factory. But here's the thing..."

My father's eyes went wide as he stared into mine.

"There was something wrong with the glue. It did something to all the people here in town. Old man Ripkin went cheap and started buying the epoxy from China, and when it got heated, it released some kind of toxins into the air. Sniffing it here outside the plant was enough to cause hallucinations. All those mornings you were out waiting for the school bus. You used to tell your mom that the clouds in the sky turned into dragons, and that they frightened you when they breathed fire."

I looked deep into my dad's eyes to see if he was teasing me, but the gaze that met me was one of absolute seriousness. "You weren't the only one. People in town reported crazy things to the Lisbon Police Department. In fact, the *Lisbon Falls Ledger* dropped their crime beat column for nearly six months because of the insane reports that came in. It was scary, believe me. And then that one day came where the Fiber-Tech crew vanished. The police searched the Androscoggin River for months looking for bodies...sent divers in to search all the way down to the dam in Brunswick. They never found anything. Son, I'm going to tell you something right now; I don't *ever* want to hear that you set foot on that property. Not even on a dare. Bad things happened in that plant. I believe that eight grown men died in there. So don't you dare cross that fence. Do you understand me?"

***

I was called into the principal's office at 8:45 the next day, just before the school bell could end AP English and begin chemistry. My head was spinning just thinking about Ryan (who had not shown up for school that day) and about that goddamn glue they used in the pressboard factory. My name was announced over the intercom to report immediately, and when I passed by the school secretary and went into Mr. Gerlack's office, my parents were sitting across from him, an empty chair placed between them so that I could join them. Next to Mr. Gerlack stood our school's resource officer, Deputy Miller, whose hands were folded neatly across his chest so that his brass badge shined above his breast pocket, his gun belt in plain view at all times.

"Ryan Alton never made it to school today," Gerlack spoke calmly despite the veins pulsing in his temples. The man looked fatigued with worry, and it made me think of Ryan's father, and if the marine veteran would be pacing their little raised ranch on Goddard Street with those meat-hook fists clenched in rage or if he would be genuinely worried for his son, who was obviously transgender and living in terror. Hearing Ryan tell me his confession seemed crazy at first (and I thought of the glue from the factory, and whether it had residual effects on members of our town), but the more I thought about it, the more it made sense. If Ryan had grown his hair long and dabbed on some blush and eyeliner, I'd never have been able to tell he was a boy. But I was still a teenager then and had been repulsed by the thought of it all, that my friend had been some kind of genetic freak and that I'd been defending and protecting him while never even knowing.

"If you know where Ryan is, you need to tell us," my father said. "This isn't a joke, Billy. Ryan could be in serious danger."

"I don't know where he is," I said with very little emotion. "I'm sorry, but I can't help you."

Deputy Miller glared from his corner of the room. "Son, this isn't a game. His parents are worried sick about him. We need to get him back home safe. If he told you in confidence where he was going, it will help us get to him much quicker and bring him back home."

"You want to bring him back home safe?" My teeth were now gritting down tight in my mouth, rows of fractal enamel grinding in anger at what was going on around me. "His old man has been beating him for years. *Years!* And all of a sudden everybody gives a damn about him?"

My mother whimpered quietly in her chair. When my tirade ended, she turned and placed her hands on mine. "Billy, please. Please help them if you know where Ryan is. He's your friend. He would have told you where he was going."

"He never said a word," I lied. "I'm sorry, but I can't help you."

***

It made me sick to my stomach when Ryan told me he was going to hide out in the pressboard factory. I tried desperately to talk him out of it based on what my father had told me, but in his mind he already had everything worked out. After his father gave him the shiner, Ryan packed a sleeping bag, some food, and some camping supplies, and hid the gear in his closet. After lights-out, he simply waited for Marcus and Nadine Alton to fall asleep before he slipped out the back door and trudged through near-darkness to the Fiber-Tech factory.

"I'll have my cell phone with me," he said just before we got off the bus and went inside the school. "I'll keep it turned off so that they can't try to call me or track down my location. I'll keep it just for emergencies."

"How will I get in touch with you if I need to?" I asked.

"We'll use tree-mail... You know, like they do on *Survivor*? Across the street from the factory is the *Town of Lisbon* sign. Behind that is the tree line abutting Summer Street. There's a birch tree right out in front of the line. If you can find some kind of waterproof container, I'll leave you notes about how I'm doing. And when my parents decide to finally accept me for who I am, just leave me a note and I'll come back home."

That was the last time I saw Ryan Alton.

***

Ryan left notes for me just as he'd promised. The first note was merely scribbling that described the factory and how he was adjusting to this big adventure he was undertaking. It was less than a page long, but still confirmed every notion I'd had about the mysterious place where eight grown men had inexplicably vanished. The note read like this:

Billy,

I'm really sorry I put you through this, and I hope someday you will understand. You have no idea what it's like being me. It's awful. I wish things were different, and unless I do something drastic, things are never going to change.

The factory isn't as bad as I imagined it. The wall facing the river has huge fractures in it, where the bricks and mortar have eroded and caved in. In the daytime the river sends in a nice warm breeze that makes the air feel pleasant, but that gluey smell never seems to go away (I'm pretty sure you know what I'm talking about). I found a generator near the back of the building and it still has gas in it, so if I need electricity I'll try and get it started.

The one thing I hadn't counted on is the mess in here. There is broken bottle glass everywhere and graffiti spray-painted on the walls. This place has seen its share of horny teenagers, I guess. There's even a nasty old mattress that somebody dragged in here at some point. I suppose it's better than nothing, and I at least have my sleeping bag to give me a barrier between the beer stains and come stains on it, but it makes me miss my bed at home and it makes me sad.

I also hadn't counted on all the blood stains. They're everywhere. Something terrible must have happened in here. When I come back home, I'm going to research this place and find out what happened.

Keep me posted about how my mom is doing. I miss you already.

Ryan

***

On the second day after his disappearance, when the cops got around to upgrading Ryan's status officially to "Missing Person," search parties were sent out and the state police arrived with their recovery team and their K-9 rescue specialists. Marcus Alton provided them with clothing from Ryan's laundry hamper so they could let the dogs get his scent and try and track him down. The stupid bastards started their search over by Upland Hill Road, over by the school we went to, thinking that Ryan would have wanted to stay somewhere near civilization where he could find shelter at a moment's notice. I suspect Ryan maybe even left clues for them (he was a bright kid, after all) to throw them off his trail. I think he would have been pleased with himself if he could have stood somewhere on the periphery and watched them run around in circles as they searched for him. People from all over town volunteered to help in the search (myself included), and by later that afternoon, after school let out for the day, a skirmish line was formed and we beat our way through the woods around the high school all the way to the edge of the Androscoggin River. Of course, we were nowhere near where he was hiding.

When I got home that evening my father pulled me aside before I could sit down at the dinner table and grab some of the cold fixings of pork loin and asparagus my mother cooked for supper. He took me out to the front porch and had me sit down on one of the Adirondack chairs. He sat in the other one and lit a cigarette, then turned and looked at me.

"Billy, do you know where he is?"

"No, sir."

"You'd better tell me the truth. I won't tolerate a liar in my home. Do you understand me?"

"Dad, I don't know where he is."

My father inhaled on his Winston and breathed up a line of smoke toward the sunset.

"Ryan's dad has been abusing him. It ain't a secret, son. This is a small town and word gets around. Do you understand that?"

44

I did. Anybody that ever knew Ryan understood that his old man was a rage-a-holic ex-Marine who loathed the fact that his only son was effeminate and weak. But hearing it from an adult aggravated the hell out of me. It made me realize that grownups knew but didn't really give a shit about him or what happened to him when he went home at night into the world of that fucking psychopath bully he had for a father. It made me understand that parents had some kind of ingrained code that they lived by: mind your business and tend to your own roost. I was free to grow and experience and live in privilege because I fit into the mold society deemed normal. Kids like Ryan knew no such luxury. Learning this made me hate my father for endorsing it and it made me hate Ryan for exacerbating it.

"Dad, I don't know where he is. But in all honesty, I can't blame him for running away. If his father really cared about him...if *anybody* cared about him, he'd have nothing to be afraid of and none of this would have happened."

***

Ryan's next note made me afraid.

I returned to the birch tree and found it tucked in the Tupperware container I'd hocked from my mom's kitchen. I went there after school that Friday and found the note waiting for me, just as I knew it would be. Ryan would have nothing but time on his hands and an urge to sort out all the shit he was going through mentally. When I read the letter, I once again felt sick to my stomach.

Billy,

I made it through the night, but I have to confess I was scared as hell. The factory in the daytime feels safe. Sunlight falls through the broken glass windows and through the gaping holes in the riverside wall, and it feels like some kind of summer camp. There's about a thousand places to hide inside the factory, and that came in very handy. At one point a bunch of policemen showed up with some tracking hounds. I was able to duck out of sight as they barged in, with their dogs sniffing and yelping. I thought for sure they had me, but I think the scent of the glue must have gotten to those dogs because after a few short minutes they became agitated and started attacking each other. They had to wrestle the dogs apart, and one of the officers blurted out, "The kid obviously ain't here. Let's move on while we still have sunlight."

But when the sun goes down and the shadows grow, it almost feels like hell. I brought my iPod and some earphones, and listening to music helped distract me, but I never really feel safe here. Something awful happened in this place. There's an aura of violence and hurt in the atmosphere, and it grows deeper once the sun goes down.

I don't know what you are going through because of me, and that makes me hurt. A lot. The last time we spoke, I told you that I thought I was supposed to be born a girl. I shouldn't have said that, and it's far too late to take it back. Billy, I've told you you're my best friend ever since we met back before kindergarten, but I want to be honest with you. You deserve it for all I've asked of you. I'm in love with you. All those times I've followed you around and pretended to do what you wanted me to, that was me secretly wanting to be every girl you ever had a crush on. I can't tell you how much it has hurt me to listen to all of your schoolboy crushes and how much I've wished on every star in the sky that it could be me you were pining for. Life is so fucking unfair. Right now you just want to be sure I'm okay and I'm safe. As I write this, I wish I could be what I was supposed to be. I wish I was beautiful and complete in the way I was supposed to be. I wish you could understand that, because my parents never will and society never will and I'm here and alone and I'm tired of hurting inside.

I don't know how this is going to end. Part of me hopes I die in here, and that I join the restless spirits that seem to haunt this place. Maybe all of this is for the best.

Ryan

***

I made it back to the birch tree three more days after that last letter, but Ryan remained silent. I thought about just going over the fence and storming the Fiber-Tech factory to find him, but I was filled with fear over my father's admonitions and fear of being followed and exposing the truth. And, truth be told, I was afraid of that place. My dad's story was enough to make my belly squirm with butterflies and poison the thoughts in my head about trying to help Ryan. By that point, the whole state of Maine was aware of Ryan's disappearance, and the FBI was called in to ascertain the odds that Ryan Alton was even still alive. I spent the course of that time sick to my stomach, wondering if I should go against my father's warnings and jump the cyclone fence into the Fiber-Tech property and find my friend, or if I should just wait everything out to see what would happen.

By that point, Ryan's parents were desperate to discover the fate of their only child. At least his mother was. Nadine Alton had given interviews to anyone who would listen to her, begging for her child to come home and that she wanted to help her boy work things out while there was still time. Nobody ever considered going back to the pressboard factory after the incident with the rescue dogs. The Fiber-Tech plant was somehow looked upon as "the bad place," and it appeared that no one in their right mind would try to find sanctuary there. To that end, Ryan was right.

One week after his disappearance I returned to the birch tree. When I arrived at the clearing behind the *Town of Lisbon* sign, I was met by the volatile shriek of two crows pecking and arguing amongst themselves over some meager quarry they'd found in the tall grass. I ignored them and went behind the tree to the Tupperware container I left for our correspondence and found a new note from Ryan. I pulled the lid off the plastic bin and unfolded the paper.

The note filled me with complete revulsion.

Billy,

I've made the change.

They will never find Ryan Alton after today. He's completely gone. I am all that is left. I hope someday I will find you and you will understand and love me for who I am.

Rihanna

I felt the air go out of my lungs as I tried to comprehend my friend's message. I kept staring at the little heart she drew over the "i" in her name and felt my knees weaken, and before I knew what happened my legs buckled and I fell down on my ass. I clutched Rihanna's note to my chest and let my eyes scan the woods around me. All I could hear was the sound of the crows, battling and pecking at each other over the meal they were fighting for. When I realized what it was, I screamed.

The crows were tugging and pecking at my friend's severed penis. Black beaks and yellow talons tugged and yanked until the sinew and blood vessels in it became exposed in a bloody mess of mutilated flesh. I watched in terror, the knot growing tighter in my stomach as my mind played tricks on me, replacing the crows with images of father and son battling each other over the younger one's identity. It occurred to me that Ryan's dad, the jarhead marine that would punch his only son in the face for believing he was supposed to be a girl, could possibly find out that I *knew* where Ryan was all this time and said nothing. I felt the world grow cold around me as my eyes went dark and I slipped into shock, wondering if Ryan's dad would be mad enough to kill me in cold blood for not saying anything.

By the time I came to, it was dark outside and the crows and the mutilated bit of flesh were long gone.

***

In July of 2002, Stanley Ripkin and his crew showed up for work at the Fiber-Tech pressboard factory. They all punched the clock and started what would be their final shift of manufacturing particle board at the little plant on the bank of the Androscoggin River. I suspect by that point the glue had eaten into the soft gray area of their brains, allowing them to conjure bad ideas and plot terrible schemes. It's a small town here in Lisbon, and in small towns gossip is king. For all I know, one of the workers suspected another of looking a bit too longingly at his wife, or that a secret enmity was brewing between other workers over a myriad of reasons. In small towns, secrets are disguised soldiers of dissent. It wouldn't take much, really, to bring things to a boil: a hot day, some bad blood between coworkers, perhaps a toxic chemical that was supposed to bond wood pulp but somehow didn't. No bodies were ever found when the Fiber-Tech plant was searched that day. Nobody knows what became of those eight men. Just like nobody knows what became of Ryan Alton, although I suspect I do.

I suspect that the glue got to his brain. Being inside that place and breathing that air must have been disastrous. There had to have been plenty of tools inside that decrepit old building, the kind that a seventeen-year-old high school kid could find after days of breathing in those toxic fumes and perform surgery on himself. At night when I drift off to sleep, I dream of Ryan Alton in that shell of decayed brick and mortar and blood, placing his genitals on a table that at one time had been the template for an 8' x 4' particle board and castrating himself with a hammer and chisel. Or maybe even a rock instead of a hammer. I can't even fathom the pain he went through, hoping to become the creature he was convinced he was supposed to be. All the while, the ghosts of those eight missing men watching and egging him on.

After I found the note, I finally went to the police. I found that I did not have the courage to jump the cyclone fence and find out if my friend was still there inside the pressboard factory. In my mind's eye, I could imagine him cowering in the corner, the place where his genitals once resided turned into a bloody mess of damaged tissue and veins and infected flesh. If Ryan thought that his self-surgery was all he needed to transform himself, he was wrong. There would be no vagina; no birth canal nor urethra to urinate through. There would only be an eternally wounded wasteland below his pubic mound, and a broken mind desperately trying to make herself whole again.

When the police arrived at the factory and searched it from top to bottom, no trace of Ryan or Rihanna was found.

***

The smell of glue makes me sick, and I have good cause. It's been five years since I last saw Ryan Alton. The Fiber-Tech factory was sold to a new owner only two months ago, and the town is once again filled with the stench of hot glue as a new crew of workers produces particle board. The stench lingers, overpowers, and I feel that wave of nausea creeping up on me all over again. Ryan Alton's body was never recovered from the factory, and his disappearance adds to the mystery of the pressboard factory. But there have been times in town where I've been waiting in line at the Rite-Aid or standing in line to order at McDonald's and noticed a young woman with long blonde hair watching me. This phantom figure always remains in my periphery, and disappears before I can make eye contact, but I know if I did, I'd see pretty blue orbs flecked in gold that once belonged to a boy I knew. I know that if I looked too long in them, my heart would break and my mind would fill with thoughts of clouds that looked like dragons that breathed fire, and that somewhere in the distance I'd hear crows cawing and fighting over some damned prey that was about to become extinct, that was about to disappear from the world without a trace. Their shrieks echo in my head and make me want to scream.

Mr. Expendable

Bruno DeAngelo was both surprised and irritated to see so many faces at his retirement party.

He let his eyes scan around the dinner tables set up in the Gleason Theater, taking in the sight of nearly two hundred friends and colleagues from his working days. Some were dressed to the nines in their fancy tuxedos and evening gowns, as if this was some kind of award ceremony. Others wore fancy suits and expensive shoes and designer cocktail dresses (there was always an air of competition among these people, always a need to steal the spotlight). Bruno glanced down at his own apparel: a charcoal-grey number at least a decade old. He'd bought it on the occasion of his wife Lydia's funeral, after her bout with breast cancer drained the life right out of her. He'd thought about purchasing a new suit for tonight, but eventually decided it just didn't matter all that much.

After forty-five years of appearing on the small screen, he could at least say he worked with some of the best in the business...and even if most Americans *didn't* know his name, they could at least recognize the face. He was the character-actor *T.V. Guide* once dubbed, "The Man Who Died One Thousand Deaths," and had appeared and died on virtually every televised drama, mystery, or crime show since 1968.

His first job had been a big one, and as his mind drifted back through time to that first gig (just after he dropped out of his senior year of high school and caught the Greyhound bus for Hollywood) a man pushed through the crowd to his table and held out his hand.

"Bruno...great to see you. Congratulations on an amazing career!"

Bruno extended his own hand and shook with the guest.

"Good to see you too, Bill. I'm absolutely amazed that you made it out here to join me tonight."

"I wouldn't have missed it," the man answered. "You know what they say... Nobody gives 'good death' like Bruno!"

This was true. Bruno DeAngelo absolutely had star quality. He had the rough, chiseled face of Rock Hudson and the body of Rocky Marciano. He could remember the way the young woman at the portrait studio all but drooled on his toes as she snapped his face shots for his portfolio, and how she'd whispered to him, "You're gonna be a star someday," as he forked over the last of his money from washing cars in the daytime and washing dishes in some greasy Hollywood dive at night. There were times in his career when he'd work with an actress and she would be wearing the very same perfume as that gal in the portrait studio, and his heart would ache to be seventeen again. He never got that photographer's name, but he'd thought about her a lot through his career. He spent many nights (as Lydia lay sleeping beside him) wondering where she was and if she would still remember him if he suddenly got the courage to go back to that portrait studio and find her.

Now, shaking hands with William Shatner, Bruno's mind raced back to the dressing room, back to when he got his first acting gig on *Star Trek*. He remembered the wardrobe lady handing him the "red suit." He remembered the way she chuckled as she explained that the red suit was the kiss of death, and that he should be expecting to get vaporized by a phaser blast before the episode was even half over. Bruno snatched the script off his table and began thumbing through it, severely dismayed and disappointed at the news. From the next room over, he could hear the voices of famed show creator Gene Roddenberry and writer Harlan Ellison bickering over plot points (and quite frankly, the little writer fellow frightened him). Shatner and Nimoy were already on the set working through their dress rehearsal. Bruno scanned through the script and found his one and only line:

"Captain, they're coming this way!"

...and then, just as the wardrobe lady told him, he gets blasted to smithereens. He scarcely had time to set the script back down when the production assistant leaned in the door and said, "They're ready for you."

Bruno was coached all the way to the set, some intergalactic planet scene where other extras dressed in rubber suits were milling about, waiting for their inclusion in the final dress rehearsal.

"You don't talk while you are on the set," the production assistant began. "You don't approach the cast members. You don't interfere with props, equipment, or set design. You may move about freely behind the yellow line while we're not recording, but once the director calls 'Action!' you are to remain on your mark and wait for your cue. Got it?"

"Yeah, I got it," the eighteen-year-old version of Bruno replied, still in awe at appearing on television's biggest science-fiction program.

The cast did two dry-runs of the scene, and then the director yelled "Action!" and Bruno died his first on-air death. His screen time lasted only five seconds, but what a five seconds it was! When the scene was over, both Shatner and Nimoy extended their hands and picked him up off the ground. Nimoy dusted him off with a smooth Vulcan hand and commented, "I hope that looked as good on film as it did in real life." Shatner smiled and nodded. "Yeah, this kid's got a hell of a future ahead of him."

It was only five seconds, but that gig led to another gig. And that gig led to another. And another. And another.

At some point Shatner had moved on, and Bruno found his eyes scanning around the room. He saw a lot of fellow character-actors mingling about and hoisting drinks and making small talk. Working stiffs, just like him, that had gotten a break in show biz but not that fabled *Big Break* that led to fame and fortune. A few of them had landed bit parts on the big screen, but those big moments were always peppered with the harsh reality that most of the footage shot of them ended up on the cutting room floor, and the brief nanoseconds they saw of themselves on-screen were instantly forgettable moments, where they were either eclipsed by the celebrity actors or the roles they were cast in just weren't all that important to the script. At least for Bruno, on those few occasions he *did* make it onto the screen, his role as "the guy who got shot/stabbed/poisoned/strangled" had some import to the movie or to the program. He was relevant even if his screen time lasted about ten seconds.

Bruno had to laugh as he picked up the pamphlet and glanced over its contents. The pamphlet read: BRUNO DeANGELO; CELEBRATING THE CAREER OF MR. EXPENDABLE. This whole retirement party had been his agent Walter Merrill's idea. Bruno had fought and protested it, but Wally was insistent that both Hollywood and Television owed it to America's favorite victim to pay their homage and respect to a man that elevated the standards of the dramatic demise. Wally had gone so far as to have his research assistant track down all the shows and films Bruno died in, listing his credits right in the pamphlet. Bruno ran down the list of character names and sighed.

"Soldier 3" — *M*A*S*H**

"Victim 5" — *Kolchack, The Night Stalker*

"Deceased Husband" — *Murder, She Wrote*

"Desert Victim" — *CSI*

The list went on and on. Over two hundred television programs and a dozen movies (and a far cry from the 1,000 deaths he was credited with). Sometimes his credit had a character's name listed, but mostly just a non-descript term to denote that Bruno DeAngelo had played *somebody*, and that somebody died before they could utter a single phrase and become crucial to the story.

And that was their trick...speaking roles pay better than non-speaking rolls. How much had the business cheated him out of by relegating him to non-speaking parts?

But I DID have some speaking parts. Not a lot, but enough to have been discovered. Enough to be recognized by people...

This was true as well, but the speaking parts came mostly *after* he joined the union. The Screen Actors Guild was just one more hand in his pocket, and based on those bit parts he kept getting, he could scarcely afford it. But at least the roles he was getting improved. He'd had speaking parts on *S.W.A.T., Miami Vice, NYPD BLUE,* and *ER,* just to name a few off the top of his head. Bruno also had a very good role in a made-for-television movie about Leon Ray Hickey, the serial killer from Albany, New York. That one was called *Cold Blooded Beast,* and had Bruno credited as "Deputy Crane." In the movie, Deputy Crane had been one of the cops that had chased Hickey back to his apartment on Ontario Street, but was stabbed to death with a butcher knife after kicking down the door and rushing in.

"You forget to check your blind-spot," the assistant producer explained (he'd been a cop himself, and had been hired onto the project as a technical advisor). "Hickey will come up behind you with the fake knife and slit your throat. You just drop on the floor and convulse as your blood leaves your body. But don't drag it out too long... We want to keep it real."

The paycheck from that gig barely covered the rent, but he gladly took it. Just like every other check he'd received. And that was back in 1981.

More guests made their way to his table and shook his hand. He recognized and shook hands with a lot more celebrity actors than he'd first calculated. Some were from shows back in the early seventies, shows that most of the current programming demographic had never even heard of. Others were folks that he'd worked with just this past season; kids, practically, that he knew in his heart had a lot less talent than he had.

So *why* hadn't it been him? Where did he go wrong in his career?

Because at some point you became a running joke. For every leading man and starlet in Hollywood, a thousand lives are broken. You were a casualty, just like a lot of other folks like you, who tried to follow their dream and failed.

It wasn't fair! It just wasn't fucking fair!

Kind of like tonight.

Bruno wasn't sure at what point he'd decided to go through with it, but now here it was, far too late for anything to be done about it.

At some point in his career, he'd just given up. He wasn't sure at what point it was, but there eventually came that final realization that he was *never* going to be a leading man, *never* going to catch that big break that he kept thinking was just around the corner. Fame was so elusive, and even if people *did* recognize his face on those off occasions where he was out shopping at the grocery store and the woman in line behind him gasped and asked him if he was *that guy*, it meant nothing. It meant that he faked another death in front of the camera, and someone recognized his face. The Facebook community was still abuzz with the episode of *Criminal Minds* that aired two weeks ago (his very last paying gig), where the victim had his head severed clean off, and how real it looked as the head rolled across the victim's linoleum floor. Gruesome. And memorable enough for that lady at the Social Security office to have her jaw drop as he passed her his retirement paperwork.

"I *know* you!" she blubbered as she stamped and signed his papers. "It looked so *real* when the killer chopped off your head. How do they do that?"

Bruno DeAngelo was never going to be a star. But just this once, this *one* time, he was going to be the last person standing.

At some point, Wally (who'd agreed to be the emcee for the evening) stood up at the lectern and began to speak. Bruno didn't pay much attention to his lifelong agent (who'd failed him time and again at landing him the prime roles... This was *Wally's* fault as much as it was his own) as the man began to rattle off some rosy speech about the great Bruno DeAngelo, Hollywood's beloved MR. EXPENDABLE, who'd died more deaths than the victims of the Alamo. The speech went on, arousing some tittering laughter and occasional applause.

And then Wally was lifting his glass in a toast to the Man of the Hour, nodding and smiling politely right at Bruno as he finished his little spiel, held his glass to his lips, and began to drink.

The rest of the audience followed suit, each lifting their glass of champagne to their lips and drinking.

Everyone except Bruno DeAngelo.

There was a standing ovation as Bruno rose to his feet and made his way to the lectern. He thanked everyone politely, gently trying to urge them all to their seats. It wasn't going to take long now.

It had been a laborious task, but one that he didn't seem to mind. Ten cases of champagne had been delivered to the Gleason Theater (named after the great Jackie Gleason, another hero of television that today's audience demographic had probably never even heard of), with each case containing twelve bottles of champagne. A quick trip back to the CBS studio's wardrobe facility and Bruno had the appropriate costume to blend right in with the catering staff. Some would have said it was his finest acting yet, mixing in with both the theater's Latino crew and the caterer's banquet team. All he needed was time alone with the champagne and with the poison he used to spike it.

He'd gotten the idea from *Monk*, the very episode where his character kicked the bucket at a wedding where a jilted lover poisoned the punch at the reception. Bruno remembered Tony Shalhoub as being one of the nicest guys he'd ever met, and was secretly thankful that Tony wasn't among the guests that were about to take their last breath. One hundred and twenty bottles of champagne (not Dom Perignon but the cheaper stuff), each tampered with just enough to inject a quick syringe of toxins, waiting to be uncorked and consumed by the unsuspecting crowd.

To hell with them! To hell with them all, with this condescending ruse to somehow make me feel better for being the laughingstock of Hollywood.

The first victim began to gasp. It was an extra he'd worked with on *Tales from the Crypt*. The man, a portly fellow that had gotten acting gigs as the stereotypical "fat guy" (as if *that* didn't seem like something to be ashamed of in Hollywood...and yet he took those gigs with a smile and carried it all the way to the bank), stood to his feet and began to jerk at his tie and collar. There was a murmur of whispers in the crowd as guests watched the man's face turn white, then purple. The man panted and gasped and wheezed until his throat finally seized on him, and then his chunky frame fell hard to the ground.

The crowd gasped, watching in terror as the waitstaff rushed over to help. And then the theater's security team was rushing in to offer further assistance. From outside the theater, the wail of an ambulance siren further distressed the evening's activities.

Walter "Wally" Merrill pushed past Bruno to the lectern and began to speak.

"Calm down, everybody... Please, if you just take your seats and calm down... Just let the paramedics do their..."

Wally's face also began to turn ash white. He coughed for a few moments, turned, and threw up his meal all over the podium. He was still hurling and choking as his knees buckled below him and he collapsed, dropping into his own vomit. He writhed for a few more seconds before his life passed from his body.

In the audience, a young starlet also began coughing and hacking. Bruno recognized her immediately, recalling the sordid tales of her falling onto a casting couch to land her first big break. She had signed a contract to appear as the heroine in a new Marvel Comics superhero movie, but that plan now winked out of existence like a falling star.

She looks like Lydia, he thought. *She looks just like how Lydia did just before she passed away on me. All skin and bones and...*

Bruno thought of his late wife, and how it was just before she died. The cancer had robbed her of everything that made her the stunningly attractive redhead he first fell in love with. Lydia had discovered the lumps while he was off filming that Stephen King miniseries in '98. He took some time to be with her during the radical mastectomy, hoping and praying they'd saved enough money away to cover the medical bills along with their day-to-day expenses while he was out of work. He could still hear himself whispering to her, "We're going to beat this," as he stroked her sweating forehead. The chemo and radiation treatments had put an end to that long, beautiful red hair of hers. Bruno had purchased a few wigs for her, but Lydia always refused them, instead taking to wearing silk scarfs or colored bandanas. He remembered toward the end how he broke down and cried, wailing, "This isn't fair! I'm supposed to die *first*," at the top of his lungs. Lydia simply looked up at him from her bed and smiled. "Sweetheart, I've spent years watching *you* die first. This time, it's *my* turn."

Another audience member clutched his chest and began coughing. Then another. Then another. People were getting out of their seats in a wave of panic, all screaming and crying and running for the doors, but falling stone dead after only a few steps. Bruno scanned about the room to see if Shatner was still around, but that slippery shit had beat feet just after offering his congratulations. He hadn't even stayed long enough for the toast. No matter. The rest of the room was awash in vomit and piss and shit as body after body collapsed and died. It was simply amazing. After forty-five years in the business, it appeared that Bruno still had a lot to learn about the way people died in real life.

Chaos reigned. The living guests were now crawling over dead bodies, bumbling and stumbling and trying to find their escape. It was, in a word, pitiful.

Just like Bruno's career. Just like Lydia's death.

The ordeal lasted almost five whole minutes (way longer than that first death scene he shot back on *Star Trek*), but for him, it was the best five minutes of his career. After five minutes, he was the only living person left in the room. Even the rescue team had fled, fearing that perhaps a toxic gas had been released, which they weren't prepared to deal with. It was thrilling, captivating to watch.

Bruno smiled as he gazed at the corpses on the floor. He had one last scene to perform, but now there were no cameras, no audience to watch.

It was Bruno DeAngelo's finest performance.

"Here's to you, Lydia," he said, and felt the tears begin to well up in the corners of his eyes. "I've missed you so much since you've been gone."

He picked up his champagne flute and took a sip.

Portrait of an Old Woman with Crows

The crows were never going to stand still, so Marie had to use quick brush strokes to capture their essence and their positions, knowing she'd have to go back and add detail. The crows cawed madly and flapped their wings as they strutted around the old woman's feet. They pecked nervously at each other as they waited for her wrinkled old hand to reach back inside the burlap sack and disperse another spray of corn kernels. The old woman paid no attention to the young lady in the green smock and denim jeans as she dipped her brushes against the blotches of oil paint on her pallet and set upon her canvas. For all Marie knew, the old woman was gazing upon the water in the fountain or at the turning foliage. Deering Park in early October was spectacular to behold, with the fiery red and gold and orange leaves creating an inferno in the heart of the city.

Marie worked with fierce determination. The painting needed to be completed by Monday in order to turn it in for her art class, and Professor Jennings wasn't the kind of teacher who would suffer excuses to allow life to get in the way of art. Beyond the looming deadline for her second big project of the semester, her son Conner needed to be picked up from playschool by noon, which meant she wasn't going to finish the painting anyway. She just needed enough time to capture the old woman's figure and the pattern of the crows around her, and to define composition and space. Details could always be filled in later, like after Conner went to bed for the night and before Josh came home from working second shift at the B&M Baked Beans plant. Josh would want a dinner that consisted of anything other than hot dogs and baked beans, and then a few beers and a bit of intimate time before settling down and falling asleep for the night. The old woman on the bench was at least fifty yards away, and after sitting there for hours doing nothing but feeding the crows by her feet, it wasn't like she gave a damn either way. If she got up now and walked away, Marie would still eventually finish her painting and get the grade she needed from Professor Jennings. The assignment had been to capture something nostalgic, and what was more nostalgic in America than an old woman on a park bench feeding the birds?

She dipped her brush against the pallet and swept up a blob of ebony to finish the strokes on her final crow. Marie had not counted how many crows there actually were, but rather embellished both for time's sake and for her own sanity. Those goddamn beasts kept flapping and hopping around and pecking at each other whenever the old crone dropped another spray of corn on the ground. On her canvas, the replication of the old woman was mostly complete; the subject was draped in a long, flowered dress and a black shawl and a hat that Marie was pretty sure was called a snood, with a black veil over her eyes and long ebon feathers jutting over the back. In the painting, the woman was holding her hand out and dropping kernels of corn on the ground while the crows gathered at her feet, squabbling and puffing out their tailfeathers to show dominance among each other.

The alarm went off on Marie's cell phone. She pulled the device from her pocket, shut off the alarm bell, and started to gather her paints and accoutrements. Conner would be moody if he was the last child to be picked up from Miss Kristina's playschool, and then she'd spend the car ride home listening to the four-year-old pitch a tantrum and wonder why the hell she'd chosen to have Josh's baby in the first place. It hadn't been like Josh put a diamond ring on her finger, or...

The old woman was standing right behind her. It was as if she'd closed the fifty-yard gap between them in the blink of an eye.

"God's eye is on the sparrow," the old woman said, her voice a chorus of bullfrog croaks and formaldehyde. Her bony hand shot out and grabbed Marie's wrist, forcing her to drop her paintbrush in the dying grass below. "But Satan's eye watches from the crows."

Marie stifled the scream from her mouth as she looked through the veil on the old crone's hat (*Yes, it's definitely a snood,* she thought for no reason at all, and then the bubble of panic burst inside her and the thought flew away). Behind the mesh fabric was a pair of glazed hazel orbs, laden with cataracts, and she found herself wondering how the old woman could even see. Eyes *that* cloudy had to be blind. Staring into those orbs made her think of wretched old goats deformed from years of inbreeding.

"You didn't ask my permission before you painted me," the old woman croaked. Her lips formed a distasteful snarl, exposing blackened gums around crooked teeth. She reached her free hand up to the ugly old hat on her head and plucked out a long, black feather. Before Marie could protest, the woman gouged the prickly nub of the quill into the skin of Marie's wrist and carved a long, bloody trail. "You will repay me for taking without asking, young lady."

Marie saw the blood spill down the warm skin of her fingers and onto the ground. Yanking her hand away from the old crone, Marie slapped her paint rag on the wound. The crows over by the bench cawed, screaming bloody murder at the offense, but when Marie turned to face her accuser and protest, the old woman was gone.

***

"Thank goodness you're here," Miss Kristina said as Marie entered the foyer of the *Amazing Tots* playschool. The unfinished "Portrait of an Old Woman with Crows" was nestled neatly in the trunk of her Honda Accord (although the *real* old woman had never escaped her mind since the assault back in the park. In fact, her heart still racing with fear pounded faster every time she looked at the bloody fabric tied around her wrist), waiting to be completed after her and Conner were home. Miss Kristina looked both frightened and embarrassed as she crossed the romper area to speak with her. The room was quiet—too quiet—and Marie noticed the other children sitting around the worktable and looking at her son in horror. Their faces were all sealed lips and wide eyes as they gathered away from him at the far side of the table and gawked at Conner. Conner's eyes leaked tears down his ashen face. Marie moved closer and noticed that her son's wrist was wrapped in gauze and a length of eggshell-blue bandage. "We were sitting at the table working on tracing the letter Q when Conner took his pencil and started gouging it into his wrist. It was the scariest thing I've ever seen. His eyes rolled back into his head, and he just rammed the pencil into his skin...like he was trying to stab a mouse or something. I yanked the pencil out of his hand, but by then he was bleeding all over the table. I got him cleaned up and put the bandage on him." Miss Kristina leaned closer and spoke in a hushed, conspiratorial voice. "As I wrapped the bandage around his arm, he kept whispering, 'This is all Mommy's fault.' It's an absolute miracle he didn't puncture any arteries."

Dread filled Marie's belly. She walked past the other children and wrapped her arms around Conner's tiny frame and squeezed him tight. "It's okay, honey. Mommy is here now. Let's get home and we'll figure out some lunch. Maybe we can have a bowl of ice cream for dessert. Would you like that, baby?"

Conner lifted his face to look at his mother. "You have a boo-boo just like mine," he said. There was no emotion in his voice, no trace of concern or remorse or fear. He could have been reading lines from a teleprompter or discussing the weather. This was *not* the little boy who threw his arms around his mother and lavished her with kisses every time she picked him up from playschool.

"I'm so sorry this happened," Miss Kristina said from somewhere behind her. "I wish there could have been something I could have done to prevent it. It breaks my heart seeing him acting like this."

Marie slipped her hands under her son's armpits and picked him up. She held Conner close as she moved past the other children and over toward the cubby area to collect his jacket and backpack. Miss Kristina was right on her heels, still talking to her (talking *at* her), but Marie was having trouble focusing on anything other than how her wound and Conner's were in the same exact location. "He's never had behavior issues like this before. This could be leading to something serious. I'm very concerned that he might try something like this again in my classroom. I can't have him hurting himself or the other children. Do you understand what I'm saying?"

"This won't happen again," Marie said over her shoulder. "We'll have him looked at over the weekend." She opened the door as the parade of parents arrived to collect their own children. Her cheeks flushed with embarrassment just thinking about the other children running their mouths off at their dinner tables that evening about what Conner Lynch did to himself at school today, and just what those other parents would speculate about her and Josh and how they were raising their son.

In the back of her mind, she could hear the old woman on the park bench laughing.

***

It took a hot bubble bath and a bowl of ice cream just to get Conner to return to the happy, vibrant little boy that he usually was. Marie decided to not mention what happened to him (or herself) to Josh, who was still sleeping up in their bedroom when she and Conner got home, and would discuss the whole thing later after their son was asleep and Josh returned from work at midnight. Now that Conner was back to normal, she could settle him in the den, in front of the television for the PBS Kids afternoon lineup (in Marie's mind, PBS stood for Public Babysitting Station, with Elmo and Curious George as ersatz conductors on the cartoon railways), and return to work on her painting.

Or did she really want to?

The thought crossed her mind as she retrieved the painting and her equipment from her Honda. Opening the trunk and reaching in, she noticed that her painting had changed—only a little bit, but enough to make her blood run cold. When she was working in the park, she'd painted the old woman looking out toward the Deering Park fountain, her outstretched hand dropping kernels of corn toward the crows...

Satan's eye watches from the crows!

...by her feet. Now the old woman was staring back directly at her, and in her other hand was the feather she'd used to assault her. Seeing it made her wound burn and throb under the new bandage she'd put on after giving Conner his bath.

You didn't ask permission.

"I don't *need* your fucking permission. And I don't have time to start a new painting. I need to get this finished and turned in so I don't fail my course." Marie yanked the painting unceremoniously from the trunk and hauled it up to her studio. If she had to, she would repaint the old woman so that her face looked back out at the water, and she would remove that feather and replace it with a hot dog or a squirt gun or a big yellow rubber dildo if she so chose. This painting was *hers*, and she would do as she pleased with it. With the portrait in one hand and her easel and box of brushes and oils in the other, she raced up to her studio room above the garage.

***

Her cell phone rang at 10:17 that evening, long after she'd fed Conner and herself a dinner of fish sticks and broccoli with cheese sauce and tucked her son into bed. Conner had remained happy and animated all evening, as if the whole episode at playschool never even happened. Marie steeled herself to not even bring it up with him, to let herself forget the whole incident, and she found herself shaken when the child in the Mickey Mouse pajamas brought it up anyway.

"I didn't want to hurt myself today," Conner said. His eyebrows furrowed with worry, causing his bright blue eyes to squint. "I tried not to, but she made me."

"Who made you, sweetie?" Marie sat down on the bed next to her son and stroked her fingers through his shaggy blond hair.

"The old woman. She showed up at school today while we were working on our letters. She told me she could teach me how to fly like the birds." The little boy with blond, curly locks and Mickey Mouse pajamas leaned forward and whispered, "Her eyes were awful. They made me scared so I did what she said."

Panic welled deep inside her. Marie's mind jumped to the nearly completed painting in her studio, where the old woman was once again facing the water. She had to use some heavy oils to correct the old woman's visage (and she added quite a few details as well, like those nasty cataracts that looked more like the eyes of a blind goat than a human's) and improved the composition of the crows around her feet. A few more hours on Saturday and Sunday and the painting would be finished, but where would the old woman be? Could she be watching right now? Did she already know the damage she'd inflicted on her son? There was no doubt that the old woman Conner was referring to was *her...*

You didn't ask permission.

***

Her cell phone rang.

After Conner fell asleep, Marie decided she did not want to return to the studio and face the portrait. Doing so would only serve to unhinge her, and that was the last thing she wanted while alone in the house with Conner, waiting for Josh to get home from work, so instead she fixed some sleepy-tea and snuggled up in bed. In the end, sleep won out and she dozed off.

She rolled over and plucked her phone off the bedside table and looked at the number of the incoming call.

It was Josh.

She pressed the on button and offered a sleepy "Hello?"

Josh's voice sounded panicked, and she knew something had to be wrong.

"Honey, it's me... Listen, I fell asleep in the locker room during my lunch break and had the most horrible dream. I dreamt you and Conner were here at the bean factory. For some reason, we were all standing up on the roof, just beneath the neon B&M sign. You were holding Conner in your arms, and you had this crazy look in your eyes. When I asked you what you were doing, you told me you were going to teach Conner how to fly. And then...and then you pitched our son off the roof. I watched Conner fall past the windows, flapping his arms like he could fly or something, and then he just splattered all over the parking lot. And you smiled. You smiled the whole time like you were satisfied with yourself. I know it sounds crazy, but I just wanted to hear your voice, and to hear that you are both okay."

"Oh, honey, I'm sorry," Marie answered, secretly thanking the stars above that she hadn't discussed with him what happened in the park earlier or what happened to Conner's wrist at playschool. Josh hadn't even noticed the bandage as he made his routine stumble from the bedroom to the bathroom to do his business, shower, and get dressed for work for the night. Life with her boyfriend meant cleaning up his clothes from the night before (the ones reeking of baked beans and molasses) and getting them into the washing machine before they made the house smell like an Elks Club barbecue. "It was just a dream. We're both fine here. Conner went right to sleep when I put him down."

Josh's voice sounded immediately relieved. "I swear to God, it was so real. Marie, your eyes looked so damned vacant and empty. It was like there was no soul looking through them. It was like looking into a bird's eyes."

That made her shiver.

Satan's eye watches from the crows.

"It was just a bad dream, sweetie. You're probably just overtired. Get home soon and come to bed with me. I miss you."

"Miss you too, hon."

After she hung up the phone she sat up, yawned, and climbed out of bed. She needed to pee, and wanted to stop in Conner's room and give him an extra kiss goodnight. Josh's dream scared her the more she thought about it, particularly after being told she tossed her child to his death off the rooftop of the baked bean canning plant.

When she entered Conner's room, his bed was empty.

***

Marie Lynch tore through the raised ranch on Hawthorne Drive screaming Conner's name as she darted from room to room. The house sat quiet in reply, an icy tomb of quaint New England décor and domestic frailties. The only sound to be heard was her heart pounding in her chest, and the accusatory caw of some lone crow in one of the treetops outside the back window. It called in a shriek that insisted, "You didn't ask permission." She raced up the staircase at the back of the house and burst through the door to her studio, where she found Conner in his Mickey Mouse pajamas, sucking his thumb and staring at the painting.

Tears of relief sliding down her cheeks, she hurried up behind him, throwing her arms around his tiny frame, and then gasped in terror as she gazed upon "Portrait of an Old Woman with Crows." In the picture, the old woman had vanished completely. Instead was a new figure, dangling from a noose that held taut from a tree limb somewhere outside the picture. The figure was dressed in a green smock and denim jeans, and Marie had no difficulty discerning that this was herself in the portrait, that the old woman had somehow changed things around. Below the cadaverous version of herself was a wooden sign staked into the ground where the crows continued their vigil. The sign was painted in blood-red letters: *This Is What We Do To Witches!*

"Come on, sweetie, let's go back downstairs," she whispered to Conner. The little boy remained frozen in place, staring at the painting. Marie knelt beside him and tried to turn him away, but when she did, she noticed that his irises had turned from blue to raven black. Feathers sprouted out of his pajama collar in long, dark plumes that made his neck shine in the overhead light.

Marie screamed in horror.

***

Her eyes flew open.

The whole thing had been a nightmare. A dream and nothing more. Her family was sleeping safe and sound in their house on Hawthorne Drive. It was nearly six a.m. on Saturday morning according to the digital clock on Josh's side of the bed, and by the smell of the lingering odor of baked beans, Josh had probably fallen asleep with his work clothes still on. This was fine. She could deal with the baked beans scent. She wouldn't even scold him over it.

She picked up her cell phone and examined the call log. The phone showed no record of receiving a call from Josh the evening before, and that was also a good thing. Just chalk it all up to a stressful afternoon, on top of worrying about getting that stupid painting done and turning it in to Professor Jennings on time. Marie realized that she'd been making such a huge deal about obtaining the professor's approval and getting a decent grade that she had put too much stress on herself. Getting the arts degree had been a luxury idea more than it had been about establishing a career. It was getting her out of her house for a few hours every day now that Conner was old enough for playschool. It was a refuge for a stay-at-home mom, who probably should have been working a part-time job to help cover the bills so that Josh wasn't always at work. All of this had just been a stress-related dream.

The wound on her wrist prickled in disagreement, and Marie had to stifle the scream to keep from waking her husband up.

The wound on her arm was real.

What happened in the park was real.

Marie sprinted to Conner's room before she could carry the logic any further.

***

Conner was sound asleep in his bed. The nightlight shined from one of the outlets in the corner, but Marie decided to flip the overhead light on anyway. Her heart racing once again, Marie found herself terrified of what she would see when the room was illuminated.

Her worries were in vain. Conner's eyes were sealed shut with blessed sleep. There were no feathers protruding from his Mickey Mouse pajamas, nor were there any signs that he had gotten up at any point in the middle of the night.

There was also no bandage around his wrist, and no puncture wound where her child had stabbed himself with a pencil back at playschool. There was only warm, pale, unmarked skin. Marie lifted his arm up to examine it close, but when she did, Conner's eyes flew open.

"I'm trying to sleep, Mommy."

"I know, honey. Just close your eyes and go back to bed. I just needed to come in and give you a kiss." Marie leaned down and planted a big, wet smack across her child's forehead. Conner tugged his arm away from her and tried to wipe the wetness of her kiss away.

"What did you do that for? You didn't ask permission."

Marie Lynch stood up and backed herself away from her son in slow, timid steps as his words echoed in her brain.

***

She staggered down the hall and up the stairs to her studio. Her mind raced in fear and panic as she fought to sort out what was reality and what wasn't. The world was spinning in chaos, and she merely skipped like a stone across its surface. The only thing she *did* understand was that it was time to destroy the painting. It was time to destroy the goddamn thing once and for all, and whatever happened afterward was going to have to be worked out and dealt with. She didn't care if she failed her art class, or if Professor Jennings berated her for wasting her talent. None of it mattered.

Marie threw the door open and flipped on the light switch. The painting sat on the easel at the far end of the room, and even from a distance she could tell that the painting had changed once again. She sidled up to it slowly, sure that some mystical hex would drag her kicking and screaming onto the canvas, but nothing happened. This time the bench was empty but the crows were still there, only they had all turned their heads to face her...

Satan's eye watches from the crows!

...and what she *hadn't* noticed before was now brutally evident. If it had been a connect-the-dots picture, she could have flown right through it without even looking at the numbers to trace the lines correctly. The crows were positioned so that they formed a large pentagram in front of the empty park bench, and just as she noticed it, she felt the ice-cold breath of the old woman on her neck.

Marie turned around and stared into those cataract-laden eyes and whimpered a timid sob.

The old woman cackled in amusement. Her laughter echoed in Marie's ears like the serenade from a murder of crows.

"I'm sorry!" Marie said to the old woman. "I'm sorry I didn't ask your permission. Please forgive me and leave me alone." Tears spilled down her cheeks, and everything went blurry. "I'll destroy the painting if you want me to. Just leave me and my family alone."

The old woman moved toward her, raising her bony old hand out in a beckoning gesture. "It's too late for that, child. You should have minded your own business and left me alone. You took away my anonymity the moment you put your brush to your canvas. Now everyone who sees this portrait of me will know I'm still here...that I never went away."

The old woman reached her other hand into the bosom of her long, black dress and removed a corn-husk doll. The cob fetish had been honed and whittled down to represent a miniaturized version of Marie. The green husks had been folded around it to resemble her artist's smock, and the golden fibers of corn hair had been pulled back into a perfect ponytail. Marie looked at the dreadful figurine and screamed at the top of her lungs.

The witch dropped the doll at Marie's feet and then Marie Lynch, devoted partner and mother, turned into a cascade of corn kernels that spilled all over the studio's floor. Outside the window, a murder of crows cawed and flapped their wings and waited for the old woman to collect their next meal in her little burlap pouch. Their eyes pierced through the window in wicked triumph as the old woman stuffed what remained of Marie Lynch in her little burlap sack.

In the portrait, a young woman with tears flowing from her eyes tried to shoo away the crows around her feet. The beasts fixed their eyes upon her, and Satan watched through them with delight.

The Ghost of John Lennon

Kasim knew a thing or two about time, having spent most of his adult life running the clock repair shop his father opened on Ventura Boulevard. He took over the shop in '68, during the Summer of Love, back when the hippie movement blossomed up north in San Francisco. It was also the same summer that his father, Mohmod al Abdul, was diagnosed with lung cancer from chain-smoking Marlboros since he and his wife Zainab came to America. Kasim had discovered The Beatles years before the doctors discovered the black spots riddling his father's lungs, but he'd suspected something was wrong when his papa's breathing became raspy and congested, leaving him doubled over his workbench as he coughed and heaved. Kasim would fold over the white cloth that nestled the cogs and springs of whatever was being fixed to keep them clean of his father's germs, all the while patting Mohmod's back and asking in a terrified voice, "Are you okay?"

At sixty-nine years old, Kasim was once again walking in his father's footsteps now that he'd been diagnosed. And trips like this, what healthy senior citizens might have referred to as a vacation or a sabbatical, he considered a pilgrimage. With the repair shop sold off to some young Latino couple (who planned on turning the old store into a tanning salon), and his own wife, Noora, predeceasing him by nearly ten years, the trip was now or never. After all, how many chances did you get in life to travel to Manhattan and follow the final footsteps of John Lennon? He knew a thing or two about time, and time was growing short.

He hadn't counted on the TSA hassling him as he checked in at LAX, questioning about his purchasing a one-way ticket and wanting to know what his plans were in New York City. They claimed it had nothing to do with racial profiling or the fact that he moved funny when he walked. He could have explained that radiation and chemo had kicked the living shit out of him, but what did it matter? It was none of their goddamn business anyway. In the words of the young man in the starched and pressed blue uniform, "It's all random, and I'm just doing my job. We have to keep *everybody* safe."

It hadn't bothered him (well, it *had*, but not enough to get angry over) that they dragged him over to a cordoned-off area beside the gate and went through his suitcase as the other passengers rubbernecked. It was that they'd taken his portable CD player and the few discs he'd brought with him and scattered them carelessly across the floor. The album on top actually made him smile. It was titled *REVOLVER*, and how funny was it that, had they been paying attention, they could have held the disc up and shouted, "See? Toldja he had a weapon!" *Because that's how America worked now.* Any asshole could legally obtain and carry a gun, and way too many of them did. But if a person of color tries to go through the airport...

Kasim hated guns. In fact, he loathed them with a passion. And so did John Lennon. The one Beatle who preached "All You Need is Love" and "Give Peace a Chance" was also the one that was shot dead outside his home in the Dakota Building on West 72nd Street. Kasim had been repairing an old Ingersoll grandfather clock when the news came on the black-and-white television mounted above the work bench, and it felt like the wind had been knocked out of him. This had been December 1980, long after Mohmod and Zainab were laid to rest in a dreary, overcrowded cemetery in Los Angeles. Kasim sat down on the floor and wept until Noora had to leave the show room out front and see if he was okay.

When they finally let him board the Boeing 787 and take his seat, he retrieved a book from his carry-on and leafed to the part about the Dakota Building. That was going to be his first destination once he checked into his hotel and caught up on some sleep. The Dakota was the first and most historic of the upscale apartment buildings in Manhattan. Lennon and his wife Yoko Ono owned several apartments in that building, and that was where his favorite Beatle had retreated so that he could sober up and be a father to his second son, Sean. In the book, Yoko mentioned seeing the ghost of John Lennon on several occasions. She claimed he would sit behind that white piano he used to record his *Double Fantasy* album, and when she entered the room, he would look up and tell her not to worry, that he would always be there with her.

Wouldn't that be something? Kasim thought as the other passengers boarded and took their seats. *Wouldn't it be amazing to see Lennon's ghost...even for a second or two?*

He was replacing his book and digging out his CD player and *MAGICAL MYSTERY TOUR* when the young portly fellow in the muscle shirt and denim shorts waddled down the aisle, stopped at his row, and frowned. Kasim could feel the suspicion radiating off this stranger, who was obviously going to be occupying the window seat beside him. Kasim offered a polite smile and stood so that the guy could stuff himself into his seat and get situated. He was anxious for the plane to taxi over to the runway and take off on time, and that meant being cooperative even if he didn't feel like it. The stranger watched him with vigilant eyes through most of the flight, particularly those moments when Kasim would pull his carry-on bag out from under the seat in front of him to swap out his Beatles discs.

Give peace a chance, my ass! he found himself thinking after the umpteenth time of catching the stranger's hateful eyes gazing on him. *What the fuck happened to America once the Summer of Love ended?*

***

Kasim al Abdul checked into the Hilton Hotel on the Avenue of the Americas and found his room on the sixth floor. The hotel was pricey and a bit more upscale than he'd have normally booked, but what the hell? This was *his* pilgrimage, and there was nobody back home to inherit any of the small fortune he'd amassed after nearly fifty years of clock repairs. There had also been a tidy life insurance check after Noora passed (she died in a car accident driving to an In-and-Out Burger to pick up their lunch one unseasonably hot April afternoon. Kasim cried as the officer in the starched blue uniform told him the news, but it hadn't been the inconsolable sobbing he'd wept when he heard the news of Mark David Chapman killing his favorite Beatle). Kasim was never one for fancy possessions or high living. He'd had friends and he'd had customers that came and went, but in the end, he discovered that the Muslim religion his parents worshipped never really measured up to the preaching of John Lennon. "Imagine no possessions," Lennon crooned in his most popular solo song. "Yes, I think I can," Kasim believed, and it was liberating. While the world around him fought to keep their rights and their material objects, they became slaves to them. Western culture was chock full of futile irony.

Kasim paid a visit to his bag of pharmaceuticals and doped himself up good and proper on Ambien before falling asleep that night. Lo and behold, it was one of the most peaceful slumbers he'd ever drifted into. *SERGEANT PEPPER* had barely reached "Fixing a Hole" when the last vestiges of consciousness floated away into a sweeping polychromatic picture show of dreams.

***

This is going to be the best day of my life, he thought as he passed through the Hilton's lobby and turned toward West 72nd Street. *I haven't felt this alive in so, so long. Not since...*

Not since he said farewell to Noora. It had rained on the day of her funeral, and he could remember standing beneath the little tent the cemetery had set up over her plot. There had only been a handful of people in attendance, her friends mostly, and he could still remember them all holding him up so that he wouldn't collapse as her casket was lowered into the dirt. At her memorial service the evening before, he'd arranged for the song "In My Life" to be played. It had been their wedding song, much to the chagrin of Noora's parents, who wanted traditional Iraqi music rather than anything Western. This had been just after Paul McCartney officially announced that The Beatles were through and that he'd formed a new solo act called Wings. The announcement had been a bitter blow to him, even though he knew The Beatles weren't getting along at all anymore. The animosity between John, Paul, George, and Ringo had been legendary. John was accusing Paul of writing "grandmother songs." The other Beatles were tired of Yoko showing up and interfering with the dynamics of the group. George was already over the hippie movement the band was spiraling into. Ringo was refusing to play. They were no longer a band. They were now strangers moving in different directions.

Of course there was animosity, Kasim thought. *The Summer of Love came and went. America was still in Vietnam and the world was in chaos. By the time the Summer of '69 came around, The Beatles were pretty much done. There would be no appearance at Woodstock or farewell tour. Only a short-lived stint on a rooftop in London in January of 1969 that would become the basis for* LET IT BE. *John and Yoko would have their famous bed-in in March of '69, and then he'd fall into his "lost weekends" with Harry Nilsson and Keith Moon and Alice Cooper.*

Kasim stopped along the way for a bagel with lox and some coffee. His hunger had returned, and he found himself savoring every bite. It stunned him to realize how many meals he'd eaten over the course of a lifetime where he never even bothered to notice how delicious something tasted. It seemed like he spent his meals just stuffing his face without thought as the music swirled around him. Now the flavors came bursting through, the smoky flavor of salmon and the salt and crushed onions of the bagel. There was a television dangling from a gantry in the far corner of the bagel shop, and on it came the report of another suicide bombing in Iraq, with ISIS claiming responsibility for the dozen or so lives taken. And from the tables around him came the bluster of white American citizens denouncing those heathen Muslims and their extremist religion. Hearing their comments reminded Kasim of the man back on his flight, who refused to lower his gaze of suspicion the whole time they were in the air. He could sense fear and hatred radiating off the people around him and decided to take the rest of his breakfast to go. Kasim exited the shop quietly and made his way toward Broadway, which he would follow right up the west side until he reached West 72nd.

He had the book about the Dakota Building in his back pocket, and he fished it out and skimmed on, reading about the famous celebrities who lived in the building at one time or another: Leonard Bernstein, Boris Karloff, Gilda Radner, Jack Palance, Judy Garland. Hollywood stars, musicians, artists, showmen. All a dying breed of opulence and fortune as life in America was still changing. The middle class was shrinking. The number of impoverished was rising. People were angry and fearful, all the time. Lennon could have had all the money in the world but that didn't stop the bullet that took his life as his wife watched in terror. Wasn't that a line from the end of *ABBEY ROAD*? The one about the love you take with you in the end? Mohmod and Zainab al Abdul were loved when Kasim saw them buried. The same with Noora. He'd loved her deeply and missed her every day she was gone.

Who would love him once the cancer finished spreading through his body and claimed him? Ever since his beloved wife passed, he'd remained alone.

Kasim pushed the book back into his rear pocket and moved along. He was so close to his destination. This pilgrimage he embarked on was moving him both physically and emotionally. It felt like everything he knew about life was wrong, misinterpreted, and after nearly seventy years on the planet, it was all finally making sense.

***

Kasim veered off Broadway onto Central Park West. The traffic was much crazier than anything he'd seen in Los Angeles, but that was okay. It seemed like there were crowds at every intersection, collecting in clusters just to help him cross safely. He tried to make eye contact with the people around him, but it seemed as if they avoided it. It felt taboo, and in those moments he was trying to establish some kind of connection with any of them, but they dropped their heads down to the heels of the people in front of them and soldiered on. He wondered if they'd have done the same if John and Yoko were passing by. Would they smile in delight and try to make John's acquaintance? Would they even recognize his presence? Would they...

The man with the Bushmaster AR-15 hustled out of the trees along Terrace Drive, by the intersection of Park Street and West 72nd. There was a collective gasp as the group of New Yorkers Kasim was crossing the street with suddenly parted, allowing the man in the green army jacket and faded jeans to push forward, his hands slinging the weapon from his back and into the crook of his right shoulder. His eyes narrowed into slits as if the sun was burning them, and his mouth was pulled into a ferocious, triumphant grin. Before Kasim could even fathom what was happening, the man drew a bead on his torso and squeezed the trigger. Kasim was still standing as the first three bullets ripped through his belly. Next, he was toppled backward into a hot dog vendor's cart as more rounds ripped through his lungs and shoulders. People were screaming all around him as the gunman moved closer, yelled, "Fuck you and fuck Allah!" and pulled the trigger again, unloading as many rounds as the clip could hold.

As Kasim's body toppled to the ground and his final breath hissed from his ruined lungs and out his mouth, he saw the silhouette of the Dakota Building resting peacefully across the street. The light above him grew brighter, and he felt his spirit beginning to rise out of his corpse.

Another figure approached, floating swiftly across the street as the frightened citizens fled off in every direction. Kasim squinted, pushing tears out of his eyes as this phantom floated toward him. He recognized her immediately as his beloved Noora. She looked young and perfect, for she hadn't aged a moment since the accident claimed her life. Noora reached her soft, delicate hand out to him, and he grasped it, and the joy of her touch filled his heart with a sense of gratitude he'd never felt before. "I've missed you, dearest heart," she said. "I've waited so long for you to come find me." The gunman sat quietly on the curb with his weapon cradled in his arms. He was slowly rocking back and forth, laughing and crying simultaneously as the line of police cars pushed past the traffic up and down Park Street. Noora pulled him to his feet, and the two spirits embraced. He'd hoped for Lennon, but Noora was what he truly needed, and he understood that love was truly what all of us need. She took his hand, and together they floated off toward Central Park and into Strawberry Fields forever.

It was just another day in America.

The Perfect Parent

"Thanks for meeting me on short notice, Tom."

Archie Ballard set his briefcase next to the empty chair and sat down across from the young author. Tom Dorsey looked every bit the writer-type: faded denims and green flannel shirt (unbuttoned to expose the Edgar Allan Poe t-shirt underneath), and dark horn-rimmed glasses. His hair was unkempt, and he had at least three- or four-days' stubble on his cheeks and chin. The pencil tucked precariously behind his right ear completed the picture of a young, ambitious author. Ballard suspected in ten years ambition would be replaced by quiet resignation, a potbelly, and a drinking problem, but for now the kid looked content. Tom smiled politely and glanced over the top of his glasses at his half-eaten hamburger and fries.

"Sorry I didn't wait for you, but I got a royalty check this morning and I was starving." Tom picked up his rum and Coke and took a sip.

"Oh, that's fine," Ballard said. He looked around Fogg's Tavern at some of the other patrons. More folks were drinking on a weekday afternoon than he cared to see, but that was how things were nowadays. Besides, he was on official business and preferred to wait until after hours for his tumbler of brandy. His drink would be waiting for him later at home—if this meeting didn't go too long, that was, but Ballard suspected it would. The information he was about to relate was so shocking, it was going to rock the young writer's world.

"It's been six months now, but I'm sure you're still grieving over Neil's death," Ballard said. "You and Neil Cooper were close friends for quite a few years. How are you taking it?"

Tom sighed, picked up his cocktail, and drank it down. When he saw the waitress approaching, he held the empty glass up and nodded to indicate a refill.

"Can I get anything for you, sir?" she asked the lawyer sitting across from him. Ballard smiled politely and said, "Just a cup of coffee, please."

The waitress sauntered back to the counter. Ballard reached down, opened his briefcase, and plucked out a large yellow document envelope. He dropped the envelope unceremoniously on the table next to Tom's half-eaten lunch, leaned back, and folded his arms.

"Well, for what it's worth, I'm very sorry for your loss. Neil was a hell of a writer. I've read at least three or four of his books, and I have to tell you...some of his stories scare the shit out of me."

Tom smiled, and Ballard could see the tears forming in the corners of his eyes. They made his gray irises glisten in the cheap overhead fluorescent bulbs. The author tried to speak, but instead removed his glasses, set them on the table, and then placed his palm over his face to conceal the growing storm inside him. Ballard had gotten the impression when he spoke to the young man on the phone that this meeting was going to go very hard for him, and with the prudence he'd obtained over twenty-six years of working cases for Johnson and Wilkes, he congratulated himself over deciding to *not* officiate things over the telephone.

"Yeah, Neil was really something. I still can't believe he's gone." Tom picked up his napkin and dried his eyes. "I'm not even sure what happened. There are all kinds of rumors going around in our authors circle that he committed suicide. But I just can't believe that. I know he missed Christine a lot, but..."

He didn't have to finish the sentence. Ballard already knew about Neil and Christine's four-year-old boy, who was now orphaned and living with his grandmother in Connecticut. And he was right: Neil would *never* have taken his own life and abandoned his son Sean. It would have fractured Christine's soul had he done such a selfish thing.

The waitress returned with their drinks and Tom immediately downed half of his third cocktail before Ballard could empty his creamer into his mug and stir.

"You'd better go easy on that," Ballard said coldly. "You need to be sober if you're to sign for what's inside the envelope."

Tom set his glass down, ran his hand haphazardly through his curly hair, and put his glasses back on so they perched halfway up his nose.

"What'd you bring me?" he asked. "Is that Neil's last will and testament?"

"Sort of."

Ballard was used to this kind of tête-à-tête. By this point in the grieving process, most loved ones were in the "greedy heir" phase, just waiting to find out what was bequeathed to them by the deceased. Family inevitably becomes vultures, wondering if treasures awaited or if they were about to be snubbed and cheated. Tom Dorsey wasn't family, but it was obvious that he was closer to Neil Cooper than his deadbeat brother in New Hampshire, or his catty, self-aggrandizing sister in New York (who'd phoned the day after Neil's passing to press him about the will). Tom not only acted as if he didn't feel entitled, but almost as if he was put off by the meeting. In fact, Ballard half-expected Tom to sign off on Neil's request and pass the buck back onto Mildred Cooper.

"Neil has named you in his will to be the custodian and executor of all his written works, both published and unpublished. Do you understand what that means?"

Tom glanced suspiciously at the yellow envelope.

"It means that Neil just quadrupled my workload. I have my own affairs to contend with. I have deadlines. My agent is hounding me every other Thursday for updates on my new novel. I have my publisher threatening to terminate our contract if I don't deliver a blockbuster manuscript... My last book was a bit of a flop, if you didn't know. I'm really flattered that he thought of me, that he trusted me enough to take this on, but if I do—and here's the thing that makes me worry—if my new book *is* a success, people will think I just stole his work and put *my* name on it. And I'm not okay with that. So if it's all the same, maybe you should designate this stuff to his agent, or to his mother. There are people out there who can help her sort it all out."

Ballard's face was stony, unchanging. It was as if he'd been expecting this reply from the young writer. He'd researched Tom Dorsey with great scrutiny before arranging the meeting, and Tom seemed like a reputable fellow. It was neither Ballard's job nor his place to make a value judgment as to how Neil's will was executed. It was merely business. It was Tom's frankness and apprehension that made him certain he was the right man for the job. After all, there were complications involved.

"I can't tell you what to do on this," Ballard said. "But I can tell you *this* much. If you really want to know how Neil Cooper died, you're going to have to sign your name on my documents here. And that includes a waiver forbidding you to disclose *any* personal information concerning Neil's death or his estate. But it's all in there.

He started a journal just after Christine died. Neil's mother insisted on the non-disclosure. She doesn't want anything damaging about her son to be presented to the general public. And I have to say, knowing what I know, that I don't blame her a bit."

Tom sat back and rubbed the whiskers on his chin. He continued to eye the yellow envelope suspiciously, almost as if he'd expected it to jump up and bite him. Ballard hated himself for having to dangle that big of a carrot to get him to consider accepting the inheritance, but he truly believed it was for the best.

"So you already know how he died," Tom said, never taking his eyes off the envelope. "Why is it such a big secret? Shouldn't his friends have a right to know?"

Ballard scooped up the envelope (causing Tom to jump backward in his seat), flipped it over, and pried the metal tabs so that the flap could open. He withdrew the stack of papers and neatly set them before the young author, slipped a pen out from the inside pocket of his suit coat, and pushed it into Tom's trembling hand.

"I have to follow the law on this, Tom. You've got questions. The answers are all here. And I can promise you this much: you're *not* going to like what you find out. I've already read through it all and I know what happened. As soon as you put your John Hancock on all this paperwork, you and I can start talking all about it."

Tom glanced over his horn-rimmed glasses at the pen in his hand. The trembling was beginning to subside. There wasn't a cat alive that curiosity couldn't lure in and devour. The young writer leaned over and scribbled his name and initials through the stack of papers.

***

"I'll start at the beginning," Ballard said, casually glancing down at his watch. He'd already known this meeting was going to run lengthy, had already planned on billing Mildred Cooper for at least two hours of legal services (he'd also known enough to order lunch anyway, and planned to cover both his and the writer's meals and write them off as a business expense). "Neil had a bit of a nervous breakdown after Christine died. After the funeral, he drove himself and his son out to his mom's place in Connecticut. He started to feel overwhelmed with the strain of having to raise Sean by himself—something that he probably never considered when he and Christine became parents."

Tom nodded, trying to imagine his friend of a solid dozen years suddenly having to wake up every morning and get his boy dressed, fix him breakfast, and keep him occupied all day, rather than rolling out of bed and heading straight for the computer to get his customary four hours of writing done. Christine's death meant that sacrifices had to be made. Tom knew that Neil loved his son more than life itself, and that meant his priorities would have changed drastically, especially during the time when he and Sean needed to be grieving together.

"Neil thought that living with his mother would help alleviate some of the new responsibilities he had to take on, and for a while, it did. He got back to work writing his final novel, as well as starting the journal I told you about. He also started drinking heavily, and his mother eventually told him he needed to sober up or get out. I don't know if you've ever met Mildred Cooper, but she's a tough-love kind of gal. Especially since she felt she was too old to be raising Tom's child by herself. Between you and me, I feel horrible that the kid is stuck there now, with Mildred having to raise him."

Between you and I, Tom mentally corrected the lawyer.

"So they moved back home, and Neil found himself wallowing in the same morass all over again. I think he really, *really* wanted to be the 'perfect parent' for Sean. He didn't want to disappoint Christine, and he certainly didn't want to feel like a failure in raising his only child. But the reality was he felt like he couldn't keep up with all his other obligations anymore. He grew tired of being overwhelmed. He needed to find a way to multitask and get work done while still being able to watch his boy grow up right." Ballard paused for dramatic effect. "So Neil had the surgery."

"The surgery?" Tom had been hanging on every word. He was still throwing suspicious glances at the yellow envelope of documents he'd already signed. Ballard noticed and nonchalantly scooped the envelope up off the table and dropped it back inside his briefcase.

"Yeah. I don't think anybody knew about his surgery, and that's probably a good thing. If he'd come to me and asked *my* advice, I'd have recommended he get a good psychiatrist instead. But by that point I don't think he was coping at all. It was like he had a squirrel loose in the attic of his mind, if you catch my drift."

"Yeah, get on with it," Tom said. He picked up his cocktail and meant to take a sip, and then paused. "Is it okay to drink again? Now that I've signed your goddamn papers?"

"Sure, why not?" Ballard glanced over at the waitress and signaled her over. "I suppose it's safe for me to have one too." He looked up at the waitress. "I'll take a whiskey on the rocks. In fact, make it a double, please."

Ballard watched her ass as she sashayed back to the bar.

"Where was I? Oh, yeah...the surgery. He went to one of them—what are they called? Not a plastic surgeon but some kind of weird reconstruction specialist. It's all in his memoir if you want to look it up and find the name. Anyway, Neil went in and told him he wanted something in particular done. He even offered to pay in cash. I guess it's pretty unlucky after all that his books were such good sellers. Had he been a nobody, we probably wouldn't be having this conversation. He told this quack doctor that he wanted eyes put in the back of his head."

"He *what?*"

Tom's own eyes looked comical, like huge saucers sitting behind those horn-rimmed glasses.

"I know. It sounds insane, doesn't it? But think about it, Mr. Dorsey: Have you ever lost the love of your life? Have you ever had to hold the frayed ends together once they've been severed? Some days it feels damn near impossible. Neil felt like he was running out of options, and the best way to be able to sit at his computer and get work done *and* still keep an eye on his four-year-old boy was to have a new set of peepers installed."

"He found a doctor that was willing to do this? That just goes beyond all ethics. People have lost medical licenses for less than that."

The waitress returned with the whiskey. Ballard took the drink, dropped a twenty-dollar bill on her tray, and told her to give them some privacy. He lifted the glass to his lips and took a healthy sip.

"Yes, he found a doctor willing to do the surgery. I don't honestly understand the logistics of it all, and the fact is that the doctor insisted upon only adding *one* eye rather than a pair. There was nothing on the level about any of it...no organ transplant list or anything like that. As for the business of optical nerve splicing or cutting and removing skull segments and creating an ocular cavity, or developing the muscle tissue that would allow an eyelid to open and shut, or working tear ducts..."

"I think I'm gonna be sick," Tom whispered. "I can't get over this. How the hell was he going to go out in public without being looked at as some kind of freak? How would he do book signings or reading events?"

"That's all easy enough to deal with. A hat would suffice."

"Did it even work? They actually put an eye—a human eye—into the back of his head? Was he at least able to see out of it?"

"Oh yes," Ballard sighed, picking up his whiskey and gulping it down. "And better than you'd think. According to his journal, for the first few months, everything worked out perfectly. He could sit there at his computer and type away, all the while watching Sean playing on the floor in his den. At first he was really happy about it, felt like the sensation of being overwhelmed was finally drifting away. And then things started going bad. Slowly at first and then eventually becoming disastrous."

Tom's cheeks had gone from rosy to pale. He thought of his best friend Coop, his companion at all the conventions and writers' conferences, shaking hands and signing books for the line of customers that never seemed to give *his* books a second glance. He imagined Coop's head shaved completely bald and could almost see that rogue eye on the back of his skull. The eye would be open wide, bloodshot and accusing, staring back at him while Neil's fans mewled and stuttered hyperbole-laden praise. It struck him profoundly to discover just how jealous he really was over his friend's success.

"Like I said, it's all in his journal," the lawyer continued. "One morning Neil was working on his final novel—I think he planned on calling it *Such Pretty Confusion*—and Sean was in the den watching some cartoon or other on PBS, and then all of a sudden Sean was standing up in the middle of the room, staring at him. But not just staring. According to what Neil wrote in his journal, Sean's face had changed. The boy's skin had turned green and the pupils of his eyes broke apart like egg yolks, making his sclera look like soured yellow crocodile eyes. He wrote that Sean was smiling the most malicious, unnatural smile he'd ever seen, like his mouth had stretched out halfway around his head and magically filled with snake fangs. Neil wrote that he nearly had a heart attack, and actually popped a vertebra in his neck from craning his head so fast to see his son with his real eyes."

"What did he see?"

"He saw his son. Exactly like he was supposed to. The boy was standing there looking at him, but he was frowning rather than smiling."

From Neil Cooper's Journal:
"Daddy, I'm hungry. Would you please fix me some lunch?"
"Sure thing, bud."
My heart was still pounding in my chest, and I actually got the chills. I must have written about people getting goosebumps and feeling dread in the pit of their belly a thousand times, but I'd never really

experienced it for myself until that moment. It was terrifying...like looking into the eyes of a demon. I'm not exactly sure what I'd have done if he was still in that monstrous form when I looked at him with my real eyes, and I'm glad I didn't have to find out. When we went into the kitchen I made Sean walk in front of me, just so that I didn't have to see him through my third eye. It simply scanned around my home from behind me as we moved from room to room, looking for unaccounted-for shadows or any other oddities I might not have noticed before with my real eyes. I had him sit down at the kitchen table, and any time I had to turn my head to fetch something I had to force that eye to close because I was too afraid to see him in that demonic state again.

"I can't get over this," Tom whispered. "Jesus Christ, this sounds like something out of one of our books."

"It gets worse." Ballard sighed and drained the last few drops from his tumbler. "The implant went in successfully, and stayed rather healthy for a while. Neil thought it was a neat trick to conceal the eye in such a way that he could still see out of it when he went out in public. He could stand in line at the grocery store and spy on the people around him. He wrote that he could watch other shoppers entering their PIN codes when they used their debit cards, or that he could catch secretive glances down ladies' shirts as they bent over to empty their shopping carts. He said that at times it made him feel like a comic book villain. Of course, Sean would be right there with him, and after that dreadful incident, whatever tricks that third eye allowed him felt cheap and loathsome. He got the transplant so that he could watch his son, but discovered that watching his son through that eye was about the *last* thing he wanted to do. And then the night terrors began."

"Night terrors?"

The journal continues:

Now that it's daytime and I've been able to process it all, what happened last night made me think of the Edgar Allan Poe story "The Telltale Heart"...the one where the young man ends up murdering the older fellow because the old guy has a creepy eye that upsets him so badly. I started taking tranquilizers to help me sleep. Things have grown worse as of late, and I'm constantly in a state of panic. Every now and again I'll be trying to write, or to get stuff done around the house, and I'll see Sean scoot past through that damned third eye. Always green-skinned. Always smiling that awful demon-grin. My daily life feels like

I'm raising a beast rather than a boy. I've taken to wearing a bandana on my head so that the eye remains covered, but even now I can hear Sean creeping around the house...tiptoeing on creaky floorboards and racing conspiratorially up and down the stairs. But what happened last night! Like I said, I took my sedative just before bed, and sometime after midnight I heard a noise in my bedroom. I was sleeping face down in my pillow, so my third eye opened, reflexively, to see what was going on.

Sean was standing in the doorway.

My son was just standing there staring at me through those awful crocodile eyes. I have no idea how long he'd been there in the room with me, but seeing him there pulled me from deep, sound sleep up to a heightened state of awake and alert. I could feel my heart thudding away in my chest as I wondered if he could see my eye open while the room was still dark. I moved my hand slowly, very slowly, over to the lamp beside my bed and flipped the switch, then turned my head to look at Sean. I screamed out loud when I discovered he wasn't actually in the doorway like my third eye saw, but standing right next to me...

"I think what we both need to understand," Ballard looked up from his second drink and examined the young writer, "is that this new organ was an alien thing. It was not to be trusted because it wasn't actually a part of *him*."

"You're saying that Neil was delusional and paranoid?"

"Wouldn't you? We have no idea whose eye was implanted into Neil Cooper. It could have been from a drug addict that overdosed and died. It could have been from someone with severe mental illness. The one thing it could *not* have been was that Sean Cooper is actually a demon, and that he was *trying* to coerce his father into taking his own life."

"Then it *was* suicide."

Ballard sighed. "The official police report claimed that Neil's death was accidental. You already know they found him at the bottom of the stairs. You know that he'd been consuming sedatives and still drinking heavily. Everything reported is as true as one can see. Unless..."

"Unless what?"

"Unless you're looking through an alien eye."

The journal continues:

I believe my son is trying to kill me. I know it sounds crazy, but when you have a third eye to look at the world with, it's hard not to see all those hidden dimensions looming around you. I can look at Sean through my real eyes and see a beautiful little boy, with golden hair that makes him look like a baby chicken when I ruffle it. I can see freckles and the missing tooth that came out when he bit into an apple last week. I can see Christine's features in his nose and cheeks, and I can see how much he hurts for her when I look into his eyes. But when that third eye sees him, all of that goes away. He isn't a child, but a thing. A dreadful thing. I see the way he's taken to sneaking up on me when I'm trying to get stuff done, or how he's taken to carrying weapons around the house with him, like he's some kind of primitive hunter...holding a dinner fork like a spear as he darts through the halls of our home. Every now and then he'll make demands like, "Daddy, I need attention!" or, "Daddy, I want you to play with me." I feel compelled to just drop whatever I'm doing and give in, hoping to keep that green monster at bay.

"Aha!" Tom cried out. "Don't you see?"

The lawyer jumped backward, surprised by the young author's outburst.

"See what?"

"Neil is talking in metaphors and clichés. 'Green monster'? Seriously? Neil was implying that Sean was jealous from not getting enough attention. And rightly so, may I add. The kid needed his father to help work through the grief of losing his mother. He needed love and tenderness and reassurance. Neil was a great guy, but he has never been a demonstrative person. He loved Christine dearly, but he was never big on public displays of affection or any of that stuff. And if you knew him like I did, you'd know that his career *always* came first.

"He could live without Christine and probably without Sean, but if you took writing away from him, he'd have taken his own life in a heartbeat. And that's what all of this comes down to. He painted himself into a corner. He couldn't be a writer *and* the 'perfect parent' at the same time. So he created all of this nonsense to justify his self-sabotage."

"If you say so." Ballard picked up the check the waitress left on the table, examined it, and then reached into his wallet to cover the tab.

A confused look spread across Tom's face.

"Let me ask you this—when the police and the EMTs arrived, did they find a third eye in the back of his head? Wouldn't *that* have made the evening news? I'd think *that* one would be pretty newsworthy. 'Bestselling Author Discovered with Third Eye.' Didn't anyone else ever see it?"

"Of course they didn't."

"And why do you think *that* is?"

The journal continues:

That little sonofabitch cut my eye out! I fell asleep last night at the computer, and when I awoke, I felt the gaping hole in the back of my skull where my eye should have been. I've been trying to piece together what happened last night, and all I seem to remember is that I put Sean to bed around 7:30, and then went back to work on Such Pretty Confusion, *trying to get the first draft completed by my deadline. I don't know how much scotch I drank, nor do I recall if I took my sleeping pill or not. All I do know is that this gaping hole in my head is hideous. And it hurts so goddamn bad I can't stand it! I can feel air touching the back of my brain, and blood and pus trickling down the cold skin of my scalp. I remember screaming Sean's name over and over again, but the little demon wouldn't come to me, so I stormed the house from room to room. I was furious and lumbered like a giant, turning over furniture and knocking pictures off the wall as I went after him. I found him hiding under his bed, cowering in fear and clutching a bloody soup spoon in his trembling hand. But the eye...my goddamn eye was nowhere to be found. Sean refuses to tell me what he did with it. But I'll get it out of him. Sooner or later, I'll get that eye back and then I'll make him pay for what he's done to me...*

"I think Neil really intended on killing his son. I believe that much. The only missing piece is what happened next. I don't know if Neil fell down the stairs while chasing Sean, or if Sean actually pushed him. Without the eye in the back of his head, Neil never would have seen him coming."

"If there *was* a third eye," Tom added. "Which I still don't believe. Without proof, all of what you just told me is nothing more than fiction. And speaking of which, now that I've signed your paperwork, fiction will be about the only thing I get to deal with for a long time." Tom lifted his glass—his fifth or sixth rum and Coke, he couldn't remember—and offered a toast.

"To Coop! You were everything a great storyteller should be. I wish I had your talent. Thanks for leaving me the yarn to end *all* yarns. Well played, sir." He tipped his head back and finished his glass. Ballard watched in silence until the young author put the empty glass down.

"I'll arrange for all of Neil's files and documents to be shipped to your house," the lawyer said. "You can expect them within five business days. But I do need to give you one more thing before I leave you." Ballard picked up his briefcase, set it on the table, and opened it. He retrieved a small, square wooden box and placed it in front of the author, then closed his briefcase and turned to walk away.

He could hear the gasp, and the screech of the author pushing his chair backward away from the table.

"What's in the box?"

The lawyer turned and looked at Tom Dorsey. The potbelly and drinking problem were definitely waiting somewhere in his future, perhaps closer than he'd originally imagined. Tom Dorsey would never be the author that Neil Cooper was, and that was probably for the best.

"Mildred Cooper mailed that to me a few days after Neil's death. In the note, she said that Sean brought it with him when he came to live with her. She said that it was *not* a part of her son when she gave birth to him, and she didn't know what else to do with it. I found that I did not have the courage to look inside, even after all this time, but I suspect you will. It's all the proof you will ever need, Mr. Dorsey." With that, the lawyer turned and left the bar.

Tom picked up the box and cupped it tight in his hands, and in his mind he could imagine his dead friend passing through vast, obscene dimensions all around him. It was the most loathsome inheritance he could imagine, and as he left the bar he found himself wondering if he would ever be brave enough to open the box and see the third eye for himself. He thought of Sean Cooper, the four-year-old boy who needed his father so badly, yet was so afraid of what his father had done to himself that he committed mutilation. He thought of how crazy Sean would have had to be to carve the alien eye out of his father's head, never even understanding exactly why it had to be done. In the end, Tom decided it was best not to look. He thought just seeing the alien eye would be enough to drive him crazy as well.

The Old Guide's Tale

"We ain't gonna catch nothing today." The Old Guide set his fishing rod between his legs, pulled out a book of matches from his coat pocket, and relit his pipe. A wisp of smoke poured out his nostrils, making him look like an ancient dragon in some storybook illustration. His eyes never left the choppy ripples.

"...The water ain't right, that is. And when the lake is in cycle, the fish won't bite."

Skinny Pete threw a glance at him before responding.

"And we *ain't* gonna catch nothing as long as you're running that mouth of yours. You're scaring the fish, dammit!"

I couldn't help but laugh. John (the "Old Guide," as we preferred to call him, on account of his lifetime of hunting and fishing in Maine) was notorious for running his mouth off. He was the one who could never keep his comments, advice, or stories to himself. And Skinny Pete, who had grown quite restless after an hour without a single bite, was looking for a better reason as to why the fish weren't tugging on his line.

The three of us worked together on the loading platform at the Postal Service. Skinny Pete and I had been planning this trip since fishing season opened. Sebago Lake had just turned over (the dermis of ice that coated the surface for the winter finally fractured and disappeared, gone like another lonesome ghost of winter) and we were hoping to catch at least a few salmon, if only to get some practice in for later on in the summer. And sitting in the cold morning air on the dock of the Portland Water District station can get quite frustrating when there's no action going on.

John is old enough to be either of our dads (myself at forty-four, Skinny Pete at five years less than me), and when Skinny Pete and I went out in public with him, we'd call him "Dad" just to bust his balls. He served in Vietnam for three tours of duty and had the bullet holes scattered across his abdomen to prove it. Both of us spent countless hours listening to his war stories at work. For John, the bigger his audience, the bigger the stories would get. I suppose with age comes the license to embellish. After all, when you're old enough to start forgetting things that happened in your life, you may as well make the stuff you do remember as unforgettable as possible. So when he was sure he had you hooked, John's smile would grow even bigger than his story and he'd reel you right in with it, the way he would a fish if one had decided to bite.

When we first started at the post office, the Old Guide had us convinced that the first part of a deer you'd eat once you shot it was its asshole. "You stuff that sombitch with potatoes and carrots, and just roast it right on the fire," he said, his grin practically stretching from ear to ear. John has the smile of an old-timer; the teeth a bit crooked and stained yellow with coffee and tobacco. But it's an honest smile, a smile of general amusement, not fixed and forced like some smiles you get nowadays.

Except this morning, John wasn't smiling. In fact, he treated this fishing trip with apprehension from the moment Skinny Pete and I started planning it. He tried to talk us out of it at first, saying it was still too cold out or that every angler in Southern Maine would be out fishing and it wouldn't be any fun. In the end, he insisted on coming with us. He never showed an ounce of enthusiasm or excitement, totally uncharacteristic of the Old Guide.

"I'm serious," John shot back at Skinny Pete. "I grew up on this lake. I know every inch of it. The water is bad... It goes in cycles. Let me ask you something. Other than us, do you see anyone fishing this lake today?"

"That don't mean shit." Skinny Pete set his own rod down long enough to light himself a cigarette. "It's still early. I bet this lake will be jumping by afternoon."

"The fuck it will," the Old Guide snapped. "There ain't nobody around but us. There ain't even a game warden around. We are all alone, my friend. Don't you think there's a reason for that?"

"Maybe there's a tournament going on today somewhere else," I offered.

The Old Guide picked up his plastic coffee cup (filled with beer, not coffee) and took a gulp. He set the cup back down, dragged the sleeve of his green L.L. Bean coat against his thick, white beard to wipe it dry, and began reeling in his slack line. His gaze at the water never broke during this transaction. It was as if he was hypnotized.

"If there was a tournament this weekend, I'd be fishing it instead of sitting out here with you two. But there ain't no tournaments going on this early in the season. I didn't want you two to be out on this lake alone. I know that this lake is in cycle." The Old Guide held his pipe to his lips and took another long drag off it. "You two don't realize it, but we're in a lot of danger out here. Skinny Pete didn't grow up on this lake like I did. And, Linus... Well, you're an out-of-stater..."

I was always thankful that the Old Guide referred to me as Linus, my pledge name from college. Since Skinny Pete and I share the same name, the rest of the crew at the post office call us Pete and Repeat, a moniker I loathe to this day. There are some that refer to us as Pete and Skinny Pete, but I'm told that when I'm not around I'm always Fat Pete or Big Pete. The truth is I prefer that over Pete and Repeat. If it really bothered me, I'd just go on a diet.

The "out-of-stater" part is true. My being born in New York has been an excuse for the Old Guide to pick on me. If I ever make a mistake, it's because I'm from out-of-state and don't know any better. I've come to learn that the residents of Maine not involved with commercial or tourist trades hate us out-of-staters with a passion. They would prefer we kept our money and our business as far from Maine as possible, which seems counter-intuitive for the state known as "Vacationland." I can still recall a time when I first came to Maine and the Old Guide treated me mercilessly, just to try and get me to go back home to New York. It took him at least a year to give up trying, and another year to quit referring to me as an out-of-stater and start referring to me as being "from away." Somewhere in those two years we became good friends.

The wind picked up and the three of us shivered in unison. Without warning, a strong gust caught Skinny Pete's baseball cap and tossed it into the water just past the dock. Skinny Pete bent down on his knees and reached down to pick it up when the Old Guide's arm shot out like a bullet and caught the back of his neck. With a tremendous yank, the Old Guide sent Skinny Pete tumbling backwards onto the dock.

For the first time since I've known him, I saw a terrified look on the Old Guide's face.

"Goddammit, Pete... Don't touch the fucking water!" John was yelling, and for a moment, I was actually too stunned and too afraid to say anything. When I could speak, I was barely above a whisper.

"Calm down, John... He's just trying to pick his hat up."

"I'll buy him a new one. I don't want either of you to go near the water." The Old Guide sat back down in his folding chair. Skinny Pete stood up and brushed his ass off, sending a cloud of dust adrift in the cold breeze. He shot an angry glance at the Old Guide and muttered something under his breath as he sat back down in his own chair. A few minutes passed by before the Old Guide decided to tell us the story, or rather, the legend of Sebago Lake.

***

"I know you two ain't gonna believe a word I say about this. You both know that I can tell a tall tale when I'm up to it. Well, I'm telling you the truth right now, so I want you both to pay attention. This lake is in cycle right now... The water is bad."

I glanced over at Skinny Pete, who was now wide-eyed with fascination. He no longer looked upset about being dropped on his ass a few minutes ago, but rather like he knew there was a good explanation coming regardless if an apology was involved or not. I turned back to face the Old Guide again. He had just finished the last of the beer in his coffee cup. He opened up his grotesquely oversized tackle box and removed a fresh can of beer, which he opened and poured into his coffee cup. He placed the empty can back in his tackle box and closed it. When he finished this ritual, he put the lid back on the coffee cup and continued.

"Every five years, this lake takes somebody's life. It's in cycle right now, as it's now been five years since the last accident. All the locals know it, including myself. That's why I didn't want you two to go fishing this morning. The lake is waiting right now. That's why you can't touch the water."

Skinny Pete laughed, breaking the heavy silence around us.

"What are you saying, Old Guide? That the lake is hungry?"

The way these words fell out of Skinny Pete's mouth made me laugh as well. I tried to choke it back, as I could tell from the seriousness on the Old Guide's face that he wasn't amused. But the more I thought about it, the sillier it sounded and the sillier it made me feel for falling for another of John's stories. The last thing I wanted was to be convinced that I should eat a deer's asshole for dinner.

"Well then, fuck you both... I'm going home." The Old Guide began reeling in the rest of his line.

"No, no... We're sorry. Please continue," I pleaded between chuckles.

He reeled his bait in, inspected it, and frowned when he saw there wasn't even a nibble on it. He cast it back out into the dark, choppy water and set his rod down.

"A couple hundred years ago, this lake belonged to the Indians. They lived here all year round. Christ, there was enough wildlife to hunt and fish that they could have lived here forever. Everything they could ever need, this lake provided for them. This was their paradise.

"Well, the chief of these Indians was named Red Bear. Supposedly, as a boy, this guy was out hunting along Sebago, gathering for his tribe, and he spotted this giant red bear out along the tree line. The bear spoke to him and told him that the spirits favored him. The bear told him that if the boy let it free, if he didn't kill it, the spirits would grant him one wish on his deathbed. The boy understood that this was some kind of magic, turned his back on the bear, and it disappeared back into the woods where it came from.

"The boy went back to the camp and told the council of elders about what had happened to him. As a result, he was given the name Red Bear, and was regarded as a holy man among the tribe. Later on, when the chief of the tribe died, Red Bear took his place."

The Old Guide took his eyes off the water and glanced at us to see if we were paying attention. When he saw that we were, he took another drink from his coffee cup and continued.

"Red Bear became a great leader. He was revered by the whole tribe as a wise and honest man. He was courageous in battle, a cunning warrior against the other Maine tribes when they fought for territory and resources. But above all, Red Bear was humble to the spirits. He was what you'd call a righteous person.

"When the French decided to come down from Canada and explore this new land for settlement, they stopped at Sebago. Fucking out-of-staters! They always fuck up everything." John stopped and threw me a glance. "Red Bear offered the French soldiers food and hospitality. Although there was a language barrier between them, the commander of the soldiers accepted the food Red Bear offered under the pretense of friendship. The French dined with the Indians at a great celebration. And when everyone went to sleep, the French commander woke his soldiers and they began slaughtering the sleeping Indians. A few women and children escaped into the woods, but most of the Indian warriors were murdered in cold blood, right over on the beach, over by where we parked the truck."

The Old Guide pointed to the patch of sand just to the right of the dock where we were fishing.

"Their blood ran right into the water of this lake. And Red Bear, after being slain by the French commander's saber, had a vision of the red bear that he'd seen as a boy. The bear spoke to him. 'Greetings, favored one. I have returned to grant your wish. What is it that you desire?' Red Bear responded, 'My people are murdered by my enemy, and I am to blame. I was deceived, and my tribe has all but died because of it. I pray my people shall flourish again someday, but that is not my wish. I wish that for every drop of my people's blood spilled by this lake, a life of my enemies shall be taken in return.' 'So shall it be,' the bear responded. 'For every drop of blood spilled, a life shall be taken. However, as in nature, all things occur in cycles... The sun, the moon, the seasons. As spirit of this lake, I shall only take one life every five years. Thus, nature shall keep its balance.' With that, the bear disappeared and Red Bear died."

The Old Guide inhaled deeply from his pipe, allowed the smoke to escape through his lips, and breathed it back in through his nostrils—a trick that, although pretty gross, was still neat to watch. As he did this, a noise broke through the silence. A truck with a boat in tow had entered the parking lot. Upon inspection, the Old Guide nodded.

"They're from New Hampshire. Fucking out-of-staters." John glanced at me, "No offense, Linus."

I shrugged in response, watching as the man in the passenger side of the truck jumped out and hand-signaled the driver to back up toward the boat launch. When the stern of the boat was in the water, the passenger unhitched the boat and slid it off the trailer and tied it to the launching dock's post. The driver pulled the truck back into the parking lot, where he parked next to John's GMC and unloaded their fishing gear from the truck's bed. The passenger joined him, and together they loaded and launched the boat. As the wind pushed them by us, the passenger tipped his hat to us and called out, "Any luck this morning?"

The Old Guide answered, "Nah, we ain't caught nothing yet."

The passenger turned his back to us to get situated in the boat. The driver was tugging at the start cord on the Mercury motor. It choked out a few coughs of smoke before begrudgingly turning over. When it roared to life, the two forgot all about us as they sped off to the center of the lake. The Old Guide jumped to his feet, pulling us both off our own chairs with his giant hands. Standing up straight, John was at least 6'4". The guy towered over us, making us two grown men look like children.

"Come on," he bellowed. "Get in my truck."

"What about our fishing gear?" Skinny Pete protested.

"Fuck the gear," the Old guide responded. "We'll get it when it's over!"

"When what's over?" I asked.

"You'll see. I told you, the lake is in cycle. These fucking out-of-staters are about to die."

There was no hint of a smile on John's face to tell us he had us hooked on his story. Instead, he had a look of fear and conviction, and I couldn't help but wonder if this was the look he had when he was fighting against the enemy in Vietnam. Within a few short seconds, he had us piled into the cab of his GMC Sierra.

The Old Guide's truck was a shrine to the Maine outdoorsman. It was decorated with magnets portraying every species of bass, trout, and landlocked salmon found in Maine. Hanging off the rearview mirror, a pine tree air freshener, a tiny wicker basket with several variations of trout flies hooked into it, and a few duck feathers fastened together with fishing line. On the back window hung the obligatory gun rack (no rifles though, as hunting season was far later in the year) which now held a rather large wooden club that one might use if fishing for bluefish or anything with teeth that might take a finger off if one wasn't careful. On the faded upholstery of the seats, several maps, hunting and fishing rule books, and several scattered audio cassettes featuring George Thorogood and Jimi Hendrix. These last few items got shuffled about as we situated ourselves inside the cab.

"It ain't an accident that I survived three tours of duty in 'Nam." The Old Guide had just opened a fresh can of beer (his coffee cup left behind with our abandoned gear). "Hell, I caught a few bullets here and there, but in the end I killed more of them fucks than my whole platoon combined. It was the best hunting I ever did. When I was a kid, I used to go deer hunting all the time, and for the most part, I never even saw a deer until my father taught me how to hunt."

He set the can down on the dashboard and picked up his pipe. He opened the door of the truck just wide enough to knock the dead ashes out of the bowl and examine the inside of the pipe when it was empty. He closed the door, pulled out his tobacco pouch, and filled the pipe again.

"Ya see...the deer knows you're out there. He's going by his senses. He can either see you, hear you, or he can smell you. And if he can do any two of those three things, well, you ain't never going to see him. But if you're up in a tree stand, wearing animal urine to throw your scent off, and you're sitting still and quiet like a mouse, that deer will walk right beneath you. All you have to do is pull the trigger."

The Old Guide swept a match against the strike bar of the matchbook and lit up his pipe.

"The enemy is the same way. Now, I've seen soldiers tearing through the jungle, whooping and hollering like assholes because they think they're scaring the enemy (or at least confusing him into thinking there's a hell of a lot more of us than there really was). Then there were soldiers who wore enough bug juice to wake the dead. You could smell these idiots a mile away. Didn't bother the mosquitoes though. They kept biting no matter what we smelled like. There were even some who would stop and take a shit in the middle of an open field. These were the assholes that we'd ship home in body bags. Ya see...the enemy knew we were there *all along*. Charlie would be hiding under a bush, counting each pair of legs to march right past him."

John stopped for a moment as he opened his glove compartment and pulled out a pair of binoculars. He handed them to Skinny Pete. "Now don't take your eyes off the two guys in the boat. You're gonna see the lake eat them alive." Then he glanced at me. "You too, Linus. Keep your eyes on the boat." He picked his beer up, took a long guzzle, and continued.

"So, when I went into the jungle, I made myself invisible. Charlie was so busy watching the soldiers who were listening to the radio or putting on bug juice or taking a shit, that all I had to do was shoot him first. The enemy was just as foolish and predictable as we were. But..."

Skinny Pete and I turned in unison, both of us hanging onto every word. A frown spread across his face.

"Don't look at me... Watch the boat!" Our faces snapped back toward the water.

"But the enemy had a reason to try and kill us. We were invading his home and trying to kill him first. Now, Mother Nature. She has no reason for killing people. She doesn't need one. Like when the tornado drops on someone's trailer house, or when the avalanche buries a family out skiing for the day. She doesn't care. She's a cold, calculating bitch that strikes without reason."

The two men in the boat had just dropped anchor out toward the center of the lake. They were too far away for us to see their faces, but we could see their doomed silhouettes as they baited their hooks and threw their lines in.

"I was a kid when I saw a man die for the first time, right here where we're sitting now. My father took my brother and I out to this very spot to show us what you're about to see. I was only six at the time, but I remember every exact detail. I'll never forget it as long as I live. It was February, and the lake had frozen to at least a foot and a half thick. There was this old guy by the name of Hunnicut that was staying at a camp right down the road from us. He'd come up from New Jersey to do some ice-fishing. He didn't know anything about the lake's history, and he had no idea that the water was in cycle, just like it is now. Why would he? Fucking out-of-stater.

"Well, my dad took me and my brother snowshoeing for the day. Hunnicut told my dad that he was going fishing, even invited him to come along. But my dad knew about the water. He could have told Hunnicut about the water, could have saved the guy's life. Instead, he let the guy go fishing. I doubt Hunnicut would have believed him anyway.

"So my dad walks us along the bank, trudging through snow that was waist-deep for us, to this spot. And we watched it happen."

I turned to look at the Old Guide again, but he motioned with his hand to look back out at the water. The men in the boat appeared to be having a grand old time. I noticed that the water was no longer choppy with spring whitecaps. It had glazed over smooth, and not so much as a ripple echoed off the boat as the two men moved around. The Old Guide glanced over at me.

"You see it too, don'tcha, Linus?" He inhaled on his pipe. "The water is getting ready." He exhaled, and the cab filled with a cloud of smoke. For the first time in my life, I felt truly terrified. My heart was pounding in my chest, and I could feel my skin crackle with goosebumps. It felt like time had stopped moving forward, and that my every breath took deliberated thought just to fill my lungs and exhale.

"Hunnicut was sitting on a folding chair out on the ice. He had five traps set around him, and a sixth hole in the ice that he was jigging a line out of. He had built a fire on the ice with some dead brush he pulled off that small island just starboard of the boat you two are looking at. Hunnicut saw us and stood up. He had the jigging rod in his left hand and a thermos of coffee in his right. He set the coffee down and began waving at us when all at once, the ice beneath him opened."

My eyes left the water again, and I watched the expression on the Old Guide's face turn blank, as if he were staring at a ghost out in the middle of the lake. For a brief instant he looked as if he were not just telling a story, but reliving it, and for that moment I was filled with dread. I almost hoped he was pulling our legs with one of his tall tales. His tired gray eyes bulged out and he continued talking, but I wasn't quite sure if he was still talking to us or himself.

"The ice didn't just open. Not a break-through like you see on the news, where some idiot snowmobiler thought the ice was thick enough when it wasn't. No, the ice came alive like a giant mouth with huge icicle teeth. Old man Hunnicut never saw it coming. It just happened. He was standing there with that goddamn jigging rod in his hand, waving like an old lady who sees you coming down the street. And the next minute, his body was half-submerged into the ice, and the fucking ice was chewing on him, eating his torso. These huge fangs of ice were ripping him apart, spilling his stomach and intestines all over the pure white surface of the lake.

"And that motherfucker screamed. Not like the soldiers in Vietnam when they got shot. Hell, I never screamed like that when I caught a bullet. Hunnicut's voice shrieked and bellowed across the lake and far into the woods. Christ, I bet they heard it way the hell out in Portland. Every time that frozen mouth opened and closed on him, he'd gasp in just enough air to throw out another scream. He did that all the way until the fangs got a hold of his diaphragm and lungs. After that, either he went into shock or he died outright. But once he stopped breathing, the ice sucked the rest of him down below the surface and the lake froze right back over again. The only thing left of Hunnicut was a few patches of red ice and the traps he'd set around him.

"My father made my brother and I watch the whole thing. When it was over, I was paralyzed with fear. I stood there looking at this patch of ice stained red with blood where old man Hunnicut was waving to us moments before. I might have gone into shock myself. My dad carried me home, and when we were inside by the fireplace, he told my mother that he was going back out to bring in Hunnicut's traps. I freaked out. I never felt more afraid in my life than when he walked out the door. Not even in Vietnam. I cried like a baby, begging him not to go back out on the ice, but he swore up and down that the ice was safe again. And when he did come back with the traps, he told me and my brother the lake's history, just like I told you."

The Old Guide turned and looked at us again, and the color was returning to his face. He inhaled on his pipe, and rubbed the whiskers in his thick, white beard as he exhaled.

"I've seen a lot of people die in Vietnam. Mostly kids the same age as you two when you started working at the post office. Hell, I've killed a lot of kids. Even babies. I was so good at it that when the war ended I was admitted into Special Forces and was shipped into some other third-world country so I could keep going. I didn't have to come home to a nation that would condemn me and spit on me and call me a baby killer like they did to the other soldiers. Can you imagine that? Fighting a war for your country and have your country hate you for it? Most Americans think that war is soldiers fighting soldiers, and leave the women and kids alone. In Vietnam, the women and children would try to kill you just as fast as the men would. Let me tell you something... Little enemies become big enemies. In combat, you never take chances. Protest my ass. If you held a gun in the face of the average American, they'll cry like pussies. They have no concept of what war is. But of all the deaths I've seen while I was in the service, nothing scared me to the point of terror like watching old man Hunnicut die." The Old Guide turned and looked at us.

"Hey, Skinny Pete, how are our friends in the boat doing?"

"They ain't catching anything, that's for sure."

The two men in the boat had been sitting there for almost fifteen minutes, constantly retrieving their lines and casting out again. The water had not made a ripple all the while they were out there.

And then it happened.

One of the men had been drinking coffee, and when he finished, he leaned over the side of the boat to dip his cup into the water and wash it out. The exact moment his hand made contact with the water, the lake exploded into action in a manner I could never have dreamed possible, except in a nightmare.

The water took the shape of a giant, transparent hand. It pushed the small boat into the air in one huge wave, sending the two men and the boat at least twenty feet upward, where it held still just long enough for us to watch them squirm in raw fear and disbelief. We could hear them screaming to us for help, although the three of us in the truck knew damn well there was nothing to do except watch helplessly. Their motions inside the boat were pathetic; the two men pitching back and forth, trying to find some form of balance as this aquatic hand held their lives in a chilling grip.

I snatched the binoculars from Skinny Pete, who let them fall out of his grip without a hint of argument. I held them to my own eyes and could see two weeping, trembling faces, their chins quivering and pleading desperately for help that wasn't coming. I had the impression of watching trapped animals, the fight beaten out of them until there is nothing left but a terrible sadness and desperation. I felt helpless, to the point of almost being insignificant, and the fear and sadness began to consume myself as well. I was not looking at the Old Guide or Skinny Pete, but I could tell from their breathing that they felt the same as I did. If I could have spoken, I would have asked God to make this vision before us stop, but my throat had knotted and I could barely choke out my own breath.

And then the water moved again, this time parting like the sea before Moses and his people, exposing the jagged rocks at the bottom of the water. They lie there dead and solid and black as night, except the few patches of green growth that made up the vegetation at the bottom of Sebago Lake. For a split second, I could hear the Old Guide's voice in my head telling us that the lake was hungry. Now here it was before us, the water opened like a giant mouth, and a watery hand holding the men in the boat, ready to satisfy its appetite.

The two men in the boat were now in hysterics, and I felt myself wondering what the view they were seeing must have been like. I pushed these thoughts from my mind, waiting to see what I already knew was going to happen.

With brute strength, the watery hand rolled the boat so that the two men were turned upside down, and before they could fall out, the watery hand smashed the boat against the rocks below like a human hand would squish a mosquito. From the confines of the truck, we could hear the terrible crunch of the wooden vessel crashing and splintering into the jagged black rocks in the depths of Sebago Lake. A moment later, the water splashed over the shattered vessel and settled back into the quiet, choppy lake top we'd been fishing out of all morning. The waves had returned and, hesitantly, the broken pieces of the boat's wooden frame floated to the surface and bobbed silently up and down among the whitecaps.

"What the fuck just happened?" Skinny Pete's face had turned a pale shade of blue, and I had to wonder if he had stopped breathing altogether during the horrible spectacle we had just witnessed.

Two small orange shapes bobbed to the surface, and for a sick moment, I thought they were the lifeless bodies of the two men from the boat. I peered through the binoculars again, only to see that they were empty life vests.

"What happened to the bodies?" I turned toward the Old Guide, secretly wishing I hadn't asked.

"We won't see them again. Nobody will," he answered. Despair crept down his spine, and he shivered silently behind the wheel of the truck. John could have prevented all of this from happening, but instead chose to educate us through the obscenity of proof. "Their bodies will never be found. The lake ate them."

Skinny Pete buried his face in his hands and started crying. I reached out to put my hand on his shoulder, but my eyes caught the Old Guide's, and I withdrew.

"What do we do now?" I asked, dreading the response.

"We get our shit and get out of here," he answered. "I'll call the game warden's office when we get back to Portland...let them know about the out-of-staters. They'll already know anyway. None of this is new to them. The state will come down and collect their stuff. They probably won't bother skimming the lake or nothing. They know about the lake. I bet the incident won't even be in the newspaper. C'mon, let's get our own gear."

The three of us collected our fishing gear as quickly and quietly as possible. There was nothing more to say about the subject, and if there was, well, we just ignored it. And as the old GMC Sierra exited the parking lot, I turned back to face the lake one last time. My eyes scanned across the cold, choppy water and back into the woods along the tree line. For the tiniest second, I thought my eyes were playing tricks on me. I could have sworn I saw a big red bear streak into the woods.

The Diary of Mary

The voices are real, and say dreadful things,
About the nature of death and the darkness it brings.
Their whispers are cruel, and their secrets are scary,
So sayeth the words in the Diary of Mary.

For the world is filled with monster and beast,
With razor sharp claws and fangs for the feast.
Yea, people are wolves and sickness they carry,
So sayeth the words in the Diary of Mary.

What am I but a tool of the almighty God?
To hunt down the wicked, the different, the odd,
And cut them to ribbons and leave their blood spilled.
I shall not rest till the sinners are all killed.
And the will of my Lord by mine eyes are fulfilled.
Then at my death, by God's side I shall tarry!
So sayeth the words in the Diary of Mary.

The Strange Medicines of Dr. Ling

Brilliant, dazzling sunlight.

It was still an hour before noon and the sun was already hammering down along the dusty grounds of the carnival's midway until the ground itself seemed to shimmer like water. Clear blue sky above the gaily colored canvas tents, and the bright, cheerful banners and flags strung out through the landscape of the fairgrounds. Clowns everywhere, masked in grease-painted smiles and silly hats and costumes, handed out balloons to passing children when not performing their slapstick antics. Animals abound in nearby petting zoos, where children giggled as sheep and goats nibbled grains and oats from their tiny fingers.

Jerry Ryan pushed his hands to his temples as he staggered past the rows of midway games, his wife Sandy traveling directly behind.

"Honey, are you okay?" Sandy asked as her husband rushed to a deserted table by the Leone Brothers Pizza stand. Jerry dropped into the seat, his shaking hands clutching at the dull, throbbing pain in his head. The migraines were getting worse, no question about it. This one felt like his brain was going to finally burst. Amidst the pain, Jerry could actually visualize his eyeballs popping out of his skull, followed by a soggy stream of blood-soaked gray matter that was formerly his brain.

The heat was making it that much worse. It seemed to permeate his skull and intensify the pain. Tears blurred his vision, forcing him to remove his hands from his temples and sweep them across his face. His biggest fear was beginning to surface, that the pain would become so unbearable that he'd stroke out and spend the rest of his life as a wheelchair-bound vegetable.

It seemed very possible, at least for the moment. After all, he could still recall being a young boy and watching his grandmother stroke out. Only, she had fallen down a flight of stairs and died in grand defiance of the whole paralysis bit. There were no stairways here at the carnival. Only sawdust-strewn pathways along the barren lawns of the fairgrounds and parking lot pavement that was now hot enough to literally fry the proverbial egg.

"I have your pills in my purse," Sandy offered. "Let me just grab you a drink. You stay right here in the shade."

Like I'm going anywhere... Jerry mumbled to himself as he watched his wife turn and wander over to the pizza stand's counter. His eyes were blurry with tears, but he could still make out the way Sandy's ass shifted so seductively in those cut-off blue jeans she was wearing.

Sandy was a sight, even for sore eyes.

In the background a marching band began to play. The sound of brass instruments blared above the steady droning beat of a bass drum, and Jerry found himself actually wishing for the stroke to come, if it would at least show him the mercy of ending this awful pain.

It felt like an eternity had passed before Sandy returned with a glass of fresh lemonade in one hand and a pair of pain relief tablets in the other. She slid into the empty seat next to her husband.

"Here, take these."

Jerry took the pills and washed them down with the drink. When he finished, he cupped his head in his hands again, trying to squeeze the pain away.

"Do you want me to drive you to the hospital, Jer?"

"Just give me a couple minutes, I'll be fine."

"How bad is it?"

Jerry sighed. "This is the worst one yet. I feel like someone hit my skull with a sledgehammer."

"At the very least, let me take you home. You can go back to sleep if you want. That always makes you feel better. Besides, you'll be more comfortable out of this heat."

Sandy stood up and offered her hand. Jerry took it and stood himself up. He grimaced as the pain seared into his brain from the blood rushing to his head. And then they were off, pushing their way through the crowd as they made their way back down the midway.

They had almost made it to the end of the strip when Jerry stopped dead in his tracks.

"You okay?" Sandy asked, gripping his hand slightly with her own.

"This wasn't here before," he whispered in a disoriented voice.

He was staring up at an extremely large horse-drawn cart (the horses nowhere in sight) parked at the end of midway. The cart itself appeared enormous; its red walls, shoddily painted, seemed even bigger than the area of their whole apartment. On the side of the cart was some stenciling that read in big white capital letters outlined in gold:

THE AMAZING DR. LING
POTIONS, REMEDIES, ELIXIRS

Surrounding the letters were miscellaneous Chinese characters and sketches of moons, stars, and dragons. Jerry's eyes followed the trailer, scanning it until he noticed the wooden plank steps leading up into its mysterious belly just around the corner at the cart's far end.

"Do you remember passing this cart when we came in?" He turned toward his wife, his eyes wide with disbelief.

"I don't remember," Sandy stammered, shrugging helplessly. "I was paying attention to you. I'm sure it was here though. There's too much going on around here to move in something this big without people noticing it."

"I'm telling you, this wasn't here before. This whole corner was empty, all the way up to the ring-toss game."

"Well, it didn't just appear out of thin air. You're probably just confused, honey. There are at least a hundred game tents around here. You're probably remembering a different corner. Now please, before the sun fries your brain completely, let me take you home."

Sandy started to lead him away, but Jerry pulled his hand back and walked around the corner toward the entrance. Still believing the cart had mysteriously appeared as if by magic, he stopped momentarily and kicked one of its massive wooden wheels. The wheel didn't budge, and Jerry found himself wondering just how big a horse would need to be to pull a monster like this.

"We're going in," he said aloud, not only to inform his wife but to verify to himself that the cart did, in fact, exist and that he wanted to go inside and talk with this Amazing Dr. Ling. Perhaps to chat a bit about this fucking unbearable heat wave or inquire which concession stand made the best corndogs. Maybe even discuss with the good doctor if one of his potions, remedies, or elixirs might cure him of these goddamn migraines once and for all.

"Honey, this man isn't a real doctor. He's a carnival attraction. Don't you get it? He can't practice real medicine without a license."

Sandy was tugging at his arm, but Jerry was already around the corner and approaching the wooden steps. He paid no attention to her. It was almost as if he was already in a trance; the last little portion of his brain that hadn't succumbed to the migraine was drawing him like a bit of iron filing to a magnet.

The door at the top of the steps was equally enormous, making him wonder if perhaps a giant lived inside. On the door was a smaller but more freshly painted version of the lettering.

THE AMAZING DR. LING
KNOCK FIRST BEFORE ENTERING!

Underneath the words was a tiny set of hand-painted dragons forming the symbol for the Yin and Yang. They curled about each other's tail with jaws open as if ready to feed.

"You're really serious about this?"

Jerry grunted out a response that resembled yes. Sandy shrugged again. "If this clown charges you more than twenty dollars for one of his little 'remedies,' I'm taking you to a psychiatrist directly after we leave the emergency room!"

He considered this for a second, and then asked himself when was the last time *he'd* seen an Asian person walking around with his hands on his head, complaining of a migraine. Never! Because obviously there *is* something to all that ancient Chinese mumbo-jumbo, with their exotic herbs and roots and extracts. All that shit has been handed down for centuries, from generation to generation. And behind this big, hulking wooden door awaits the mysterious and wonderful Dr. Ling, who will know how to relieve migraine headaches!

He lifted his hand, formed a fist, and pounded on the door.

The door creaked open by itself, as if by the hand of some unseen spirit, and Jerry pulled his hesitant wife by her arm into the trailer. It felt like stepping into an entirely different dimension. Despite the dreadful heat outside, the trailer felt cool and tranquil. Inside the cart was entirely empty, void of any signs of life. There were no windows inside the room they had entered, and when the door closed again as if by magic, they were standing completely in the dark.

Sandy let out a frightened gasp, gripping down tight on her husband's hand. And then a small light bulb above them clicked on. It filled the room with light once again, but this light was extremely soft, shallow, casting shadows all around them.

Suddenly, a small, elderly Chinese man was standing in front of them.

"Greetings," the man offered politely as Sandy tried to back herself toward the door. "Do not be afraid. I am Dr. Ling. Welcome to my home." His words were choppy, and laden with Cantonese dialect.

"You live in here?" Jerry asked, feeling a bit startled by their host's unexpected entrance.

Dr. Ling stood at least one whole foot shorter than Jerry. He was adorned in a flowing purple robe with a black sash knotted delicately around his waist. His head was shaved perfectly bald except for a long jet of fine, neatly braided black hair that protruded from the back of his scalp. A pair of fluffy, grayish-black eyebrows rested between his wrinkled forehead and his mysterious, piercing eyes. Around his lips, a Fu Manchu style mustache and pointy beard. No different than any actor playing the villain, even in the worst Asian whodunit. Hell, he could even stand on any street corner in Chinatown and somehow fit right in. There he'd be *Mr.* Ling, but here, in this mysterious, oversized horse-cart in the heart of the carnival, he was Dr. Ling. Just how amazing he was had yet to be determined.

Dr. Ling raised a long, wooden tobacco pipe to his lips and inhaled. When he exhaled, smoke rushed out his nostrils like a pair of crazed serpents.

"It is a bit modest, I suppose, but it is home nonetheless. Is there something I may help you with?"

To Jerry, it had felt like his headache had left him the moment he stepped into the room. Now, hearing the doctor speak, the pain flew back into him, and he found himself on the verge of passing out.

"Won't you please sit down?" Dr. Ling spoke, noticing his discomfort. From out of nowhere, a red velvet couch appeared behind the young couple. Too afraid to question it, Sandy plopped herself down, followed by her husband, who was in too much pain to take notice.

"I have headaches," Jerry announced. "Terrible migraines. It feels like something is chewing my brain apart."

Dr. Ling walked over to where Jerry was sitting. He leaned forward just enough so that his slanted eyes were gazing directly into Jerry's own. The old man's gaze was long and terrible, leaving Jerry shifting about nervously.

"That is a very accurate description, sir. How long have you been having these troubles?"

"Since I was a kid. They come and go from time to time. Only lately they've been getting worse."

"I see. And you have seen doctors for treatment? By doctors, I mean practitioners of Western medicine."

"Yeah, but nothing really seems to help." Jerry cringed. The pain was now unbearable.

Dr. Ling stood up and puffed again on his pipe.

"That is how it is with Western medicine," the doctor said, waving his left hand dismissively in front of him. On the palm of his hand was a tattoo of a bright red dragon curled into a semicircle. As his hand passed by, the dragon appeared to move, but only for an instant. It was a quick illusion that Jerry paid little notice to.

Sandy saw it but said nothing.

"Western medicine only good for treating symptoms. Never concerned with cure!"

"So you can cure me?" Jerry lifted his head from his hands, his teary eyes pleading for help.

"Dr. Ling is practitioner of Eastern medicine," the elderly Chinese man continued. "My remedies do not cure diseases. Rather, they remove them from the body entirely. And once they are gone, they cannot return!"

"How much is this going to cost?" Sandy could keep silent no longer. The rational part of her felt like she was watching her husband being led into some sort of con game, one where his headache might be cured through the power of suggestion or hypnosis, but not a permanent fix. Sandy refused to sit idly and watch Jerry get his hopes up, especially when the pain was as bad as it was.

Dr. Ling waved his right hand, and on this palm was a tattoo of another dragon. This dragon was green with yellow stripes and faced upside down. Sandy again noticed, realizing that if Dr. Ling was to cup his hands together, the two dragon tattoos would form the same Yin and Yang symbol she'd seen on the door.

"Something this terrible, I fix you my own personal remedy. Fifty dollars, I remove your headaches forever!"

The pain flared again, and Jerry grunted out loud. When the surge passed, he looked up at Sandy.

"Pay him the money."

"Jerry, are you out of your mind?"

"Give him what he wants! I don't care. But I can't go on like this any longer."

Dr. Ling bowed his head, remaining silent. His razor-thin lips curled upward into a smile.

"He isn't a real doctor, don't you get it? You're willing to throw away fifty bucks on something that isn't even guaranteed to work?"

Dr. Ling drew on his pipe and exhaled.

"Oh, I guarantee my medicine will work. If your husband isn't completely satisfied, I'll give your money back, and you're free to go."

Jerry thrust his arm out and grabbed Sandy's pocketbook. She clutched down on it, still protesting.

"What about side effects? Can you guarantee that there won't be any side effects?"

"Give him the fucking money!" Jerry threw her a look of utter ferocity.

"There are side effects in all medicines, my dear lady." The old man cupped his hands before him, revealing the tattoos forming the symbol for the Yin and Yang as Sandy quietly predicted he would.

"In nature, all things are in balance. A harmony of co-existence. All medicine is devised to, in some way, break up this harmony and remove the elements that are bad." Dr. Ling swept away his hand with the tattoo of the red dragon. "This leaves the other element to either find something new to co-exist with or to die altogether." He closed the hand with the green dragon. When he opened his hand again, the dragon, the tattoo itself, had changed. Now the dragon formed itself into its own circle. But strangest of all, the green dragon now had a long red stripe flowing down its back to the tip of its tail.

Abruptly, the doctor slapped his hands together and rubbed them back and forth, causing the couple to jump in surprise.

"So, do we have a deal?" Dr. Ling extended his hand, and the altered tattoo was back to normal.

"Yes...yes...please! Just make the headaches go away!" Jerry extended his own hand and shook the doctor's hand.

"Well," Sandy exclaimed, jumping up to her feet. She opened her pocketbook and removed her wallet. "I hope this makes you happy." She reached into her wallet and removed fifty dollars, crinkling the bills as she pulled them out. "I'll be waiting outside. And when you come out, I don't want to hear *any* complaints about headaches!" She dropped the money in her husband's lap and turned towards the door.

"Ah, miss, won't you stay and watch? You may not believe in strange medicines, but perhaps you'll change your mind after your husband's illness is removed." Dr. Ling offered her a sinister grin, and for a terrifying instant, his pupils grew fiery red like the eyes on the tattooed dragons. It was a wicked stare that left her hypnotized. The moment passed and Sandy found herself sitting once again at her husband's side.

"Now then," Dr. Ling announced. "Let us proceed!"

He swept about the almost empty room, lighting candles in sconces along the walls. As the room lit up, it began to fill up with shelves and tables covered with mysterious bottles and jars and bowls and containers until the room resembled that of one inhabited by some apothecary from dynasties long past. An ancient magic filled the cart, flowing with forces of darkness and light, scented by powders and roots and extracts of secret and terrible origins. Inside the cart itself, it felt like thunder was rolling nearby, and strange winds were howling about. The Amazing Dr. Ling placed his pipe in his mouth and began mixing ingredients.

Jerry closed his eyes and gritted his teeth, trying to ride out the terrible pain in his head. He thrust a hand out for Sandy to hold, and she took it, squeezing it tight as she watched the doctor produce the antidote to her husband's ailment. To her surprise, she couldn't take her eyes away.

Dr. Ling was finished within seconds. He stood before the couple with a small vial of formula in his hand, and the room magically emptied itself once again of the tables and shelves of mysterious ingredients. Even the candles in the wall sconces had blown out, leaving only the soft, dim light of the bulb overhead. As far as carnival attractions went, the illusions taking place inside the cart were astounding.

"Drink this!" Dr. Ling commanded, handing the vial to Jerry.

"And then I'll be cured?"

"This will manifest your illness into a physical form. When the transformation is complete, I'll call it forth and remove it from your body."

Jerry took the vial and drank.

And then he started screaming.

"Oh my God... It hurts! It fucking hurts so bad... *make it stop!*"

Sandy whimpered out loud and pulled her hand away from him to cover her mouth, horrified at watching her husband squirm and convulse.

"Plea-he-hese, make it stop!"

The pain was beyond description. It felt like an animal was clawing its way around inside his head. He could feel the jabbing barbs of tiny, razor-sharp claws digging into the tissue inside his skull. And when the claws moved, the rips and tears they produced burned like fire.

"Oh God! *It's killing me!*"

Sandy screamed.

"Do something!" she yelled at the doctor. "My God, what have you done to my husband?"

Dr. Ling stood silently, waiting.

Something broke loose up inside Jerry's nostrils, and a mixture of blood and pus gushed out his nose. He let out a horrible gasp and fell to the floor, shuddering in a seizure that gripped his whole body.

Sandy jumped up and knelt by his side, wanting desperately to help him, but Dr. Ling placed a hand on her shoulder and guided her back up to her feet.

"Do not touch him!" Dr. Ling ordered.

Tears rolled down her cheeks.

"What have you done, you asshole? What did you do to my husband?" She sobbed helplessly, covering her eyes with her hands.

"You must trust me, young miss. Your husband will be fine... Now sit down!"

She did, keeping her eyes covered to avoid looking at Jerry as the pain consumed him.

At last, the doctor moved. He held his tobacco pipe before him in his right hand, and began to wave his left hand over it. The pipe disappeared, and in its place appeared a long wooden flute. When the transformation was complete, he placed the flute's reed into his mouth and began to play.

The music was soft and sweet, like an old Oriental lullaby. Sandy removed her hands from her face and watched as he filled the room with music.

Eventually Jerry's spasms ceased, and he managed to sit upright. The blood and pus were still trickling from his nose, but the rest of his face looked calm, pacified.

The notes from Dr. Ling's flute grew stronger, the melody quickening to a crazed crescendo. Jerry moaned once, his eyes rolling back into his head so that only the sclera was visible. It looked like he was actually losing consciousness. Sandy wanted desperately to comfort him, to reach out and hold him, but she could not. The music was hypnotizing her as well, subduing her to the chair.

Louder, still, grew the notes. The haunting music swirled about them, echoing off the bare walls of the cart.

And then the malignancy birthed itself. A tiny red dragon thrust its head out of his right nostril. Its demon head yawned and screeched, showing off its needle-sharp teeth.

Sandy screamed again. The sight had been too horrific for her to bear. She simply closed her eyes and screamed until all the air left her lungs.

Dr. Ling continued the insane melody on his flute. The tiny dragon, no more than three inches long, was listening to the music as though it was listening to some foreign language that only it could understand. It crawled its way completely out of Jerry's nostril and dropped onto the floor. Sandy gazed on in horror as it scampered across the floor until it was standing at the feet of Dr. Ling.

The old man bent down and snatched up the dragon by its tail. When he did this, the music stopped, and the trance over Jerry and Sandy died away.

Both of them sat upright: Sandy on the chair and Jerry still on the floor. They watched as Dr. Ling held the tiny creature up into the air and examined it.

"Ah, my little friend," he spoke to it. "Let us place you somewhere safe."

Dr. Ling placed the flute between his lips (it had already changed back into his tobacco pipe again, but they hadn't noticed) and reached his free hand into a pocket somewhere inside his robe. When his hand came back out, it was holding a small glass jar that resembled a saltshaker. Dr. Ling opened the jar and placed the dragon inside.

The dragon roared furiously inside its tiny prison. Each tiny huff it made sent a blotch of foggy steam up the inside of the glass. It swirled angrily about on its tiny legs, the claws on its feet making a rapid clinking sound as it moved.

Jerry made his way to his feet and stared at the dragon in the bottle, eyes wide with disbelief.

"That...that was inside me?"

"It was, but in another form. Would you like to keep it?" Dr. Ling pushed the bottle toward Jerry.

"No. Jesus Christ, no!" Sandy was now standing behind him, peering around him cautiously to look at the bottle.

Dr. Ling nodded. "How do you feel? Is your headache better?"

He started to say yes, but instead looked down and noticed the bloodstain on his shirt. He turned to look at his wife, who started sobbing when she saw him.

His face was covered with blood.

Dr. Ling placed the jar with the dragon in it into his pocket and smiled.

"Pay no attention to the mess. I will take care of it."

He waved his arm out in front of Jerry, and the blood vanished. Every last drop melted away, evaporating into thin air the way everything else in the room had done at one point or another. Even the chair they'd been sitting on had vanished.

"Now, if you are satisfied, I'll bid you both 'Good Day.'" Dr. Ling bowed gracefully, and as he did, the door to the cart swung open, sending in a wave of the scorching afternoon heat. Without a moment's hesitation, Sandy grabbed her husband by the arm and was pulling him through the open door and down the wooden-plank steps, into the safety of the real world.

When they rounded the corner and took off down the midway, the Amazing Dr. Ling's medicine cart vanished as well.

***

It was well after midnight when the pain had awakened him. Jerry sat upright in bed, rubbing the area directly between his eyes and groaning in agony.

Terrible pain!

He'd thought for sure that he'd been cured once and for all. He'd felt fine all day...once they had left the carnival, that is. Better than fine, in fact. Seeing that horrible dragon in the glass bottle had been proof enough.

The feeling of tiny claws digging into his brain.

A wave of horror flushed through him.

Maybe the dragon came back!

"Oh my God!"

Sandy was awake instantly, switching on the lamp on her nightstand.

"What is it? You don't have a headache, do you?"

"Oh, Jesus... Oh, Jesus, *no!!!*"

The blood erupted once again out his nostrils, this time accompanied by the terrible crunch of cartilage snapping as the missing half of the whole manifested itself. White hot pain burned through him, and he began to claw frantically at his nose.

Sandy screamed, jumping off the bed and cowering into the corner as her husband convulsed in agony. She watched in terror as the other dragon, the green dragon, emerged from her husband's left nostril. It slithered out his nose and landed in a bloody-green plop on their bedspread. It offered one vicious little roar, then it scampered off into the darkness.

Sandy crawled over to the bed and stared at her shaking husband.

"Jerry...honey, are you all right?" she whispered in between sobs.

"I...I can't see," he whispered back. "Oh God, I'm blind... It took away my sight!"

Panic struck, and Jerry Ryan began to wail out loud.

"I can't see!"

For that had been the real prize that Dr. Ling had wished to claim. The Yin and Yang were once again a complete entity. Without the other, the one meant nothing. But together, they formed something complete, something important. Somewhere, at some carnival off in the distant future, some poor soul would be waiting to have his sight restored, even at the price of a few bad headaches. He'd even pay handsomely for it (a lot more than just fifty dollars), with a smile on his face and hope in his heart for a miracle. Such is the way with strange medicines.

And as Jerry entered, terrified, into his new world of cold, permanent darkness, he could hear the haunting melody of a flute playing somewhere in the night.

The Three Billy Goats Sothoth

It had been so long since Aelrick had heard the sound of human footsteps crossing his bridge he had almost forgotten what it sounded like.

He was the *last* of the trolls, and when the ancient ones had fallen into hibernation and mankind came and knocked down the old wooden bridge, *his* bridge, Aelrick had known the gates of the dominion had closed forever. The planet had moved on. And mankind, with their ambitions and technologies, had taught themselves above and beyond the dark magic and alchemy they'd once clung to. His old wooden bridge that gave passage between the flatlands and the mountains was replaced by beams of steel and paths of smooth, bonded stone. It was a blasphemy, in Aelrick's opinion. He could not understand why the Ancient Ones no longer concerned themselves with how mankind was corrupting the landscape and turning themselves into the New Gods.

Nowadays he merely slept beneath the bridge, casually listening to the roar of car engines above as man raced back and forth in his pursuit of defiant convenience, concerned only for himself. Even the trees along the mountainside whispered their displeasure at those ridiculous beasts, and the animals choked and gagged on the breaths of their metal chariots.

And, not that he would admit it, he was deathly afraid of them.

So when the day came that the engines ceased, and the once-noisy bridge was blanketed with a malignant silence, Aelrick began wondering if he might creep his way back up to the surface, back to the gates of his bridge, to investigate.

It was the sound of approaching footsteps that startled him.

It had been so long.

Aelrick spilled out from his nest beneath the cold, iron girders and scrambled his way to the road.

"Who's that clip-clopping over my bridge?" he screamed aloud, and found himself wondering if those were even the words he'd used to say.

The shroud of mist along the highway parted, and there before the tired old troll marched the first of the billy goats.

"Old fool! It is I," the first goat announced, its voice rolling off the vast expanse of nothing where the roar of traffic used to reside. "I am the Harbinger of Truth and Light. Have you not read about me in the Necronomicon's pages of Revelation? I have come to prepare the way for those who would escape the wrath of the Ancient Ones. I am the Clearer of Paths, and I must cross your bridge and make my way into the yonder mountains so that I may guide what is left of the pure and righteous to shelter and safety."

"You may *not* cross my bridge," Aelrick replied. "Mankind has made a mockery of this world, and I shall be damned to let any of them flee from the wrath of the Ancient Ones. Turn back, lest *you* wish to spend eternity falling prey to the monstrous appetite of Cthulhu himself!"

The old goat snuffed and stomped its feet on the worn, cracked macadam.

"Have you not felt the changes already begun?" the old goat spat. "Have you not witnessed the return of the Colours out of Space? The Ancient Ones are awakening, and it is for *them* to decide who is saved and who is cast aside. I implore you to move so that I may cross!"

The troll gazed into the heavens and found his mind spinning as he now understood the cosmos was also spinning in dreadful misalignment. Had it been so long since he last left his nest to gaze at the night sky? For all his mind, he could not remember a time when the patterns of the stars were not pacifying in their constant celestial locations. Now they reeled in chaos, vomiting themselves into terrible new patterns. Aelrick grew hypnotized as he gazed upon them, and when he closed his eyes, the spell broke. He turned and faced the first goat.

"You may *not* cross," the troll insisted. "Even mankind knows that goats are deceptive beasts. That is why in man's own misguided religions, you are a symbol of evil. You have disrupted the silence of my home and have awakened me from my slumber. Turn back! Turn back or I shall have to kill you and eat you for my dinner!"

The old goat lowered his head and began to cross the bridge. Without warning, the troll produced a dagger and spilled the blood of the animal, slitting its throat from one side to the other with a terrible wave of his hand.

Aelrick was smiling as his teeth bit down into the animal's flesh and swallowed his first taste of warm meat while the dying animal watched him.

After he'd fed, Aelrick returned to his nest and dozed off. In his weary mind's eye, he could still see the cosmos circling in chaotic orbits. How had he *not* felt that something was amiss? The crossing of those infernal metal beasts the humans traveled in had practically stopped overnight, and yet the enveloping silence had not grabbed his attention for only Yog knew when. With his belly fuller than it had been in centuries, the old troll yawned and curled into a ball, and he'd almost fallen asleep when approaching footsteps brought him back to consciousness.

"Another intruder!" he sighed. He crawled out of his nest and scrambled up to his bridge as the light of the blood moon crested over the mountain top.

"Who's that clip-clopping over my bridge?" Aelrick demanded.

Once again, the mists along the highway parted, and another goat stepped forward.

"Old fool, it is I," the second goat announced, its voice rolling off the vast expanse of nothing where the roar of traffic used to reside. "I am the Harbinger of Plagues and War. Have you not read about me in the Necronomicon's pages of Revelation? I am the Bearer of Woe and Misery. The trial of mankind has begun! It is I that corrupts the lands with wars and rumors of war. I am the producer of maladies that squeeze the life out of man until he panics and begs for mercy. I must cross this bridge and await the judgment of the righteous. I have killed many, many men throughout history, and once they cross this bridge, they will earn the right to judge me. They will slay me if they must. It is their reward for pleasing the Ancient Ones. I must cross this bridge and meet my fate. I ask you to please stand aside."

"You may *not* cross my bridge!" Aelrick replied. "For the last hundred years alone, I've watched mankind flourish in spite of his wicked ways. Where were the Ancient Ones when mankind blasphemed the world with their dreams of becoming gods themselves? They have plagued the world with terrible machines and filled the skies with the darkness of progress. This is *not* the world as the Ancient Ones had once perceived it."

The second goat snuffed and stomped its feet on the worn, cracked macadam.

"Have you not heard the cries of the suffering? Have you

forgotten the mercies of the Ancient Ones? You, too, shall be judged before this apocalypse is over. The Ancient Ones are returning to feast, and to reclaim their reign over this world. It is not your lot to defy them or alter the cleansing this world has waged upon itself!"

"Turn back, or I shall have to kill you and eat you for my dinner!"

The second goat lowered his head and began to cross the bridge. Without warning, the troll produced a hammer from his cloak, and proceeded to bash the beast until its skull shattered and its body tumbled lifeless to the ground. As the goat's legs and tail produced their last twitches, the troll proceeded to flay off its skins and hang them along the sides of the bridge to dry. The rest of the goat was torn apart and left on either side of the road for the wolves to feast upon.

"Whatever other intruders happen upon my bridge tonight will have to turn and flee from the wolves," Aelrick said to himself as he scampered down the hillside to his nest underneath the bridge. The troll once again curled into a ball and fell into the deepest of slumbers. He dreamed of the Ancient Ones, and how they once ruled the planet in fearsome wrath with their slimy, phosphorescent appendages and cavernous mouths of soulless blackness. Where had they gone? Where had they been for all these millennia? Were they sleeping at the bottom of some vast ocean floor? Or had they returned through space and time to whatever hell they were birthed from?

It was just before dawn when Aelrick was awoken by the sounds of the third chorus of footsteps. He crawled out of his nest and scrambled his way to the bridge.

The sun was just beginning to peak over the eastern mountaintops. And with the dawn came the call of the Ancient Ones, who were undoubtedly cresting from the depths of the cold Atlantic Ocean. Seagulls screamed and fish shrieked at their return. And from the west came the clip-clop of the third goat.

"Who's that clip-clopping over my bridge," the troll announced, and found his knees beginning to tremble beneath him. The Ancient Ones *were* returning...that much was obvious. But had he somehow interfered with their return to glory? Had he callously thrown himself into the wheels of fate? Had he perverted the gospels of the Necronomicon? Surely the Ancient Ones would forgive him after abandoning their sentry so long ago. He'd remained at his post, after all. Even when man had forged these terrible highways and blighted the landscapes with billboards and skyscrapers and polluted the earth for the sake of convenience, he had remained at his post. Even when he was no longer effective at stopping them.

"You fool! It is I," the third goat announced, its voice rolling off the vast expanse of nothing. He was much larger than the first two, and his horns curled with sinister perfection. When he spoke, he sounded not like the others, who bleated in the old animal-speak. This goat talked like the humans, and its voice echoed off the stones of the mountainside. "I am the Harbinger of Nothingness. I have come to blot out all that remains of the Old Ways. And you, Aelrick, are as much of the Old Ways as mankind ever was!"

A swarm of rats appeared at the goat's feet. They scampered and prowled about along the cold, desolate highway. Every now and then, the roar of the Ancient Ones bellowed over the mountainside at their rebirth. From behind the rats came the sound of the Human Parade, the last of the chosen survivors who were being led to the Mountains of Madness, where they would remain in sheltered safety until the Ancient Ones could feast upon the blemishes of the earth. It was as it had been written in the Necronomicon's pages of Revelation.

The old troll smiled in dreadful defiance.

"None of them shall pass," he sneered. "This is *MY* bridge! The Ancient Ones have tasked my kind to defend it, and defend it we have for as long as we could. I have never strayed from my post, even when mankind built their metal beasts and tried to run me down. And now *they* are the ones fleeing, and by their own hand. You cannot save them! Turn back, and turn *them* back, or I shall eat you all for my dinner!"

The third goat snuffed and stomped its feet on the worn, cracked macadam.

"Can you not see that the Ancient Ones are *here*? On the other side of this mountain is the face of mankind's destiny. Those who are not on the mountain behind you by daybreak will be snuffed out of existence. It is not up to you who lives or dies! These things have been preordained through time and space and existence. For all you know, you are unbalancing the scales of fate. If some of mankind does not survive, the dominion of the Ancient Ones will die as well. You will defile the symbiosis that the universe has created. That is *not* your lot to decide!"

The troll rubbed his chin in deep thought. Before him came the screams and cries of mankind, hoping and praying for refuge from the coming Armageddon. From behind him came the fierce, unforgiving bellows of the Ancient Ones, arising from the murky depths of slumber to once again restore balance to the planet.

Aelrick looked at the goat and smiled a wicked smile.

"Perhaps *I* am a god after all!" he declared. "Perhaps the fate of this world rests in *my* hands alone. It has been so long since I've been able to stand up against man in his metal beasts as they crossed my bridge. But here they are on foot once again, and the reign of those infernal automobiles is over. It would take so little for me to destroy this bridge, and all of your followers will meet the same cruel and terrible fate as everybody else!"

The third goat lowered its head and began to stomp his way across the bridge. But before the troll could reach him, long, thin tentacles began to berth themselves from its face. Its eyes rolled back, exposing the terrible, unseeing sclera of an awakening god, and its horns grew out into long, poisonous lances.

Aelrick barely had time to scream before Cthulhu erupted from the third goat's body, and gored him into a savage, bloody pulp.

From beyond the mountainside, the Ancient Ones roared their approval.

A Taste of Green Voodoo Healing

He was going to New Orleans to die.

There were so many layers to Daniel's condition that it was impossible now to pull them apart and examine each different tier individually. There was always the pain. Following him around day and night, around the clock despite the morphine and the sedatives. The pain of his body in response to the chemotherapy treatments, and the subsequent radiation treatments when the chemo failed to bring him into remission. The pain of his lungs trying to inflate with his every inhalation, only to cause his lung tissue to crumble and break apart, allowing him to slowly cough out his own organs in small, bloody pieces.

And then there was the real pain.

The absolute horror of feeling his body turn against him, withering away against his will. Daniel had spent the first few years telling his family and friends that he was a fighter, that he was going to beat the disease no matter what it took. He wore his battle scars with pride. The loss of hair from the treatments, the ever-changing wardrobe as his body shrank from robust to gaunt, then to emaciated, and finally to skeletal, even the mahogany cane he now used to move himself around as his joints creaked and snapped out loud. It was like feeling...reduced. Reduced from a normal human being to a wretched freak, to a prisoner in a decaying body while his still-normal mind was left trying to cope with his situation and not go crazy. The only pain worse than the burning in his lungs was feeling his heart breaking knowing that his family and friends were no longer praying for him to get better, but that they were secretly praying for him to die quickly and painlessly. And, of course, the heartbreak of having to say goodbye. So when loved ones were around he laughed a lot, hugged a lot, and always spoke of the good times. He fought his disease hard, and with all he had.

As time passed, the mind fought harder as the body failed. The laughter died away slowly. The hugs were followed by tears. Goodbyes became harder, to the point where Daniel found himself ending departures with friends by saying, "Thanks for everything," and, "I love you," just in case. Just in case...

Fighting battles and winning wars were two separate things. The war had already been lost. And to his deepest loathing and sorrow, he realized that the fighting he was doing wasn't against a disease. It was against acceptance. Accepting that he had no control, nor any possibilities. Life had become for him a frozen stage of transition. So when Dr. Metzger gave him a final consultation, informing him that all the avenues of treatment were exhausted and that it was time to make peace, time to close the open doors, Daniel found himself happy.

He also found himself packing a suitcase the moment he got home. If he couldn't beat the disease, he would cheat it. No dying in his own bed, surrounded by loved ones watching helplessly. No teary final farewells. No drowning in a morphine haze as the cancer finished the job it started. Just a note saying his goodbyes for him.

Fuck the cancer! He was going to go down with a bottle of bourbon in one hand and a cigar in the other.

He could be in New Orleans by Saturday. He would live to see Mardi Gras.

That was his final fight.

***

Driving was a nightmare, but it was the only way for him to travel. Flying was out of the question; the cabin pressure alone would have flattened his lungs completely. Daniel had considered taking a train or a bus down, but the thought of sitting still for hours on end, trying not to vomit or hack what was left of his lungs out, made him sicker than his symptoms ever could. Best to keep occupied, to hold onto the illusion of control for as long as possible. He had to quit the morphine cold turkey to do it, and the pain was almost intolerable, but it was the price he had to pay for buying his freedom. Daniel followed Route 10 south and turned his aqua blue Ford Escort onto Canal Street. He felt the hot tears streak down his face as he entered the French Quarter and glanced around the busy, tourist-filled streets of his dying ground.

Daniel thought he'd gone to heaven.

He had no trouble at all finding a table in the near-empty bar.

The Diablo Lounge, a blues joint on St. Charles Street, was beginning to fill slowly, but he'd entered early enough on Sunday afternoon to get a seat in a darkened corner facing the stage. A jukebox near the bar hummed noisily with a Robert Johnson tune. "Got My Mojo Working" rang out in the unctuous voice of the dead blues man. Daniel poured himself a glass of Pouilly-Fuisse from the bottle the waitress had left with him and raised a toast to the sentiment.

Many nameless faces came and went as the day passed by. The air had grown thick with the odors of stale cigarette smoke, Creole cooking, and the lingering scent of fresh, clean young women as they sauntered by. His lungs ached from it, but Daniel didn't care. His brain ached worse with the thought of how his mother and father would react when they opened his note and read it. All those nights they had spent at his bedside as the malignancy ran its course. Mom always there with his medication and the cool, wet washcloth to wipe the sweat off his tired face. And Dad constantly holding his hand and reading to him, trying to keep Daniel's mind occupied so that he could rest easier.

He'd been selfish to leave them, but it didn't matter now. It couldn't be helped now. Daniel would never survive a trip home at this point, and he knew it. He'd punished them for long enough with his disease. Just watching him dying had been enough of a drain on them. But he really hadn't escaped for their benefit. He'd left for himself. Daniel could only hope that they understood.

The Diablo Lounge was alive and well by sundown, and absolutely jumping by seven p.m. when the band came on. A jazz quartet called The Swinging Foot had taken the stage. Their leader, a lanky pianist with a coppery suntan and long, stringy black hair was leading his bandmates into a raucous dance number that had the crowd on its feet. The dancers (mostly young women) all had shiny plastic beads strung around their necks. Tourist kids, mostly. College students blowing their parents' cash to get drunk and crazy and flash their tits around in pursuit of those damn silly beads.

Daniel had finished off the bottle of wine ages ago, and was already at the halfway point in a bottle of bourbon. By the time The Swinging Foot had begun its third song, he was almost down to the bottom of this new bottle, and the room was spinning quite wonderfully inside his head. He'd almost succeeded at drowning out the pain, but the sorrow still lingered.

"I'm dying," he told himself aloud. "I'm really fucking dying." The tears began to form at the corners of his eyes. "I really have to say goodbye to all of this." Daniel closed his eyes as the tears began to fall, but the image of the bright lights and the dancing people continued to flash in his mind.

"Is that why you are here?" asked a soft, silky voice to his left.

Daniel opened his watering eyes and looked up at the woman who had addressed him. She was an exotic-looking woman with rich, cocoa skin and long, frizzy black hair that slinked down her spine to the lower part of her back. Her shiny brown eyes stared down at him, and a smile spread across her lovely face.

"Most people come here to be alive, dearie. We have enough ghosts here in New Orleans (she'd pronounced it Naw'lins) without you adding to their numbers." The woman slipped the purse she was wearing off her shoulder, set it on his table, and floated down into the empty chair across from him.

"My name is Ruby," she said, and her slender hand reached across the table. Daniel had assumed she meant to shake his hand and extended his own, then retracted it when he realized she was reaching for his bottle of bourbon. Ruby lifted the bottle to her crimson lips and drained the last of the alcohol.

"I'm Daniel," he retorted, taken aback by her lack of shyness.

"Oh, honey," she said, placing the bottle back down onto the table. "You look as though you're dead already." Her glowing eyes ran up and down his withered frame. "Were you planning on dying alone down here? Where are you from?"

The waitress came over and picked up the empty bottle. "Can I bring you anything else?" she asked, a smile across her face. Undoubtedly, she was relieved that he now had company to care for him. How she had frowned when he first dragged himself in, looking like death warmed over. The Swinging Foot was wailing away on a bluesy number, the bassist thumping away like mad on his standing double-bass.

"Tell Louie to send us out a bottle of Green River, please, and we'll be on our way." Ruby slid her chair around the table so that she was beside Daniel. She traced one of her rich, brown fingers down his earlobe and whispered, "Pay her, and we'll go back to your place."

Daniel pulled his wallet out of the back pocket of his khaki slacks and plucked out a wad of crisp, new twenty-dollar bills. He shot an embarrassed glance up at the waitress, who was making corrections to his current tab. She smiled again and told him his balance, and he placed the money on her tray. Without a word, the waitress turned and walked off toward the bar to fill Ruby's order.

At first Daniel had felt very awkward about the whole money situation, and how he would be paying for this "Death Trip" he was taking. He'd handed his credit card to the innkeeper at the hotel where he'd checked in to stay (the Chateau Ste. Marie, an old bordello that had been refurbished into a cozy little inn) with a twinge of guilt, knowing deep down that he'd never have to pay his credit company for the things he would be charging. He would simply...succumb. That was as good a way of phrasing it as any. And once he "succumbed," they wouldn't be getting one red cent from him ever again. This thought, at the time, sent shivers down his spine, but after he signed the guest registry, he found the experience to be quite liberating. He'd spent all of Saturday night in his tiny room with a bottle of whiskey (which he also charged) fantasizing about a shopping spree that included a new car, new clothes, wine, women, and song, and fell asleep that night a happy man. Daniel found he'd had absolutely no problem hitting the cash machine in the lobby the next morning and taking out five hundred bucks in crisp new twenties.

He watched the waitress cross over behind the bar and whisper to the bartender, who in turn went into the back room through a large oak door labeled "Office." He felt Ruby's hand fall into his lap and begin to massage the growing bulge in his pants as the bartender reemerged with a bottle wrapped up in a brown paper bag. Daniel looked at Ruby.

"I don't think I have the strength to give you that," he said, nodding down toward his crotch. "And not just because of the alcohol."

Ruby's lips parted in a smile of teeth so white that it stood out against her dark skin in terrifying contrast. Her eyes glistened in the pale, smoky light.

"Oh, don't you be worrying none about that, dearie. I think I can help you take care of that."

The waitress walked over and silently handed her the bottle, then disappeared again into the jubilant crowd.

"I think a little voodoo healing might do you good! Are you ready to go, er... Have you told me your name yet, honey?"

"Daniel," he repeated, standing up and offering his hand again for her to shake, but he staggered back down into his seat as the alcohol hit him.

"Daniel Trembly," he finished, and found himself laughing in spite of himself at the coincidence of his surname and his shaky condition.

"Well, Danny." Ruby stood and helped him up to his feet. He could smell her warm, sweet skin as she wrapped her arm around his shoulder, her other arm tightly clutching the bottle in the brown paper bag. Together, the two parted their way through a sea of sweaty flesh as The Swinging Foot rumbled through some wailing blues number. Daniel was certain he heard the pianist sing a lyric that sounded like, "Lost soul in the Bayou/Time to make your stand... Time to learn to sing the blues/and shake the Devil's hand!"

***

The walk back to his room in the Chateau Ste. Marie was filled with delicious, playful flirtation, and for the first time in a long time Daniel had forgotten about his disease and found himself smiling. Ruby never came out and told him she was a prostitute, but then, some things didn't need to be mentioned. This was why he'd come down to New Orleans. If she demanded whatever was left of the five hundred dollars in his wallet, he'd pay it gladly, so long as she stayed the night with him. She was extremely beautiful in an exotic sense, and the thought of seeing her naked sent shivers and thrills through his own intoxicated body. Time and again he found his hand slipping down her backside and squeezing her ass. Ruby simply laughed.

"That's right, sugar... You'll be all mine by the time I'm done with you," she told him with a wink as the doorman outside the Chateau opened the door for them.

***

Even with the air conditioner running, Daniel's hotel room felt sultry. He entered the room and dropped the key card onto the dresser, but his coordination was poor from the alcohol and the card tumbled to the floor. He stumbled across the room and dropped onto the bed. Ruby followed, snatching the key card off the carpet and placing it back on the dresser.

"How you feeling, honey?" she asked, pushing her way past the bed and over to the table by the windows. The table was flanked by two large wicker chairs, one of which she pulled out and sat in, dropping her purse onto the table as she did. Daniel rolled onto his back and faced upward toward the ceiling.

"I'm fucking dying," he said. And then he howled with laughter as if it was the funniest thing he'd ever said. Shit, he'd been on some big-time drinking benders back in his college days, and had uttered that very phrase at least a hundred times. But he'd always managed to be alive come the next morning. This time there was no guaranteeing that. The thought should have frightened him, but at the moment he didn't really care. At the moment he was happy, regardless of the fact that the room was spinning and his head was beginning to hurt.

Ruby rummaged through her purse, pulling out miscellaneous items and placing them on the table next to the ominous bottle in the brown paper bag. One of the items was a large, thick candle, which she placed on the center of the table and lit with her cigarette lighter. When she was satisfied, she stood up and breezed past the bed again and darted into the bathroom.

"Didn't you just hear me?" Daniel hollered out to her. "I said I'm dying, so if you're planning to fuck me, we should get started pretty soon!"

She slid out of the bathroom with a pitcher of cold water in one hand and a pair of transparent plastic cups in the other. She set these items over on the table, next to the items she'd left there. Afterward, she turned and faced him and began to unbutton her blouse. There was no trace of a bra underneath, and the blouse fluttered down past her luscious breasts into a silky heap on the floor.

"Oh, don't you worry, dearie... I'm going to take good care of you. I promise." A smile lit across her face and she sat back down in the wicker chair. Daniel tried to lift his head to watch her as she removed the bottle from the paper bag, and then the small leather medicine pouch from her purse. His head swam, and he dropped back down onto the bed as she dipped a spoon into the medicine bag and extracted a portion of white powder. He watched her shadow, cast from the candle's flickering flame, as it danced on the ceiling. He watched it moving as she mixed drinks for both of them.

"You never even asked me what I'm dying from," he announced to the ceiling. Even if he hadn't drunk a drop of alcohol today, he was almost certain that he'd be intoxicated by the warm, sweet scent of her skin. And if that wasn't enough, whatever she was about to give him would probably finish the job quite nicely.

"I already know," Ruby answered as she lifted a pair of green, swamp-water colored drinks and carried them over to the bed. Being careful not to spill them, she sat down on the bed next to his prostrate body. Her long, black hair tumbled down her topless chest, allowing only glimpses of her warm, purple-brown nipples. "And it's nothing we're going to worry about yet. Here. Sit up and drink."

Daniel fumbled himself up until he was sitting beside her. Ruby handed him one of the plastic cups. As she did, she shifted her head so that her hair flew back, exposing her breasts, and began to drink from her own cup. Daniel lifted his cup to his lips, then stopped himself for a cautious sniff. He wasn't certain, but he believed that if his cancer had a scent, the green solution he was holding in his hand was probably close.

Ruby laughed out loud at him. "Drink it down, you silly boy," she urged him.

"What is it?"

"Absinthe," she told him, then took another sip from her cup. "It is the river of Green Voodoo."

He was going to sip his drink, but decided that if he did, he might not be able to finish it. So he closed his eyes, took a breath, and chugged it down. When he looked up again, he had a faint green mustache over his top lip. Ruby laughed again and drank down her own cup. Then she leaned forward, pressing her breasts against him, and began to kiss him and lick the sticky solution from his trembling lips.

***

Clarity and hallucination melded as Ruby stood to her feet before him, and long, angel-like wings unfurled behind her back. She leaned forward and helped Daniel pull his shirt off, exposing the pale white skin of his chest. He tried to stand before her but the world was careening madly around him, and he lost his balance. Ruby pushed him back down so that he was again prostrate on the bed, unbuttoned his pants, and helped him slide them off. His naked body felt cold despite the humid warmth within the room.

"You just relax," she told him as a radiant halo appeared around her head. "I'm not ready for you just yet."

Daniel watched as the angel before him floated across the room, stopping momentarily to unfasten her skirt and let it drop down to the floor beside her blouse. Again, she was wearing no undergarment, so he could immediately see the warm, glistening skin of her thighs and the rich, velvety fuzz of her pubic mound.

"Does anybody know that you're here?" she asked, smiling as she caught him admiring her sensuous body.

"No," he whispered, his eyes wide and staring. Every single nerve in his skin wanted him to reach out and touch her. "I mean, I left my parents a note, telling them that I was leaving to die alone, so they wouldn't have to watch." He grinned up at her as he watched the angel hovering over the table, searching through her purse. "But they have no idea where I went," he babbled on. "I had to put a note in my wallet so that when I do die, they'll know how to contact my parents and send me home."

"Is that right?" Ruby beamed at him, pulling a long, shiny object from her purse. "Well, I don't think that you'll be needing that note for too much longer. We're going to cut that darkness right out of your body." She raised the object for him to see. It was a surgical scalpel.

He watched her for a horrified moment; Ruby, with the scalpel in her hand, floating above him in midair, her brilliant halo glimmering in the candlelight of the darkened room. Her wings, adorned with long white and gold feathers, billowed out behind her. She smiled at him.

"I'm not going to hurt you, my love," she whispered, her brown eyes hypnotizing him. "You have to do the surgery yourself."

"Are...are you some kind of voodoo lady?" he asked as she floated down to him. He had thought she was a prostitute when he'd met her back at the Diablo Lounge. Now he just didn't know. Now there was no reality. There was only her, with the beauty of an angel and the smile of the Devil.

"Close your eyes," she told him.

***

There was no way for Daniel to pinpoint the moment when Ruby had coaxed his spirit to leave his body. There had been the oddest sensation that gravity had doubled on his body, then doubled again, until it felt like a thousand, thousand hands were pulling him down onto the mattress.

"Come forward," she whispered. "Come to me..."

And then he was rising upward, floating like a helium balloon. Had he been conscious through the ordeal, he might have likened it to an out-of-body experience. He felt himself levitating upward until the mass of flesh that was his body beneath him felt distant.

Ruby had reached out to him, and he could still see her as an angel with her wings and halo. He felt his spirit-hand reach out to her, where she slipped the cold steel handle of the scalpel into his palm, and then squeezed his hand into a fist. Daniel thought for certain that the instrument would fall through his ghostly hand, but to his surprise it stayed and he could actually feel it.

"Now, turn over and cut that filthy blackness out of your body," she commanded.

Daniel felt himself turning over in midair until he was facing the empty shell of his body lying on the bed. Just as he'd imagined, he saw hundreds of rotten, scaly hands holding his body down. It looked as though the hands had dug and clawed their way right through the mattress, as though the bed were nothing more than raw earth. It had been frightening enough just watching this terrible spectacle, but two of the hands were gripping his throat, and for a split second he felt as if he couldn't breathe.

"Just relax," Ruby told him, "and let the scalpel dive into the skin."

He closed his phantom eyes and let the knife hack away at his flesh, making long, vertical incisions just below each of his nipples. To his amazement, he felt no pain.

In what felt like no time at all, he'd made openings into his chest large enough to see the blood-soaked bones of his ribcage. Beneath this he could see his own heart throbbing away, keeping the blood flowing through his body. He could see his lungs expanding with each inhalation, then contracting, forcing the air out of his body's open mouth.

"I can't do this!" he whispered.

"I can't do this!" the empty body beneath him mouthed in response.

Daniel turned his spirit-head to Ruby for help and saw her naked body down by his feet at the end of the bed.

"You can!" she uttered. "You must. If you leave your body like this, you'll be dead very soon."

"What do I do now?" he asked, his flesh-body beneath him parroting the question seconds later.

"Take the knife and cut a slit right between the ribs. Then you just slip your hand inside your lungs and rip out whatever you feel squirming inside."

As if the scalpel was obeying her order, it dipped down in between the ribs over his left lung and made a fresh incision. Moments later, to his absolute horror, his free hand plunged into the bloody tissue of his lung.

It felt like he'd dipped his hand into a vat of live eels. Panic swept over him, and Daniel found himself wanting to pull his hand back out, but before he could, one of the eel-like creatures curled around his finger and bit him.

"Ouch!" he yelled in surprise.

"Ouch!" his flesh-body repeated.

With a look of determination on his spirit-face, he found himself fishing around inside his body for the culprit. When he caught it, he yanked it up out of his chest cavity.

The creature, roughly six inches long, had indeed resembled an eel once he had it out into the light. The creature swung its head around to face him, its needle-like teeth gnashing in fury, and then it began to melt into a thick, cloudy vapor, and then...

It had formed into the face of Erica Campbell, a little girl that Daniel had gone to elementary school with as a child. She wasn't the prettiest girl way back then, but she wasn't ugly either. In fact, seeing her face now, she was almost pretty, or at least would grow up to be.

But all the other boys and girls treated her as if she *had* been ugly. How they'd teased her, tormented her. He closed his phantom eyes and remembered a younger version of himself, and the day that Erica had asked him if he'd go with her to the sixth-grade dance.

How much nerve it must have taken her. She'd cornered him in the hallway on the way to the cafeteria, and before he knew it, she was spilling her guts in front of everybody, telling him how she had a crush on him and begging him to go to the dance with her. He remembered how all the other kids were watching, some laughing and tittering, others making snide remarks.

"No!" he'd bellowed at her. "Not in a million years!" He'd been angry at her for putting him in that situation, especially in front of his friends. Poor Erica ran away crying and had avoided him from that day on.

Erica's face transformed back into an eel and made to bite him again. Daniel threw it aside to the foot of the bed, where it became a piece of dead, malignant tissue. When the phantom-Daniel turned back to the flesh-Daniel to continue, Ruby snatched up the dead flesh and stuffed it into her mouth, dribbling its blood down her chin.

The surgery continued into the night: Daniel pulling the slithering, black eel-flesh from his lungs, watching the memories they became, then tossing them to Ruby for her to consume. Most of the memories were of people that he'd wronged in his lifetime, or of those who had wronged him. The eels that bit at him the hardest were the ones that involved the most hatred. Daniel saw Mr. Morrison, his high school Social Studies teacher. Daniel had wronged him one night at a party, where he'd spread some vicious lies about the teacher to some girls, just to try and impress them enough to maybe get down their pants. It hadn't worked, of course, and in the end, Mr. Morrison had found out about it.

He saw others as well: a previous boss that had fired him, a co-worker that had falsely accused him of something, an old girlfriend that he'd caught cheating on him. The eels squirmed on inside his tired, aching lungs until he reached the last, the most painful.

And the most terrible.

There was a face at each end of the last slithering black creature, and when he pulled it out and examined it, they morphed into the faces of his mother and father as they read the note he'd left for them. The note telling them that he was leaving to die on his own.

Daniel looked into the tired old faces of his parents and watched as the tears began to flow. And then his mother swooned into a faint, leaving his father grasping desperately to catch her and not fall himself.

Ruby was laughing as she viewed all of this.

"I shouldn't have left them," the spirit-Daniel said aloud.

"I shouldn't have left them," the bleeding pile of flesh that was his body mimicked in response.

"It is time to go back," Ruby told him from behind, and immediately the multitude of cold, dead hands holding his body down released him, melting back into the mattress where they'd sprung from. His body gave a great lurch upward and, without warning, its arms thrashed out until its fingers grasped the spirit form of himself and pulled the two entities back together as one.

The oddness of his body and spirit reuniting was awful enough, but the sudden realization that his chest was still ripped wide open...the feeling of the warm, moist air against his bare lungs made him scream. Daniel's hands shot out to his chest and felt his lacerated skin, and pulled his blood-covered fingers away in dread.

The angel form of Ruby floated down to him, her smooth black hand covering his mouth to silence him.

"The hardest part is done, my love," she told him in a soothing whisper. "You just lay still now, and let me help you."

Daniel tried to protest, but felt his body slacken against the bed. Ruby mounted his lower body, and he felt his penis penetrate her. He closed his eyes and the world around him seemed to be spinning much slower than before this nightmare had begun. Her hands began to gently pull the lacerated skin back together, and then she ran her tongue slowly over the wounds. The feeling it gave was a mixture of pain and ecstasy as he felt the wounds burning underneath her tongue, fusing the lacerations back together in patches of warm scar tissue. And as he felt himself mounting into an intense orgasm, he lost consciousness, his body floating away as the angel finished healing the wounds that relieved him of his disease.

***

"How are you feeling?" she asked when his eyes opened. Daniel felt like he'd slept for an eternity but could tell it had only been moments when he looked up at her. Ruby still had her wings and halo, and when she pulled herself off him, he felt his still-erect penis slide out of her vagina.

"Thirsty," he panted into the darkness. "I'm very thirsty."

Ruby was at the table again, and was mixing him another swamp-green cocktail. When she returned, he sat up and took the plastic cup from her. As he drank, his free hand traced across the healed flesh of his chest. There were tacky smears of blood still matted on him, but the skin itself was perfectly healed.

Daniel looked up at Ruby standing above him and noticed the smears of his blood on her breasts and across her face. It should have sickened him, yet seeing her wearing his blood made her more exotic than ever.

Ruby bent down to him and lifted his cup up to his lips, and he emptied every last drop in a few quick swallows.

"Am I cured?" he whispered to her.

"Almost, my love," she answered.

Ruby turned to cross the room, and Daniel noticed the feathers of her wings beginning to fall off and flutter to the floor. The moment the feathers brushed against the carpet, they crumpled up and formed into rats, which began to scurry off into the darkness.

Daniel gasped, watching the rats scamper around her feet.

"You don't need to worry," she assured him. "I've told you already, the worst part is over." Ruby paid no mind to the rats scurrying about the room. Her once-brilliant halo was fading, her wings raining down feathers, leaving a crumpled set of bare, scaly branches protruding from her back.

"You're going to live."

Daniel could hear zydeco music from one of the clubs across the street drifting lazily through the window. Neon lights flashed outside as the city reveled in its night life. The rest of the world seemed alive and well as his nightmare stretched into forever.

"There's one more bit of cancer I still need to remove," Ruby told him. She held the scalpel in her slender black fingers, looking deep into his terrified eyes. "A worm. Nesting inside your head. I need to take it out for you. Then you'll be perfect."

She lifted the scalpel against his temple and began to dig.

There was very little pain as the blade broke through the skin, and Daniel closed his eyes. She was no longer an angel, this much he knew. He simply kept his eyes closed and tried to focus on the image of his parents as they'd appeared reading the note he'd left. They had wept, and he felt himself weeping as well, knowing in a blinding epiphany that even if Ruby *had* cured him, he'd still never see them again.

He was still being reduced. Right down to an empty shell.

She removed the scalpel, and the worm bore its way out of his brain, out through the hole she'd made for it. The worm had Daniel's face on it, screaming as it birthed its way out of his head and into the light.

A set of long, black fingers plucked the worm out of Daniel's skull and tossed the writhing creature into Ruby's mouth. She chewed with a smile on her face and swallowed his soul, washing it down with a fresh cup of absinthe.

The part of Daniel that had loved life and feared dying was gone. As were his emotions and memories, his thoughts and worries and doubts and cares. She had given his body life and taken his soul in return.

Ruby wrapped her arm around his body and lifted him into sitting position. She held the cup to his lips for him to drink. There was nothing left inside of him to protest.

Daniel's eyes watched in a blind stare as Ruby stood and dressed herself in silence. Next, she picked his pants off the floor and fished his wallet out of the back pocket. All the while, her image morphed into the demon that she really was: horns sprouted from her forehead, and her forked, serpentine tongue shot out of her mouth, carefully licking the remnants of his blood off her face. She opened the wallet and casually removed the note he'd written, regarding whom to contact in the event of his death. With a sinister wink and a low, terrible laugh, she held the note to the flame of the candle on the table and let it burn. The other contents of his wallet, his driver's license, credit card, and the remainder of the five hundred dollars, she carelessly dropped into her purse. Then Ruby left all that was left of Daniel in his hotel room.

The remainder of the absinthe she left for him on the table.

***

Ruby had told him that New Orleans already had enough ghosts, and this was true. At sunrise, the zombie figure of a once-dying man left the Chateau Ste. Marie and joined the mass of a million other soulless beings in a parade of flesh. A parade of flesh that would search on for an eternity, looking for a river of Green Voodoo Healing.

Two Slugs in the Belly

The eastern side of Dome 12 smelled like broken sewage lines and obscene mating rituals. Even from three miles away Krieger could smell the stench filling his monorail car as the train passed over the last of the clean, habitable tenements in the colony. Within a few minutes the train would cross over Lake Denebola and into the farthest station under the dome. Krieger already knew the living quarters there were nothing more than scattered one-occupant pods meant for the outcasts banished from regular colony life. He'd been sent there way too many times to count, by either the Colony Council or Minister Adelaide herself. Krieger wasn't the only private investigator in the colony, but he was the best. Thorough, efficient, and most importantly, discrete. If they were sending *him*, it meant they were operating outside Dome Law.

The eastern portion of the dome was what they used to call a shantytown back on Earth, and he knew it like the back of his hand. Nearly an earth-year had passed since the last time he'd been there, but news of the growing tensions between the humans and the Sabikans had already circulated to Capitol City. Things were getting uglier by the day, according to the news reports. His target, a human named Doolah Quar, had gone into hiding, refusing to return to the capitol and disabling her Computex system, rendering her unreachable. It would take an hour, perhaps two, but he'd creep through the streets of the eastern side—with little notice or fanfare—locate Doolah Quar, and have her back on the outbound monorail before the stars of Orion could flicker blue.

He was halfway over Denebola before he picked up the file and started leafing through it.

Denebola. *The Lion's Tail.* The picture inside Quar's dossier was of a middle-aged black woman with long hair snarled into dreadlocks and eyes that indeed looked like the piercing gaze of a lioness.

According to the file, Doolah was originally from Earth (Jamaican descent) and had arrived at Dome 12 via the Colonization Lottery System. Krieger already knew this information was propaganda. She was a both a midwife and an abortion technician back on Earth. The dome had several perfectly staffed medical centers that could handle pregnancies and abortions, but after the Colony Council agreed to open Ganymede's domes to the refugees from Sabika, all bets were off. Once interspecies mating began, there was a seventy-two-hour window between fertilization and "host catatonia." Loss of neurological and motor skills, eventual paralysis, and finally a painful death as the Sabikan spawn devoured their way *out*.

"We're going to ask for your complete discretion on this," Ramu told Krieger as he passed the file across the desk. Behind him, three other members of the council watched in silence, their heads down toward their polished boots like guilty children. "We can't have word of what's happened going beyond these walls. It's Minister Adalaide's daughter. She's caught two slugs in the belly."

Two slugs in the belly. Back on Earth, that meant that the villain in some black and white cinema reel was just gunned down in cold blood. Here on Ganymede, it meant that a Sabikan had spilled its seed inside some poor prostitute or some lonely, desperate woman who was seduced by the alien species. The Sabikans looked very much human; you wouldn't be able to discern any noticeable differences with full clothing on, which made it all the easier for the Colony Council to permit their sanctuary inside Ganymede's habitat domes. Here on Ganymede, cinema reels were an archaic remembrance of the past from a planet that was beginning its next big extinction phase. Doolah Quar was lucky that the doctors in Dome 12 wanted nothing to do with aborting zygote slugs, especially once they discovered how lethal they became when removed from the womb. Krieger estimated that Quar saved more lives in Dome 12 than all the doctors there combined.

Always twins. Two slugs in the belly because Sabikan evolution perpetuates repopulation as a defense mechanism against extinction.

A pleasant female voice came over the monorail's p.a. system.

"Welcome to Eastern Station, the outermost territory in Dome 12. Be sure to obtain all your personal belongings, and please dispose of any trash in the proper receptacles. For departure schedules, please visit our Computex domain page on your portable mainframe device or speak to our friendly, courteous staff. Thank you for choosing Dome Transit!"

Krieger took one last glance at Doolah Quar's photograph and found his eyes gazing into those piercing lioness orbs.

"Time is ticking, Doolah," he said as he closed the file and shoved it into his hipsling. "Seventy-two hours goes real fucking fast when you're this far away from the sun."

***

The streets were lined with filthy pedestrians, both human and Sabikan, donning torn clothes and huddling around barrel fires. It always frightened Krieger to watch this, as the trees inside the domes were meant to produce oxygen and filter out the carbon emissions. Burning them prematurely was just as dangerous as, say, the ruptured sewage system that was supposed to bring waste to the treatment plants for filtration and recycling. Here on the eastern side, sewage now ran directly into the lake, which further threatened the dome's ecosystem. It was one of those things the Colony Council never seemed to care about.

Because fixing it takes money from their pockets.

But the minister's daughter—*that* mattered.

Ramu never mentioned just how far Tirese Adelaide was in her gestation. He only said that time was invaluable in righting her situation. They'd already had his and Doolah's return tickets purchased and ready for him inside her dossier.

Krieger hustled down the streets, basking at the changing colors of neon glow that wavered over the darkened landscape. Up close it looked a lot like an apocalyptic version of Times Square in New York City back on Earth, only on a smaller scale. There were no domescrapers here on the outskirts. Rather, the tallest buildings were three floors maximum, and those buildings were mostly dedicated to public works: a courthouse, a prison complex for those too unfit for civilian life, an energy plant, the sewage treatment facility. There were storefronts and gin-joints as well, but these buildings were single-floor units. Many were closed now, seeing that there was little need for commerce in an area where hardly anyone held a paying job. The places that *were* open either bartered in trade or made their money through illegal means.

Why the fuck would Quar want to live here? She should be making enough money in her trade to live in one of those domescrapers back in the city, back where civilian life remained civil.

He thought of the photograph he'd now committed to memory, the one with the lioness eyes which professed that she'd eat you alive just as soon as look at you.

It's the job. It must get to her. She's not that much different from you, after all… Cleaning up other people's messes and doing all the dirty work. You've got a bad liver and a horrible case of insomnia from all the shit you've slung over the years. So she stakes a claim to a vacant pod out here, where she probably gets most of her clients anyway.

The file had no direct living address for her, but the greatest concentration of eastern dwellers convened just ahead on Marley Drive. Fitting for a Jamaican immigrant, if the street was named after the legendary reggae singer back on Earth. But Krieger knew better. It was named after Captain Alex Marley, who piloted the first shuttle here to Jupiter's largest moon. The Colonization Project was supposed to happen on Mars, but back home on Earth it was decided that they wanted an outpost further out into the solar system, where it would serve as a more centralized hub for space exploration. And, as Krieger also knew, Jupiter was ripe with natural gases and resources that could fuel the Earth's needs a million times over.

At least until the new extinction phase began unexpectedly.

Krieger wondered if there were any forms of life left on his home planet.

There was movement ahead. A crowd had formed outside one of the watering holes, a gin-joint called *Neptune, Baby!*, and Krieger was almost certain he saw a tall, black woman with dreadlocks pushing her way through the front door with two young white men following directly behind her. Krieger was still a block away, and couldn't be certain it was her, but he had a gut feeling.

It was how she walked.

She stalked like a lioness.

***

"Doolah Quar?"

"I'm off the clock, mon." Doolah leaned over to one of her men-in-waiting behind her and said, "Be a doll and go get me a Martian Tourniquet on the rocks." She looked back at Krieger and glared through those wild, lioness eyes. "It's after business hours, and I ain't got no business with you, whoever you are. Come find me tomorrow if you need me to visit your little lady and fix your problems."

The young man was already off to fetch her drink, and Krieger couldn't help but admire her. Back on Earth, they'd have called her a cougar. She was easily old enough to be the kid's mother. And why not? She absolutely radiated sexual confidence and prowess. The other young man was sitting in the chair on her left, and his eyes kept shifting from giving him dirty looks to trying to gaze beneath the descending vee of her Dermex top into the luscious depths of her cleavage. It was a cinch that both young men were human; no way in hell Doolah Quar would risk mounting a Sabikan and risk catching two slugs in the belly.

"I have orders from Capital 12 to bring you back to the city with me. Your skills are needed immediately, and I'm to stun you and drag you unconscious if you refuse to cooperate."

Doolah smiled, and the burgundy lipstick on those lovely lips parted into an animal grin. He almost expected to see fangs rather than perfect incisors.

"Someone important got less than seventy-two hours to go, huh? Who it be? Tell ol' Doolah who shacked up with a Sabikan."

"I'm not allowed to say. Confidentiality. You should know that. It's best if we don't ask, don't tell."

"Fuck dat, mon! I ain't going nowhere until tomorrow. This be *my* night off. I'm here for Happy Hour. I'm gonna get drunk as shit and then, if these two boys are lucky…"

The first young man had returned with her drink. He set it down on the table in front of her, and then kissed Doolah's neck just below her right earlobe. The drink fizzled like molten lava as red as Mars itself. Krieger wondered how much alcohol it contained.

"…then both of them are gonna have their way with me. They can compete to see who's more studly, who can give me a better orgasm. And the whole time I'm gonna try not to think about the two slugs I removed from some poor girl dat got raped three blocks from here, right behind the supermarket in 'dome daylight.' Do you know what happens to slugs when they hit external oxygen before their membrane is complete?"

Krieger remained silent.

"They evaporate into an acidic vapor cloud capable of eating the flesh off your fucking hands. Breathe it in and it kills you immediately. I nearly died today because of some Sabikan rapist, and that sonofabitch is still on the loose somewhere outside. So if you can't even tell me who—"

"Adelaide's daughter," Krieger said, slowly reaching inside his coat pocket for his weapon. "I'm estimating she's already seventeen hours in, and Adelaide wants to be sure she's managed with no witnesses and no questions asked."

The second of the two young men pulled out a pulsar gun and aimed its laser sight directly between Krieger's eyes.

"Doolah is telling you to fuck off, buddy," he said coolly.

Doolah threw her head back and laughed, and Krieger couldn't help but become intoxicated by her beauty; her warm ebony cheeks and smooth, perfect neckline plunging down into her expansive bosom. Her dossier said she was in her fifties, but she could have passed for thirties easily. Whatever tricks she used to stay so young would fetch a very pretty nickel back in the city.

"What's so funny?"

"I don't know who put you up to this, but Tirese Adelaide isn't even inside Dome 12 anymore. She done absconded with a life-suit and made the Defector's Sojourn. She prolly dead now somewhere in the wastelands outside."

Krieger knew the Defector's Sojourn. It meant risking being pulled apart by the moon's enormous magnetic field while trying to cross on foot from one dome to another. Many had taken the sojourn but only a handful survived. And if they did, their brains remained scrambled for a very long time.

"Why'd she try to escape?"

Doolah stopped laughing and turned to her boy with the weapon.

"Put dat thing away before someone gets hurt." She turned to Krieger. "I don't know why she left. If you're dying to know, go find yourself a life-suit and go out and ask her." Doolah's eyes narrowed into slits, and her smile evaporated. "But I'll tell you this much... Doolah think that the Sabikans are planning to take over the colonies. We hear things all the time out here on the eastern side. They've had enough of us humans running everything and they tired of seeing me killing off their spawn to protect those they've impregnated. I'm getting death threats all the time these days. That's why I left Capitol City. I'm safer out here where there is no law."

Doolah picked up her drink and took a large sip. The kid with the gun shifted uncomfortably for a moment, then slipped his weapon back into its holster. The moment he did, Krieger leapt over the table and cold-cocked him. Doolah Quar tumbled backward, spilling her Martian Tourniquet down her cleavage as she tumbled onto the floor. The other boy, the one who had fetched her drink, had already turned tail and was sprinting off toward the door to find a bouncer. Krieger ignored him and took another swing at the first boy, catching him square in the jaw with a fist of clenched knuckles and dynamite. The kid's head flew backward (his eyes rolling in their sockets like marbles) and then he dropped unconscious onto the velvet carpet. Doolah was on her feet and moving toward the door when Krieger's hand shot out and grasped hers. His free hand reached back inside his coat pocket and hauled out his pulsar gun. He had it aimed at her midriff as the first boy returned with the bouncer.

"You're breaking the law, buddy," the fat guy in the sleeveless Dermex hollered above the music and the growing din of spectators circling them. "I can legally execute you if you don't let her go immed—"

Krieger pulled the gun away from Doolah's belly and fired a stun shot at the dude's head. The guy's knees buckled and then all three hundred pounds of him were dropping to the floor. The kid watched this happen, and then his bladder released in front of the crowd. His piss was still hot on the floor as Krieger pushed Doolah past him and out into the darkness of "Dome Evening."

***

"I know who you are," Doolah said as the monorail departed the station to make its trek back to Capitol City. The glass panels of the geodesic sphere around them were still translucent, allowing starlight from the outer constellations to shine through. To the west the sphere of Jupiter's massive surface was beginning to come into view, with its never-ending panoply of volcanic activity and gaseous eruptions. Even from his seat on the train the panorama was breathtaking. By morning the glass panels would resume their ultraviolet glow of "day mode" and the streets of the city would fill with life again. "I seen you plenty of times back on the eastern side. Always doing the dirty business of the Colony Council. Always chasin' down enemies of democracy or deadbeats who owe the government money. Every one of them is shady as fuck, you know."

She was sitting in the chair directly across from him, her breasts stale with the perfume of her spilled drink. Doolah noticed his eyes traveling down her neck to the swells of her bosom, barely contained in the material of her Dermex top. When she was sure she had Krieger's attention, she casually unzipped the Dermex until her breasts were nearly popping out, produced a handkerchief from her bag, licked at it lasciviously with the tip of her tongue, and proceeded to wipe away the sticky remnants of her spilled drink. As she did, she leaned forward and whispered conspiratorially. "Here's the thing, hot shot... I know *lots* of people. I've fixed a lot of mistakes and a lot of people still owe me their lives. So you just remember that when this is over, you best start watching the shadows, because my people are gonna be waiting for you. I'll swear my life on it."

It was Krieger's turn to laugh.

"Your life don't mean shit," he said. "Not if what you told me is true. If the Sabikans are planning to take over, you're gonna be the first to go. They ain't gonna want no abortion technician around if they mean to mass-populate. You'll be running for a life-suit and making the Defector's Sojourn too."

Doolah sat back, dropped the handkerchief, and folded her arms across her bosom. The hint of ferocity still resided in her pouty lips. Krieger ignored it and reached inside his hipsling to remove her dossier. He flipped it open and started leafing through it, feeling her glare burning at him like vaporizing slugs. "You know, Doolah, if they do try an uprising, we'll *both* be dead real fast. Only, your death will probably come seventy-two hours *after* mine. If you take my meaning."

She remained silent, nudging her medical bag occasionally with her foot (they'd had to detour to her pod to get it before returning to the station).

It occurred to him that he should have patted her down before climbing aboard the monorail, but her outfit left very few places to pack heat. A blade perhaps, but he was constantly watching her movements and his pulsar gun was always within reach. He was about to ask about her past on Earth when his Computex device rang with an incoming call.

It was Ramu.

"Did you locate Ms. Quar?"

Krieger looked at the desirable black woman across from him and frowned. Doolah the seductress had already zipped her top back up, hiding her cleavage away behind the Dermex. It made him feel like an awkward teenager, realizing just how badly he now wanted her.

"Maybe. Tell me something... How much time does Tirese Adelaide have left before the slugs go cannibal?"

Doolah Quar sat up and dropped her arms to her sides. It was as if she'd been waiting for this moment to happen, and he couldn't decide if she'd been bluffing about the minister's daughter or if that sonofabitch from the Colony Council had been lying.

Why would he lie though? Tirese Adelaide had always been a rebellious little shit. Sacking up with a Sabikan to piss her mother off seemed like something any child of privilege would try to pull.

"We think she just passed her twenty-hour mark."

"Are you sure?"

There was a hesitation.

"What kind of question is *that?* Of course, we're sure. Hers and the Sabikan's alibies check out."

"Tirese Adelaide fled Dome 12 completely, didn't she? She risked a horrible death and made the Sojourn on her own. Did she reach Dome 13? That's the one nearest to ours."

Another pause, this time longer. Doolah was now staring wide-eyed out into space, as if she was trying to mentally picture the minister's daughter hobbling over the cratered landscape of Jupiter's biggest moon, the weight of her life-suit three times as heavy because of the moon's magnetic field. The moment passed, and then the voice of Minister Adelaide came over the receiver. Her voice sounded cold and terrified.

"If you have Doolah Quar with you, bring her here immediately. *I'm* the one who's pregnant."

***

"Walk faster."

They'd exited the monorail into Capitol Station, and already people were swarming the platform in their morning rush hour ritual. Krieger moved with authority, his left hand grasping Doolah's right arm with unnecessary ferocity, steering her through the sea of pedestrians toward the exit ramp.

"There's no need to be forceful," she said through gritted lioness teeth. "I'm coming with you at this point. I ain't gonna try and run away."

"That's real good, because we're being followed."

"Are you sure?"

Doolah made to turn around and glance behind her but Krieger pushed her arm harder. She stumbled for a moment, and then her lovely legs corrected themselves as they stepped onto the ramp.

"I noticed them back at your pod when we went to get your supplies. Three men, all of them wearing navy blue Dome Security jumpsuits. Only, I can't tell if they're human or Sabikan."

She glanced up at one of the hemisphere mirrors dangling over the concourse and saw one of the men. "Dome Morning" was still hours off, but he had on dark sunglasses anyway.

"The one closest to us is Sabikan," she whispered.

"How can you tell?" Krieger reached into his coat, wrapped his palm around the handle of his pulsar gun, and squeezed tight.

"The sunglasses. You don't know shit about Sabikan anatomy, do you?"

"Fill me in," he said, redoubling his pace so that they were almost jogging.

"They're part reptile, like chameleons back on earth. Their skin can change colors if they will it to. You wouldn't notice on their extremities because they disguise themselves to fit among us. But if you ever see them under a blacklight, their skin becomes see-through. And their eyes change as well, especially when their heart rate goes up. Their sclera glows yellow like a lizard's."

Krieger felt the panic welling up in his belly. With the exception of the hemisphere mirrors over the concourse, there was no way of keeping their pursuers out of their blind spot. He listened hard for the sound of shoe heels clicking closer behind him, but with the hustle and bustle of pedestrians moving around him, it was impossible.

"Something's about to go down," he said, steering Doolah around a corner toward the commissary. There was a custodial closet ten meters away, and the moment they rounded the corner, he was sprinting (dragging Doolah behind him) toward the closet door. They closed the gap in a few quick paces, and then he was shoving her through the door and barging in after her, his pulsar gun now out and pointing toward the ceiling. He reached toward the switch by the door and shut the light off.

They watched in silence as the first Sabikan trotted past. Krieger felt his eyes focus hard on the alien's skin, waiting to see if it would somehow change as Doolah mentioned. Now that he knew their secret, he desperately wanted to see for himself—as well as buy a flashlight with an ultraviolet bulb to make their detection easier.

Moments later, the second passed, this one also wearing sunglasses. There was a moment when he swung his head toward the closet (practically staring right at them), and Doolah had to yank her arm away from Krieger and cover her mouth to keep from screaming. The Sabikan turned his head forward and continued moving, and Krieger could see the alien had his pulsar gun drawn and ready.

If they're wearing security uniforms, they have access to all the cameras in the building.

"We're getting out of here!" Krieger uttered between gritted teeth, and his hand found Doolah's arm once again. He bolted through the doorway, dragging the lioness behind him before she could protest, and hurtled directly into the path of the third Sabikan. The alien's face flashed with absolute surprise. Krieger spun the gun around in his hand and hammered the butt-end of the weapon into the alien's temple. The sunglasses spun off and fell to the floor, and for a brief moment his eyes burned the yellow of tainted egg yolks. Krieger belted the alien again, and then the two were sprinting toward the exit.

***

They caught the first available Dome-Cab, Krieger handing the driver a fifty-jank and telling him to hightail it to the Capitol Center. The two huddled down low and spoke in whispers as the driver rounded corners and flew up the entrance ramp onto Jupiter Highway.

"If what you said was true, then the fucking revolution has already started. Those goons sure as hell have no beef with me. It's *you* they're after."

"Well, fucking *DUH,* that's why I didn't want to leave the eastern side."

"You don't get it. You're not safe here inside this dome. You're going to have to go into exile after you fix the minister. She's going to have to call the Colony Congress into order and declare war. You're going to be making the Defector's Sojourn if you want to live after today."

Doolah's eyes narrowed.

"Fuck that, mon! Doolah Quar ain't going nowhere! Dis is my home, and I'll blast every last Sabikan in the fucking face before I let them put me down."

"Will you shut up for a moment and listen? We don't even know how far they've infiltrated the congress. We have no idea what plans they have in motion or what weapons they've secured. What we *do* know is that they know who *you* are and exactly what you look like. You stand out in Dome 12. We need to get you somewhere safe before you become public enemy number one." Krieger sighed. "Let's just get you into the capitol and take care of Minister Adelaide."

He closed his eyes and slipped his hand up to massage the bridge of his nose. A killer headache was forming somewhere within the center of his skull, and if he didn't get sleep and a real plate of food soon, he was going to pass out. He thought of Minister Adelaide— middle-aged like Doolah but exuding the white hair and stress lines on her face of those with *real* authority and responsibility. She'd run election platforms on *family values* in Dome 12, endearing herself to a fan base of colonists that clung to the puritanical ways of Earth. A huge portion of those folks turned on her when she voted in the congress to allow refuge to the Sabikans. Now they were going to get their chance to revel in the stupid glory of "We Told You So."

He thought of Tirese Adelaide, probably discovering that her mother copulated with one of the aliens and fleeing Dome 12 in shame. He wondered if she made it to Dome 13 or if her dead body was slowly being crushed into nothingness by the massive gravitational weight of magnetic polarity and the pressure of vacuous outer space.

"You could come with me," Doolah said, and he could hear the terror of acceptance in her voice. Perhaps the lioness was on the verge of breaking. "You be a good-looking man. Come with me and I'll spend all my nights making love to you. You ain't been able to take your eyes off me since we met—come discover the rest of me." She pushed her body into his, mashing her breasts against his arm. Her softness and proximity made his nether region engorge. "Doolah will keep you good and satisfied for as long as I can."

"Maybe. Let's just deal with Adelaide first, and then see what she has to say. For all we know, you could slip up and kill us both when the slugs evaporate."

"Not today," she said, and Krieger could tell that she was thinking that it might be for the better if she did.

Krieger found himself thankful to be male.

***

The inside of the capitol was bustling with life. The sky panels were filling with "Dome Sunrise" just as the door swung shut behind them, and Krieger was once again steering Doolah Quar by her elbow as they raced through the halls. He could feel the faces of strangers turning and watching them as they plowed through the pedestrian traffic but paid them no attention. Nobody wore sunglasses inside the capitol, so there was no way to tell just how many faces were Sabikan.

It felt like they were being hunted. If Doolah was a lioness, then some greater predator had picked up her scent and was somewhere close by, ready to pounce. Something wild, with eyes that burned yellow when excited.

They reached the elevators at the middle of the concourse and Krieger jammed the UP button until the door opened. When it did, he pushed Doolah inside and scrambled in after her, hitting the button for the fourth floor and then the DOOR CLOSE button before any other citizens could enter. Doolah gripped her bag's handles tight until the skin of her black flesh turned ashen.

She's tough, Krieger thought. *She's ready to break down and cry, but she won't. She won't because she's a lioness and will never show weakness.*

The elevator landed on the fourth floor and the doors slid open. Krieger let go of Doolah's arm and pointed down the hall. There was not another being in sight. It was too damn quiet. Ambush was coming; Krieger could feel it in his pounding heart.

"Third door on the left. I want to go in first and make sure she's there and alone. If she is, you do your thing and get rid of the goddamn slugs. When you're done, we'll talk to her together and convince her she needs to act."

She said nothing and followed him quietly down the hall to a door labeled *The Honorable Julie J. Adelaide.* Krieger wrapped his hand around his pulsar gun and pulled it out of his coat. He looked one last time at Doolah and opened the door.

Inside was a nightmare.

Minster Adelaide was stripped naked and tied down to her desk. Ramu and the other Colony Council members were also naked, forming a ring around her. Ramu's skin was purplish, and Krieger could see the network of capillaries and veins pulsing with blood beneath the epidermis. The Sabikan closest to them moved at a speed quicker than Krieger could have dreamed possible, moving past and throwing the door closed behind them.

"I'm afraid we've miscalculated," Ramu said, drawing an open hand over Adelaide's belly. "You're just in time to witness the birth of my offspring."

Minister Adelaide had already slipped into catatonia. There was nothing left of her but a vacant shell with two parasitic fetuses waiting in her womb. Krieger's eyes passed down over her sagging breasts to her belly, which now writhed and wriggled with motion beneath her skin. Somewhere in her abdomen were two slugs, with tiny razor-sharp teeth that had sprouted less than twenty-four hours ago, beginning the phase of chewing their way out of her uterus and through the lining of her abdomen.

Two slugs in the belly, he thought coldly. *That has to be the most disgusting thing I've ever heard.*

Doolah stepped in front of Krieger and stared down the naked Sabikans. A wicked smile stretched across her face as she stole their attention away from him. They eyed her lasciviously, and Krieger watched as each of the aliens' genitals suddenly engorged with arousal. He was shocked to discover how much longer they were than human genitalia. *No wonder alien conception is such a problem,* Krieger thought. His eye caught Doolah staring at the alien sex organs, and for the briefest moment, his heart filled with jealousy and disappointment. He was sure that if she wanted to, the lioness could satisfy every single one of them and still have leftover energy.

"I can still save her," Doolah said. The look of the lioness had returned to her eyes. Those perfect orbs gleamed bright with defiance and hate. "Please. Our people can still live in peace together."

"That time has come and gone," Ramu said, moving around the desk. "We tried to assimilate quietly, peacefully, but we've reached an impasse. We can procreate within our own kind, but when we try with your species, you put our children to death. We're ready to take over the colonies."

The other Sabikans nodded silently in agreement.

"And we want you to help us," Ramu said to her. "We think you'll make a wonderful host."

Doolah Quar moved like a fierce jungle cat. She turned on Krieger and pounced, pulling the pulsar gun out of his hand and knocking him to the floor. Before he could get back to his feet, Doolah was aiming the gun down at the defenseless woman on the desk.

"I'm sorry, Ms. Adelaide," she said, and her eyes flashed dark. She pulled the trigger twice, blasting away the bare patches of skin over either side of the minister's ovaries. There was a moment when the room filled with flash and gun smoke, and then Ramu and the others turned a hideous, angry shade of red as they watched their progeny aborted. In the next moment, a terrible hiss emitted from the dead minister's belly as the two slugs evaporated and misted their way out of her bloody abdomen. Ramu covered his mouth and nose and darted toward his clothing. The others were running to find their weapons. Doolah aimed the pulsar gun at each one and squeezed the trigger until the alien council members fell dead one-by-one onto the floor.

When Ramu was the only one left, she hoisted the gun toward him and waited.

"It won't matter," Ramu sneered triumphantly. "The revolution has already begun. Even if you kill me, there are so many others. One of them will eventually get you and impregnate you. We're taking over, Doolah. We can't be stopped!"

Doolah Quar smiled one last, terrible smile as Krieger watched helplessly. She lifted her arm slowly, deliberately, until the barrel of his gun rested against her right temple.

"You'll never have *me*," she replied. "*Viva la Resistance!*"

She pulled the trigger, and the heavens gained another star as her lifeless body hit the floor. A spray of blood and bone fragments showered everything around her as the lioness set herself free.

Krieger dove down, snatched up the weapon, and finished Ramu. When the alien also fell lifeless to the floor, he sat down and wept. It was preposterous to believe in a "happily-ever-after" for him and Doolah, where they escaped this death room together and remained together, but until that moment, there had at least been hope. Now there was only loss and a thirst for vengeance against the Sabikans. His tears flowed freely as he thought of the heart of the lioness, and wondered if perhaps the same heart beat within Tirese Adelaide. Unstoppable things had been set into motion under the dome, and the colonists would need a new leader to guide them. He wondered if he could get out of the city alive and, if he could find a life-suit, how long it would take to track down the minister's only daughter. If she was still alive, Tirese Adelaide was the new minister, and would have to lead the rebellion against the Sabikans.

The only thing left in his future was to make the Defector's Sojourn and continue the resistance.

I am Denebola, he thought as he escaped into "Dome Morning." *I will be the lion and hunt them all down.*

Sunset at Devil's Gulch

Dayton could hear the coyotes circling, growling and yipping under the setting sun. They must have caught his scent just after Maggie died. The horse thieves had opened fire on him and his mare when he came upon their den on the western edge of the prairie. Maggie had taken the lion's share of the burning lead. But the mare had been a fast one, and he'd managed to elude the thieves by pushing her through the tall grass and thorn bushes down into Devil's Gulch. He could still hear the pounding of hooves thundering past him up on top of the hill, and deep down, he knew they would eventually double back and find him. They would find him, sure as his daddy was gunned down by them very same sonsabitches when *he* went after them to get their horses back.

Maggie died quick. The roan mare had at least half a dozen bullet holes up and down her flank, and judging by the amount of blood pouring out of her, one of the bullets must have nicked an artery. It had been a miracle that the beast could even stand after the first round or two hit her, and an even greater miracle that she hadn't thrown him clear off and left him to fend for himself. The dust from the prairie had coated her hide, mixing with her blood into muddy cakes around the bullet holes. The color of these cakes blended in with her velvet red fur. Maggie had made it down to the bottom of the gulch on all fours, but had stumbled and fell at the bottom of the ravine. She drew in a few frantic breaths, and then her spirit galloped away.

Billy Dayton had been struck in the belly. It burned terrible, but he was fairly certain the hit hadn't been lethal. No, he'd survive it, but the coyotes were getting nearer. And with the sun setting in the western sky, the hot prairie would cool off fast. He'd have to build a fire to stay warm, but that would most definitely give away his position. The Travis brothers would see the smoke rising and close in quicker than the coyotes. And they would want blood.

He still had his pistol in his hand. He'd fired four or five shots, and one of them had taken the life of Glenn Travis, the youngest of them horse-thieving bastards. The lead ball had caught him right in his lower jaw, and there was the briefest moment where Glenn had spun around in surprise after the hit, and Dayton could see the kid with the lower half of his face completely gone. His eyes went wide with surprise and then he hit the ground hard, his body rocking and convulsing in the throes of death. Dayton had time to squeeze off a few more rounds before the Travis boys were going for their rifles and mounting their own horses. Dayton looked down at his pistol, opened the wheel, and glanced woefully at the one last bullet tucked in the chamber.

Just one.

He could hear the voice of his daddy.

That one bullet is your final blessing. Don't you ever, ever fire off all six shots. You always leave that one last bullet, just in case.

The sun was now beyond the hillside, and the tall shadows crept toward him. He could feel their coolness caress his face and the hole in his belly. Just like with Maggie, the prairie dust had caked and coated the hole, but it had at least managed to stop the bleeding. If he could make it back to Tipton, Doc Mulligan would be able to get him right again. He could almost see the face of the Irishman, and smell the cheap whiskey on his breath as his instruments extracted the bullet and sewed him up again. Tipton was at least twelve miles away, and it may as well have been twelve hundred.

There was no leaving Devil's Gulch alive.

The cold. The coyotes. The Travis brothers. And that one last bullet. One of those things would set his spirit free. Then the coldness would consume his body. And then the coyotes would eat for the night. The Travis brothers would take his iron and the billfold in his britches pocket, and anything else they wanted, and the dust would eventually bury his bones.

That one last bullet is a blessing.

Dayton closed the bullet wheel and turned the chamber to that one last bullet. If he was going to leave this world, he would at least cheat the Travis brothers in claiming his death. One of them had gunned his daddy down in cold blood and left him for dead here in Devil's Gulch. He'd heard rumor that the Travis boys were notorious for using a long bone-handled knife to dig out their slugs, just to melt them down and make new bullets. The eldest, Martin Travis, had gone so far as to boast that the rounds that had killed his daddy had also taken down Marshall Goudsward, and "Dirty Dog" MacLeod before *him*. All talk, of course, as Robert Dayton's body had never actually been recovered. For all he knew, he could have been sitting on Daddy's bones right now.

Something spooked the coyotes. They'd been cautiously crawling and sniffing their way down into the gulch, but then suddenly stopped in their tracks. By the fading light, he could see the pack of dogs suddenly cock their heads up to listen, and then they all turned tail and fled back up the hill again. Dayton lowered the gun and listened, and then he, too, could hear it: the sound of horses galloping hard back toward the gulch. The Travis brothers had gotten wise to him and were returning to finish the job. Dayton lowered his head and the tears began to fall, leaving cool trails down his burning cheeks.

"I'm sorry, Daddy," he whispered. "I'm sorry I failed you."

He lifted the gun and squared the barrel between his eyes. One bullet. Truly a blessing.

There was a rustling in the distance, and Dayton lowered the gun a second time. The last of the evening light was dying, making it hard to focus, but he could still tell that something was approaching. He could see the tall grass and brush bending as the approaching thing came forward. It plodded and skulked toward him, floating along the bottom of the gulch like a phantom in the dust. Dayton raised the pistol ready to shoot, ready to give up that last bullet, when he recognized his daddy. Robert Dayton loomed above him, enormous holes in his forehead and eye socket where his left eye used to be. There were telltale signs of knife gashes where one of the Travis brothers had indeed carved their lead pellets out of his skull. A third wound sat in the middle of his chest, along with a third set of knife wounds. The ghost moved slowly, balefully, but there was no mistaking the rage in his father's face. His one good eye was narrowed into a slit, gazing his crazy dead-man's gaze.

Dayton stared up at his father, unsure what to do.

"Daddy?"

The ghost thrust his hand out, as if to take his child and help him up. But when Dayton tried to grasp his daddy's hand, he felt nothing. Instead, he pushed himself up to standing, and then began to follow his father as the senior Dayton began floating back along the bottom of the gulch.

They had barely gone fifty paces when the boy noticed the wooden crate. The ghost had walked right up to it and pointed his dead finger at it, his angry gaze never leaving his face. And in his mind, the boy could hear his daddy speaking...

That one last bullet is a blessing. Did you save it, boy? Did you save that last bullet like I told you?

Dayton still had the pistol clutched tight in his hand. From above the gulch, he could now hear the sound of the Travis boys, hooting and hollering as their horses came to a stop at the top of the hill. It wasn't long now. Devil's Gulch was about to claim life once again. Only now, Dayton felt the spark of hope returning to him.

The crate had been left forgotten at the bottom of the gulch. When the railroad line was laid between Tipton and Silverado, the company had blasted through the mountains at the southern edge of the prairie. A case of TNT had been stolen (whether it had been the Travis brothers or some other thieves he didn't know, didn't really care at the moment) and hidden down here at the bottom of Devil's Gulch. Now here it was, a second blessing that the good Lord saw fit to share with him.

Robert Dayton lifted his head and looked upon his boy with his one good eye. In it, Dayton saw the unmistakable badge of fatherly pride. The rage in his face lifted, just for a moment, and then the ghost began to fade away.

"Daddy... Daddy, don't leave me!"

The Travis brothers were halfway down the hill. Three of them left, out for blood and vengeance for their dead brother, who was undoubtedly being picked apart by vultures back at their lair. They'd left in such a flurry that they'd never bothered to cover him up, more or less give him a proper burial. If they made it back, they'd find nothing but a bloody carcass covered with flies, and goddamn him, he deserved it. As did the rest.

Dayton grabbed the crate by the rope-handles tethered to either side of the top and began dragging it back toward Maggie. He let go of the crate, sending up a cloud of dust around his dead mare. And then he was scrambling off into the brush to wait.

The Travis boys came in fast, each packing a gun in either hand. Six guns waiting to tear him to pieces, and then a long, bone-handled knife to extract the bullets so that the lead could be reused. They whooped and chided, trying to get him to come out, but Dayton waited patiently.

"Look, there's his horse. I told you I got 'er!"

"Yeah, if you're such a great shot, how come you didn't shoot *him* instead of the horse? We coulda sold the horse if she was still alive."

"Hey, whattaya think's in that box?"

Thank you, God. Thank you for this one last bullet...

Dayton pulled the trigger, and then the crate exploded in a blast that rocked the gulch. The basin of the gulch filled with ferocious light and heat, followed by a boom that echoed all around him, making Dayton scream and cover his ears. And then body parts were raining back down from the sky. Flesh and blood fell on him and all around him, in the form of severed arms and legs and organs and charnel. Maggie's carcass was also blown to bits, adding bone and fur into the mess. The tall grass and brush quickly caught fire, and then it was day again in Devil's Gulch.

Dayton opened his eyes. In the burning firelight, he could see three pairs of boots scattered about the ground. That was all that was left of the Travis brothers. By now, their horses had surely been spooked away (as were the coyotes), but that was fine. The fire would continue to spread once the night breeze picked up. If he could climb back up to the top of the gulch, he could remain warm and safe until the dawn. And if God saw fit to bless him one more time, maybe one of the horses would return. Karma was a wheel that never stopped turning.

He scanned the floor of the gulch once more, but his father's ghost was also long gone. Dayton crawled out of the gulch, thinking of the rage in his dead father's eye, and wondering if he would now spend eternity punishing the Travis brothers through the burned-out hell of Devil's Gulch. The thought made him smile.

154

And So Shall the Gods Feast

Bethesda Point is one of those small coastal towns that never appears on any map, nor warrants any amnesties to those foreign to its soils. Their landscapes (Bethesda Point's in particular) can be deceptive to the eyes of passing tourists and migrant travelers. At a glance, one would see the trappings of a quaint New England village: the lighthouse overlooking Bethesda Sound, the tiny wharf and marina—where rests the tired old lobster boats and dinghies, victims of the cold, black Atlantic and fodder for barnacles and rust—and a few scattered neighborhoods of cozy little homes built claustrophobically close together where the fishermen and their families reside.

These houses seem to follow some haunting generic pattern, as if they had all been built by the same pair of hands under harsh, despairing conditions. Most of them, more or less, are decorated with piles of lobster traps in their yards and the trademark storm lanterns on their front porches. Towns such as these do tend to let tourists stay for a spell (a brief spell at that, but money is money and the townies *do* need to eat), but never do they allow people to come in and settle. Nor do they ever give leave to their own if they can help it.

Towns like Bethesda Point have their own secrets and they share their own superstitions. Their citizens prefer not to have strangers in their midst, particularly those who might bring with them some unnamable malignancies that curse their existence.

These towns have horrors of their own to contend with.

***

There was a great deal of speculation among the citizens of Bethesda Point as to why Jerrod Hartley had been removed from his position as innkeeper—extricated by force, no less; the man had been bound in a straightjacket and escorted away, still kicking and screaming, by local authorities—but most of the folks in town conceded that it had something to do with a stranger that had found lodging for the night at the Oceanside Inn, where Hartley was employed.

Oceanside Inn, one of the few hotels that remains open after the tourist season ends, rests at the southern edge of the small coastal town. The proprietor, Mr. Daniel Cain, had embarked rather early in the season for his winter home in the islands, leaving Hartley responsible for the establishment over the cold, bleak months of the year. No explanation for his early departure had been offered, leading Hartley to believe that it had something to do with the near-death experience his employer had had just off Bethesda Sound on his latest fishing trip. It wasn't until after Cain had embarked on his voyage that Hartley found a handful of rough illustrations in his employer's quarters, depicting some loathsome sea-beast. The beast was sketched out in shaky lines depicting the form of a semi-human torso and arms that unfolded into hands that resembled more closely two sets of giant, bulbous lobster claws. And where the head should be, an octopus or squid with long, lashing arms covered with tentacles. And more bizarre was the captions coupled with these sketches. Barely legible, each illustration had the same quote underneath:

Ng'thuth Verdiem Olg!

Followed by its English translation:

And So Shall the Gods Feast!

Hartley dismissed all this immediately as imaginative rubbish and filed the sketches away in his master's vault in case Cain should want them upon his return.

***

This had been the arrangement for almost a score of years. Hartley, a portly fellow in his late fifties, was a trusted, respectable employee, very capable of overseeing the duties that come with running such an establishment. After the incident, the citizens of Bethesda Point were left puzzled as to what could have driven a decent person like Hartley to such a horrible fit of madness.

"What a pity," they would exclaim when discussing the incident. "Crying shame, what happened to 'im." But if asked what exactly *had* happened, shoulders would shrug and eyes would roll, and silence would echo a resounding "I don't know." And after a moment's hesitation, they'll tell you in a whisper that "the poor bastard went insane."

That is precisely what happened to Jerrod Hartley.

It had been a cold, rainy Saturday evening when the stranger had arrived at the Oceanside Inn. A tall, gaunt man in a raincoat and fedora—soaked to the bone from traveling in the elements—the stranger stood momentarily in the lobby, absorbing the charm of its decoration. Several species of salt-water fish, stuffed and mounted, adorned the walls of the room: tuna, mackerel, cod, even a small but sizeable great white shark, all trophies of Mr. Cain's battle to tame the dark and mysterious swells of the Atlantic. In the sitting area was a leather couch and matching chair, with a table made from a lobster trap placed strategically in between. And above the doorway next to the admittance desk was the captain's wheel from Cain's previous vessel, *The Starmaiden* (which had fallen to those deadly swells off Bethesda Sound, leaving Cain barely alive). The stranger then walked up to the counter, where Hartley was drinking his tea and reading a copy of *The New Englander*.

"Evenin'," Hartley offered, setting the magazine down.

"A room, please." In the pale lamplight the strangers eyes were a cold, black pair of orbs that seemed to stay open forever. They gazed at the innkeeper as he pulled a key off the row of pegs on the wall behind him. The stranger's vacant, unblinking stare made Hartley uneasy.

"Certainly," Hartley responded, and then pushed the ledger, already opened, toward the man. The ledger, bound perfectly in a rich, ruddy leather, slid effortlessly across the desk, where its pages were met with the plopping droplets of water that rolled off the stranger's hat and coat. Hartley saw this and, with an embarrassed smile, reached across the desk and tugged the book back, allowing the water droplets to fall onto the wooden desktop.

"You picked a dreadful night to be out traveling," Hartley said as he watched this new guest pluck the quill pen from its sheath, dip it into the jar of ink, and scratch his name onto the dampened page of the ledger. "Are you here on business, sir?"

"I'm here to visit my father."

"Perhaps I know him. I daresay that I know almost everybody in Bethesda Point. Tell me his name, and I'll send an errand boy to alert him of your arrival."

The stranger leaned forward and snatched the key from Hartley's hand. As he did so, his eyes seemed to change. The blackness had given way to a burning yellow, as if his pupils had ripped open, exposing a venomous layer beneath. There was a terrible moment when those eyes looked directly into his own, and Hartley felt his chest tightening as the air rushed out of his lungs.

"That won't be necessary," the stranger informed him. "My father has been dead for quite some time. I'm only here to pay my respects." He held up the key and examined it. "Room thirteen. Splendid." And then the stranger was lurking down the hallway toward his room.

It was quite some time later when his heartbeat slowed down, and Hartley was able to breathe with some regularity. And the name the stranger had signed into the ledger? Mr. Jonathan Angell.

"That's 'ow he signed it, ayuh..." the citizens of Bethesda Point will tell you. "Of 'coss, they had to take the book in for evidence and all. Not that they'll ever find this Mr. Angell," they'll insist. "He was a daemon and vanished into thin air!"

At least that's what they heard Hartley screaming as they took him away.

It was sometime after midnight when Hartley felt himself awakened by the presence as it floated down the hallway. Not a human presence, for it traveled in vaporous clouds that took no material shape. They drifted about in wisps, as if a low, rolling fog had ushered its way down the residence hallway and into the lobby.

Hartley would later explain to the authorities that he had no idea what had awakened him. This unnatural occurrence made no noise— no footfalls or creaking floorboards, no noticeable sound of lungs drawing in or exhaling breath, not even so much as a sniffle or cough or suppressed yawn to indicate life other than his own in those dead hours of the night. And yet he felt it. Some form of radiant energy had passed by him where he had fallen asleep in his chair behind the desk. Hartley could only describe the sensation for what it was: a trace of static that had shocked him back into consciousness, forcing the hairs on his neck to prickle on end, sending shivers of goosebumps across his flesh.

Hartley watched this vaporous occurrence in horror. As this menacing fog floated nearer to him, the flames of the oil lamps began to flicker (some blowing out completely), filling the room with sinister shadows that would rise along the walls like swiftly approaching devils amidst those monstrous stuffed fish, and then shrink down again before they could strike. In those terrible moments, Hartley could only shut his eyes and grit his teeth and pray silently for this unholy episode to depart.

When he opened his eyes again, peeking through squinted slits, Hartley saw the final remnants of the fog floating effortlessly under the crack of the main door and into the night.

"God only knows why 'e chose to follow it," they all say. "The damn fool should have just stayed put back at the inn. Or better yet, just gone into his room and locked the door for the night, with his bible and his cross in his hands. Curiosity killed the cat..."

Jerrod Hartley cannot answer why he left the safety of the inn to follow the cursed thing. At this point, his story becomes a babble of incomprehensible events in broken sentences of stuttered words. Stark-raving terror fills his eyes, and strands of drool fall from his quivering lips as he relives this frightening episode.

After the spell of the passing fog finally broke, Hartley removed one of the few still-burning oil lamps and rushed down the hall to locate the source of this unnatural entity. Although it had been of little surprise to him to discover that the source had emanated from behind the door of room thirteen, the trail of footprints (ectoplasmic in nature, he would insist) leading from the room and down the hallway had left him in a state of shock. The footprints were not made by man, but by a beast. They had been shaped like the hooves of a goat, only with claws: two razor-sharp talons that had dug into the hardwood floor where the footsteps had fallen, protruding where toes should have been.

Only a fool's courage or a lunatic's curiosity could force a man to follow such a beast, and yet Hartley donned his coat and hat and wandered into the darkened streets of Bethesda Point, searching for the trail of this apparition and not knowing in the slightest what he'd do when he found it.

It wasn't until Hartley had turned onto Maple Street that he discovered his antagonist. By now the rain had stopped, giving way to the deathly yellow rays of the waning moon which hung in the sky just beyond the rocky ledges of Bethesda Point. Hartley could see the figure (which had manifested itself once again as Jonathan Angell) lurching forward in the moon glow.

"Such an abomination cannot be human!" Hartley cried as they dragged him away. "T'was the Devil himself. I swear it!"

The mysterious Mr. Jonathan Angell prowled along Tipton Street, traveling toward the graveyard. Hartley followed at a distance, darting back and forth between the shadows, his frightened heart pounding in his chest, his eyes never removing from the murky silhouette belonging to the tenant of room thirteen.

In horrid fascination, Hartley watched as Mr. Angell approached the iron gates of the cemetery. The figure halted and examined the bars of the gate. As always, the gates to the cemetery were locked and chained before sundown, warding off would-be intruders and grave plunderers. From behind him, the sound of roaring waves smashing into the jagged walls of the cliff that formed Bethesda Point. And all around him, darkness, which even now seemed to drown out the moon glow, just as the waves had once drowned out *The Starmaiden*.

Mr. Angell glanced quickly about the darkened streets, his eyes once again a venomous burning yellow as he surveyed the nightscape. Hartley felt his body trembling as he closed his eyes and waited for the stranger's gaze to pass over him, praying that he would go unnoticed. When he opened his eyes, Hartley watched in terror as the once-human figure dissolved into the vaporous cloud again, and floated effortlessly through the iron bars, drifting into the darkened rows of tombstones beyond the gate.

"If the fool had only turned and fled right then!" the people mumble to themselves as they tell their story. "God only knows what possessed him to follow."

Hartley cannot answer. At this point his eyes will roll back into his head and he'll begin to spit and thrash about. Perhaps something does indeed possess him.

It was when Hartley saw the figure reappear in human form that he felt his legs carrying him toward the rear wall of the cemetery. It took a bit of effort for him to scale the stone wall, his bulky frame tiring easily from lifting and pulling himself over. Once inside, Hartley had to prowl cautiously through the darkness until he could again locate the stranger. On his hands and knees, he scrambled back and forth among the crypts and mausoleums, passing by the rows of crooked slate markers and marble statuary of weeping angels. The grass was cold and wet, muddying his hands and the knees of his pants.

And in the darkness, beasts passed.

Rats!

The dreadful rodents paraded by, all of them traveling in the same direction as if being summoned by the fabled Piper of Hamlin. Tails brushed and whiskers flickered in the dying moonlight as these creatures swept by the frightened innkeeper. Every now and then several would stop and stare at Hartley, their eyes also a venomous yellow, watching to see if he would follow. Their stare was hypnotic, and his mind began to melt away into a trance, and when he was under their spell, they beckoned him to follow.

Hartley slinked and crawled along the muddy earth, following the rats in their terrible journey. Time and again he would accidentally bump into one of the stone markers, and a yelp would rise up in his throat. It was as if the rats felt his pain, and they would stop and glare at him before his lips could utter a groan. And then they were crawling forward again, Hartley following in agonized silence.

Their journey ended at a small, bone-white headstone, the name of the tomb's inhabitant weathered away to a smooth, flat surface. The rats marched around the stone, squeaking in a terrible voiceless dirge that rang out into the never-ending sea of darkness. Hartley could feel the presence of the approaching stranger, and crawled back into the shadows, his body shivering in damp chill.

Mr. Angell halted before the headstone and waved his hand into the air. "*Ng'thuth Verdiem Olg!*" Angell whispered to the rats. "And so shall the gods feast!" Immediately the rats silenced, falling dead in their tracks. And then they began to melt, dissolving into vapors which seeped down into the muddy earth.

The stranger watched, a pleased smile spread malignantly across his face.

"Yessss..." he hissed into the cold night air. "Go forth, my children, and fetch me a soul to feast on!"

Hartley watched in pure, wide-eyed terror as the scene unfolded.

The stranger began to transform. His clothing slid away as the fleeting remnants of his human form dissolved, replacing his figure with that of a beast. A monstrous daemon with red, scaly skin and bat-like wings which unfolded around him. Horns—long and curling like a ram's—sprouted from his head, and a pointed tail protruded from his twisted spine. Its legs were long and goat-like, with fur spreading from its pelvis down to its hoofed feet (and there were indeed the razor-sharp talons for toes, as the footprints in the hallway of the Oceanside Inn suggested).

As this macabre transformation continued, the mound of grass over the plot began to bubble and rise, and then the rats were crawling their way up and out of the muddy earth. Globs of filth and mold clung to their furry bodies as they erupted from the soil. So many of them, as if digging their way out of the very bowels of hell, leaving a sizeable hole all the way down to the coffin buried below.

The rats, once free from the ground, paraded around the phantom stranger, their eyes filled with glowing venom, suggesting a rage no human could ever fully understand. A rage, and a terrible knowing of what was to follow.

The beast leaned over the hole in the ground and began to inhale, and a bloodcurdling howl filled the night. Hartley tried desperately to look away and found that he could not. His hands covered his ears to drown out this terrible shrieking, but it seemed to deafen him nonetheless, as if the sound burrowed its way into every pore in his body. And then he saw it.

A spirit arose from the hole in the ground. The soul of the departed being raped of its final resting place, as the daemon breathed it up out of the earth. Hartley could not detect any features of this phantasm, no appendages or facial expression or hint of gender. Only a cloud of white mist that shrieked and wailed like a banshee as the daemon plucked it from its grave and began to consume.

A whimper escaped Hartley's lips, and a shiver of dread raced down his spine as he saw the beast's eyes find him in the darkness. And then Hartley was scrambling back through the cemetery (practically hurdling the stone wall) and racing through the darkness of Maple Street back toward the Oceanside Inn.

"He was screaming bloody murder," they say. "Loud enough to wake the dead as he entered the lobby of the inn. The poor bastard woke every last person up with his screaming. And the screaming didn't end until the constables came and dragged 'im out."

But if you ask them, the people of Bethesda Sound, not a one of them can honestly say they ever laid eyes on the stranger in room thirteen. Not even for a second.

Except for Jerrod Hartley, who now resides in a padded room, and violently refuses any visitors. The innkeeper now removes his clothing and stuffs it along the crack under the door before trying to sleep and insists he be cremated at the moment of his death, and have his ashes scattered into the wind, rather than be buried in the cemetery on Maple Street.

If the gods must feast, he prays it will not be upon his soul.

The Church of Thunder and Lightning

"You haven't told me where we're going yet," Tony announced.

His big, hairy fingers clutched the van's steering wheel as tightly as possible as he drove, all the while trying not to take his eyes off the road. The rain was coming down in torrents now and he no longer felt sure that he could keep the WRVT news van in control on these back roads out here in East Jerkwater, Nowhere. The van was a clunky old dinosaur, with its telescoping antenna that always threatened to topple the vehicle over on its side whenever it was extended. Tony always seemed to get stuck with it on remote tapings because, well, he'd been with the station way back when it was first purchased and was one of the few people who actually knew how to handle driving it. It was bad enough that the station wouldn't let him drive one of the newer vehicles—the SUVs with the pre-installed navigation units and the four-wheel drive—but having the little blonde tart with no credentials and big ambitions of one day becoming the lead anchor on the evening news giving him directions on the fly, well, that was just ridiculous.

Lindsey sighed and shoved the map she had unfolded on her lap onto the center console.

"I've already told you," she snapped at him, her thick-lens glasses sliding down her nose so that her eyes glowered over the rims. "This is part of the 'Strange Religions' special I'm working on."

Tony's eyes shifted briefly over to the passenger side of the van, sizing her up, then he rolled his eyes as he turned his gaze back to the road.

"I hope this ain't gonna be like them crazy fuckers down in Moultrie... You know, the ones that was shaking them goddamn rattlesnakes with their bare hands." Tony rolled his eyes again, and a hint of perspiration forming above his bushy black eyebrows glistened in the dim light of his dashboard panel.

Outside the window, a flash of lightning lit up the coal-black sky.

"Just keep your eyes on the road, okay?" Lindsey pushed her glasses back up her nose and brushed a lock of her curly blonde hair out of her face. "And try not to breathe so hard. You're fogging up the windows."

Jesus, she was a pain in the ass. She'd only been at the station for a few years, immediately jumping from college intern to on-screen reporter in the blink of her long, lovely eyelashes. There was speculation among the boys back at the station that she was blowing her way up through the ranks (with tongue planted firmly in cheek), but it wasn't like Tony to pay attention to petty gossip. The fact that she was eye candy was trumped by the fact that she was very good at the business, and would have rocketed up the corporate ladder anyway. And here she was, calling the shots like she owned him when he was old enough to be her father, and probably had worked for the station longer than she'd been alive.

Tony's hairy right hand left the wheel and switched on the defroster. Lindsey pulled the map over and began examining it for the umpteenth time.

"The rattlesnake people are small potatoes compared to these people," she confided. "These people *want* to die. They want to be touched by the Finger of God."

"Sounds crazy enough to me. Do I want to know how you found out about them?"

Lindsey glanced up, and her glasses once again slid down her pert little nose.

"A good journalist never reveals her sources."

She reached into her purse and pulled out a small compact, and began applying makeup. Tony risked a glance at her, his eyes wide with incredulity.

"Finger of God? What does that mean?"

"You'll see..." she said, now rubbing dark crimson lipstick across her bottom lip. Outside, lightning flashed, followed seconds later by the low rumble of thunder.

"Don't see why you're putting makeup on," Tony said, shaking his head. "It ain't gonna last once you set foot out there in this rain." His hands had doubled their grip on the steering wheel. "How far we got until I turn off this road?"

"At least another five miles," she answered, putting her compact away and examining the map yet again. "Just keep looking for a sign that reads 'Crawford.' That's where we're heading." She threw an annoyed glance at him. "And for your information, I have an umbrella to keep me dry."

"These idiots really want to die?" Tony took one hand off the wheel and ran it through his greasy black hair, as if the thought gave him a headache. "Jeezum Crow, Lindsey, you'll never get that past the censors if we catch one of 'em dying on tape. You know that, right?"

"Oh, would you just relax? They aren't going to die. More than anything, they're just trying to prove their fanatical devotion to God. We're just going to interview a few people, and video some of their ceremony, and then we'll be on our way."

"But you said..."

"But nothing!" She sighed heartily. "There's the sign right up ahead. See it? It says to turn right onto Route 127."

Tony made the turn gingerly, then accelerated slowly up the road, eyeing the homes on either side of the street. The two sat in silence for a few moments as the van rocked and splashed its way into the storm. When the silence began to grow uncomfortable, Lindsey turned to him and spoke.

"Have you ever seen someone die?"

"I've seen a lot of people die."

"Anyone close to you?"

Tony sighed and watched as his breath steamed up the windshield. He took his hand off the wheel and wiped the fogged glass until it was clean again.

"My wife Renee passed away eight years ago."

Lindsey felt her cheeks grow flush. "Oh, I'm so sorry. I didn't know you were ever married."

"It's okay. She passed from breast cancer. I held her hand when she slipped away. She was on enough morphine that she never felt a thing. It was a good death, especially after all the pain she went through. She didn't struggle or anything. She just stopped breathing, and..."

He glanced at her, then took a moment to run his hand through his hair. He couldn't decide whether she really gave a damn or not, or if she was just in journalist mode, conducting some kind of facetious little interview with him just to pass the time. He gave her the benefit of the doubt.

"It wasn't like it is in the movies or anything, if that's what you think you're going to see," he said. "Her soul didn't come out of her mouth and float off towards the heavens or anything. No angels hovering over her bed waiting for her. Renee was alive one moment, and then she was gone. She shit and pissed all over her deathbed. The nurses call it 'voiding,' as if that somehow gave her back her dignity or something." Tony paused, and Lindsey could tell by the quiver in his voice that he was close to tears. She waited for him to speak again.

"If these idiots actually, honest-to-goodness, want to drop dead, then chances are it's going to be violent and terrible. I'm not sure why you're so excited to see it, but I can guarantee you it won't be like you think it's going to be. I'm not sure if it's just a morbid curiosity for you, or if you just think this is a 'neat' story to cut your teeth on as a journalist..."

"Nobody's going to die!" she repeated. "These are just a bunch of religious kooks. People love hearing about shit like this. It makes their own lives somehow seem normal. It's a compelling story. No different than that Jim Jones guy...you know, the jerk who got his worshippers to drink the poisoned Kool-Aid?"

"Or David Koresh, or those bozos who were waiting for the comet's trail. Yeah, I get it. You're a bright girl, Lin... It just seems like you should have more class than this."

Lindsey smiled. "You've been in this business long enough. You should know that if you want to get ahead, you've gotta give the people what they want."

"Even if what they want is to watch people die in the name of their God?"

The town of Crawford looked like some sort of lonesome afterthought, carelessly dropped into an isolated valley miles from nowhere. Tony drove the van past a sparse row of farms and cottages that, had it not been for the telephone and power lines, would have resembled 19th century rural America.

"Not even a single satellite dish in sight," Tony marveled. "I doubt they can even pick up our station way out here."

Lindsey had already put the map away and was consulting a small piece of paper with hastily scribbled directions on it under the cab's overhead lamp.

"No wonder they're all anxious to die," she said, keeping her eyes down on her directions. "Without cable TV, what is there to look forward to in life? I mean, out here in the sticks. Religion is probably their only form of entertainment or something."

Tony chuckled nervously, and ran his hand through his hair once again. And then, without warning, he threw his hand back on the steering wheel and slammed on the brakes. The van hydroplaned for a few seconds, and he felt his heart actually skip a beat as he mentally prepared for the van to lose control and careen off the road, sending them tumbling blind into whatever waited out in the darkness beyond. The tires finally found traction and the van skidded to a halt, sending Lindsey crashing forward until her seatbelt went taut and jerked her backward.

"What the hell are you doing?" she shouted.

"This town is deserted!" he shot back. "Look out there... There ain't a goddamn set of house lights on in any of these homes."

Lindsey looked out her window at the row of houses on her side of the street. Indeed, all the lights were out.

"Maybe there's a blackout. Maybe they just lost a power line or something, or they're worried about the storm," she offered weakly, staring out her rain-beaded window.

"Lindsey, these homes are all pitch-black! They don't even have any candles burning or anything. If there was a blackout, they'd at least make an effort to light up one room of their houses. Don't you think somebody would be at home at seven o'clock on a Sunday night?"

She looked down at her watch in disbelief, then slapped his arm.

"Dammit, we're going to be late!" she shouted, and Tony shifted back into drive.

The parking lot to the church was nothing more than a patch of grass, but as they pulled in off the road, there was scarcely any place to park. Rows and rows of silent automobiles getting ambushed by the pelting raindrops. It was as if the entire town had come out to attend church service. And as if that wasn't enough, the church itself left them both gasping.

There was a solitary exterior light hanging over the front doors of the building, which cast a dim puddle of light over all the parked cars, but when the lightning flashed again, they saw everything.

The building itself was an enormous slate-gray monstrosity, looming like a thunderhead waiting to explode in the darkness. Its dilapidated clapboard sides were adorned with sets of tall stained-glass windows, each of which were eerily lit up from the inside of the church. And the focal point of each of these windows was a long, yellow-tinted lightning bolt twisting down from the top of the sash to the bottom. From inside the van, it looked more like some giant lunatic funhouse than a church. It looked like a stone demon, or a sleeping god with the rows of cars bowing before it.

"What do you suppose they do in there when the weather is nice?" she whispered just a tad louder than the pouring rain.

"I dunno," Tony responded, his eyes still fixed on the church. "Maybe they have bean suppers or play bingo or something." He glanced over at Lindsey. "Do they even know we're coming to film them?"

"Yeah, yeah. C'mon. Let's get the gear and get in before their service begins."

The church was deserted. The two passed down the center aisle, glancing at the rows of pews where jackets and purses and umbrellas and other miscellaneous personal items were casually abandoned. At the foot of the alter lay a handful of long, thin metal poles that curiously resembled six-foot long fencing epees. Lindsey, with her wireless microphone in one soaked fist and her umbrella in the other, stared uneasily at the metal rods, then back down at the items in her hands.

Tony stared up at the altar, contemplating the mural painted across the back of the pulpit. It depicted a crucifix planted on the top of a mountain, with the image of Jesus transfixed onto the wooden slats. All around him were dark, ominous storm clouds with bolts of lightning erupting in the direction of the cross. Long, yellow lines of electrical current were arcing out until they touched his crown of thorns and the tips of his fingers. It made Tony think of the famous Michelangelo painting of David on the ceiling of the Sistine Chapel, only with lightning bolts where God's hand should have been. The thought made him shiver. He took the lens cap off his Hi-Def digital camera, flipped the record button on, and began to shoot the painting.

"Where do you think they went?" he asked, his voice echoing off the great empty walls around them.

"Oh, shit, we're missing it," Lindsey cried. "C'mon, keep the camera rolling and follow me..."

Lindsey darted toward a door at the rear of the building and burst through into the pouring rain. Tony followed, the camera bouncing up and down on his shoulder as his short legs trotted to keep up. He kept the camera on her as she sprinted, all the while trying to paw her umbrella open and get it over her head. Within seconds, they were both standing in the rain out behind the church, and immediately the two could hear the sound of people singing hymns somewhere out in the darkened distance.

Thunder roared and lightning crashed, and the field behind the church lit up like a nightmare.

The churchgoers were dancing and parading around the storm-ravaged field, each of them brandishing one of the six-foot metal poles they'd seen inside the church. The elderly, the middle-aged, thirty- and twenty-somethings...even the children were parading about with their metal poles pointed toward the heavens, waiting for the lightning to strike, waiting to be touched by the Finger of God. Many were speaking in tongues, so their gibberish sounded like a ward of psychiatric patients rather than a congregation of worshippers. Tony stopped and gawked at them, his heart racing in his chest as he prepared himself to probably witness one of these lunatics get struck by lightning.

"Are you getting all this?" Lindsey screamed above the storm. She'd been expecting something like this all along, but the shock of actually seeing it happening before her left her almost dumbfounded.

"Yeah, but I'll get it better when I get the floodlight on."

"No!" she screeched at him. "Leave the light off. They don't even know we're here. Let's keep it that way for as long as we can."

"The video copy won't be any good without it. You won't be able to see anybody unless the sky lights up when the lightning..."

"No lights!" she repeated, struggling against the cold rain with her umbrella drawn above her. "Let's just keep this as natural as possible."

"You didn't tell them we were coming, did you?" Tony stopped dead in his tracks. The lightning flashed, turning the stormy night sky into day again, and a roaring bolt from the heavens connected with one of the parishioner's poles. The bolt arced as it contacted the metal, causing a shower of sparks to fly about the crowd. An accompanying boom shook the earth, crashing loud enough to wake the dead. The electrified man danced about for a moment or two before his muscles contracted and his figure went completely stiff. When the bolt passed through him into the ground, his knees buckled, and the darkness came pouring in before his dead body could fall to the ground.

The hymns being sang in the darkness ceased momentarily, replaced by the sound of a loud voice preaching to the congregation.

"Praise God! Praise Brother Jesus! Let thy will be done, O Lord!"

"We need to get closer," Lindsey shouted over her shoulder. The adrenaline was coursing through her now. Fear was gone, replaced by an urgent need to not miss an instant of what was going on around her. This was her ticket to real journalism. This was her big break.

"Are you fucking crazy? Someone just died out there!" Soaking wet from head to toe, Tony had been out there long enough and had seen all he needed to see. He could smell the smoke now, and the scent of burning flesh floating all around him, followed by the odor of urine and feces as the fallen corpse began to void all over the field. And never far from his wary subconscious, the realization that the camera on his shoulder was every bit as dangerous as the goddamn metal poles the parishioners were carrying. Everybody out behind the Church of Thunder and Lightning was in real, mortal danger, and that included Lindsey and himself. All of this was wrong, and a quick thought passed through his brain...

I wish we were back with them goddamn rattlesnake shakers!

"Fine, give me the camera," she snapped, dropping her umbrella onto the ground. It bounced against the soggy earth once before a gust of wind snapped it up and blew it away.

Lightning struck again in the field, and another pole-carrying worshipper was snuffed out of existence in a blinding flash of light. His agonized scream pierced the night despite the roaring thunderclap that stripped his life away.

From the darkness, the sound of voices began to wail and call out in triumph, shouting "Alleluias" and "Amens" into the face of the storm. And then, the more haunting shouts of "Please, God..." and "Take me, O Lord, I'm ready!"

"Take the fucking camera!" Tony screamed at her, holding the equipment out to her in his wet, hairy fingers. "I'll be in the van waiting for you."

As she took the camera, the sky ripped open again and a bolt of lightning fell to the earth, and a little girl in a bright yellow dress was touched by the Finger of God.

Lindsey gave him a disgusted look, then pushed ahead toward the field, the rain pouring down on her and the camera. In the darkness beyond her, Tony could see the silhouettes of the worshippers dancing around, their poles waving about into the air. A few had set their poles down long enough to drag the dead bodies out of the way, and then returned to their ceremony in the hope that they should be next to be touched by the Finger of God.

Tony never looked back as he ran toward the van in the front parking lot.

***

It was hours before the storm finally passed. Hours of Tony turning over the ignition and starting the van, planning to just drive away and leave Lindsey behind, then shutting the engine off again in a fit of anger. He found himself thinking of Renee on her deathbed, how he ran his fingers through her hair as he watched her chest rise and contract until her breathing ceased, and then watched the little green line on the EKG machine go flat. Then his thoughts drifted back to Lindsey, out behind the church running around with his Sony Hi-Def camera on her shoulder in the middle of a horribly lethal thunderstorm. Christ, she'd been gone for what felt like an eternity. And every bolt of lightning, every crash of thunder in the field behind the church made his heart race and his eyes wet with tears. Renee's death had been a blessing, one he'd prayed for after watching his partner in life suffering for so long. Now he was praying for Lindsey. He found himself trying to bargain with God (the way he'd tried to bargain for Renee, when she'd first been diagnosed), offering whatever promises that came into his mind. Anything to keep the Finger of God away from her.

How she'd ever found about these freaks he couldn't imagine, but then he'd felt the same way about the rattlesnake shakers. Seeing them dancing around, shaking live copperheads with their bare hands, had given him an instant case of the willies. But at least they could take snakebite serum if they managed to mess up and get bit (and one or two *had* gotten bit before that ceremony was over). These jerks had no options once the lightning struck. There was no cure for death, that much was certain.

And no cure for stupid either. Not just for these people, but for Lindsey as well. The little blond tart with her master's degree and lust for big-time journalism, she didn't even care one bit if any of these people died tonight, so long as it bettered her career. Tony made a mental note to tell their producer that he was all done working with her after this little escapade.

If she was still alive, that was.

There wasn't enough alcohol to consume that would make him forget about this assignment. This was the one he'd be carrying with him to his grave.

Tony watched as the congregation (what was left of them) left the church. They were smiling and laughing under the dim light from above the church doors as they made their way to their cars and drove off into the darkness. None of them seemed to acknowledge his presence or give a hint that they had perhaps run into his colleague out behind the church. As the parking lot emptied, Tony finally worked up the nerve to go out and look for her.

The smell of death and electricity was immediate, and shades beyond terrible. It seemed to linger in the warm, humid air, as if the clouds above had trapped the malodorous stench and pressed it back down against the earth. He felt himself holding his breath as he sidled his way around the building and into the darkness behind the church. The dread of panicked anticipation crept over him as he found the row of laid-out bodies in the darkness, waiting to be buried by the light of day as the storm drifted off to wherever storms go when their hearts have emptied and died. There were so many, far more than he'd have dared to believe.

He had no problem finding Lindsey, as the video camera's LED light continued to blink on stand-by mode. Its red flash winked like a serpent's eye in the darkness. Tony wondered in terror what he would see if he picked up the camera and switched it to playback mode. He wondered if he would see exactly what she had seen before the lightning burned the life out of her body. How the camera could still be working was a mystery, but then, didn't the lord work in mysterious ways?

Tony wrestled the camera from her cold, dead grip and made his way back down to the van, weeping as he struggled to decide whether or not he'd watch the footage. The video would now be considered evidence, and legal authorities (as well as the company insurance department) would want to view it to make whatever determinations that needed to be made about Lindsey's death. There was a brief moment where Tony considered just smashing the camera on the ground and destroying the footage, but he decided against it. Who was he to piss off a God of such terrible vengeance?

He opened the van's door and set the camera on the passenger seat where Lindsey had been sitting. He closed the door, sighed, and took out his cell phone. His fingers trembled as he dialed 911. He took a breath and waited to speak to whoever might be waiting on the other side to respond to his emergency call. The air around him felt warm and humid and made him shiver. There was an awful second where he was sure the sky would rip open once more, even though the storm had passed, and a bolt of lightning would find him. It filled him with terror, and made him wonder what the Finger of God might feel like.

Cattle Cars

"Keep the camera rolling, okay?"

Ruben adjusted his backpack and faced the German forest. The foliage was already changing, filling the landscape with vibrant color. The mountains were behind them, with snow-covered Alps pushing into Switzerland like the teeth of an old saw. He and Yasmine had entered from France, taking a bus from Dijon over the Rhine River and across the border. They hitchhiked to Freiburg and stayed in a hostel overnight, both of them studying the map and replenishing their food supply for the journey. Ruben insisted on hiking the rest of the way, promising they'd only have to camp out only for a night, but hinting that she should be prepared for a second night if necessary. Yasmine was shooting with her Sony handheld. She swept the video camera across the snow-covered crests before turning back to her fiancé. Ruben waited until she lifted her free hand and counted backward from three with her fingers.

"We've just entered the forest outside of Freiburg, Germany. This was the home of my great grandparents until March of 1939, when the Third Reich consolidated their reign over the country and the Jews were rounded up for..." Ruben stopped talking and looked pensively at the camera. Yasmine signaled to continue, but Ruben ignored her. He unslung his backpack, set it on the ground, and unzipped the main compartment. Moments later, he pulled out an ancient Minolta 8-millimeter camera—a 'Super 8'—that ran on D batteries and used celluloid film.

"This belonged to my grandfather, Josef Haim. He came to Germany in 1979 to retrace the trail his father had taken on the train from Freiburg to Dachau. Zaydi had meant to shoot a documentary. He spent a lifetime wondering about the man he'd never gotten to know personally. My dad was only seven years old when his father left, and has never learned for certain what happened to him. My great grandfather, Levi Haim, was taken prisoner outside the clock shop he'd worked in and was whisked away without my great grandmother even knowing. After three days of terror and uncertainty, Gynnifer Haim fled with her brother into Switzerland, her being three months pregnant."

"What's on the camera?" Yasmine interrupted.

"I'll get to that, I promise. None of what I'm about to tell you is going to make sense, so I'll start with the most recent developments. This Minolta…It arrived in our mailbox three months ago. No return address or letter of explanation. The postmark on the package was stamped in Freiburg, Germany, so somebody in this town had to have found it and done some research. Pan in closer, please."

Yasmine zoomed in on the Minolta. Ruben spun the Super 8 around until the battery compartment came into view. He pulled the tab and opened the compartment, and then turned the tiny door until it faced Yasmine's camera. Inside read the words PROPERTY OF JOSEF HAIM, BROOKLYN, NY. Yasmine gasped as if punched in the gut.

"Somebody mailed this to *our* house? How would they even know your connection to your grandfather? There has to be hundreds of Haims all over New York City."

"They Googled us," Ruben shrugged. "All I know is that when it arrived, there was still film inside the chamber. I brought it to a video expert and had him import what was on the celluloid onto a digital file."

"What was on the film?"

"Believe me, it's best we don't even talk about it until we've finished our trek and checked into our hotel. I really don't want to scare you."

"Ruben!"

He stuffed the Minolta back inside his pack and slung it over his shoulders. "C'mon. Daylight's wasting. I want to get to the graveyard and set up camp before nightfall."

"The graveyard? Seriously, I'm not sleeping in a fucking graveyard, thank you very much."

He chuckled as he adjusted his pack and buckled the harness strap around his waist. "I should have phrased that better. It's not a cemetery," Ruben raised his hands to make air-quotation marks with his fingers. He smiled, and brushed a long, dark lock of hair away from his eyes. "More like a graveyard for decommissioned railroad cars, the last five cattle cars of the Gottlieb-Deutsche Railway

Company, to be specific. The line we're looking for goes right through this forest, all the way to Dachau. My great grandfather was transported on one of those cars."

Yasmine clicked *stop* on her video camera.

"Are you out of your mind? You really need to see the railroad car that took your grandfather…"

"*Great* grandfather!"

"I can't believe you talked me into this. Do you have any idea how morbid this sounds? And who the *fuck* sent you that movie camera? You need to tell me what's on it. Right now, or I'm not taking another step!"

"Calm down. I have the video on a thumb drive in my backpack, but I'd rather you not look at it until we're out of this forest, okay? I can already tell you're nervous. But I swear to you, we're safe. The German government owns this forest, and there are ranger stations every ten miles. And even then, we're only going to have to camp out for one night. If you'll just be patient, I will show you after we set our tent up, okay. We still have a long hike in front of us."

"You said we'd be following a railroad line. There's no tracks *anywhere*."

"Look beneath your feet. You're standing directly on top of the G&D Railroad line."

Yasmine looked down, and her belly filled with dread. The iron rails were gone. She was standing on the rotted remains of wooden railroad ties hidden in the tall weeds and moss. Nature almost always claimed victory over all things manmade.

***

Yasmine pressed record on the video camera and asked from behind him, "Ruben, where are the rails to this 'railroad'?"

Ruben turned and looked over his shoulder. "I've read theories that claim that the Nazis ripped up the rails to recycle the iron for weapons as the allies moved in on Berlin. The problem with history is that it's recorded by the winning side."

"And what about the cattle cars you mean for us to find before the sun sets here in southern Germany?"

Ruben turned and started walking forward deeper into the woods, talking loudly over his shoulder so that the camera's mic could still pick him up. The truth was he had no idea how many miles they had to cover to find the abandoned freight cars, nor how many miles beyond that it would take to reach Dachau. What mattered to Ruben, what he was not telling his fiancé, was what he'd seen on the footage from his grandfather's camera. What mattered was the grainy black-and-white faces peeking out between the wooden slats of the cattle cars, captured on celluloid long after the Holocaust ended. They looked like ghosts.

***

The late afternoon sun peeked down through the turning foliage, reminding Yasmine of Central Park. It made her think of her and Ruben strolling one of the trails together, each carrying a latte smelling of caramel or pumpkin spice. His hair had been longer then, and he'd sported that mustache and goatee that tickled when he kissed her. Ruben reminded her of a younger version of Jeff Goldblum, and thought it was probably the reason she fell in love with him. Now all she had was the goddamn video camera, and she already decided it was her nemesis. That, and the early autumn mosquitoes that hummed around her head incessantly.

Ruben discovered she'd fallen behind and waited for her to catch up. Instead of asking, "are you okay?", he asked, "is the camera still rolling," which made her irritated at herself for saying "yes" when he proposed to her.

"Still rolling."

"Great grandmother Gynnifer came to America a year after Levi was taken. She never remarried, always believing that Levi would one day come and find her. My grandfather, Josef, wasn't even a year old when the steamship reached Ellis Island." He reached inside the rear pocket of his jeans and fished out an old black-and-white photograph of a woman holding her baby and signing a ledger while a bald, middle-aged clerk looked on. He held up the photo, and Yasmine zoomed in. Ruben continued with precise enunciation. "After the Holocaust, there was a push for Jews to marry and repopulate our people. But in America, when they talk about the 'Baby Boom', they're referring to the population explosion after the American servicemen returned to the women they left behind. Gynnifer never loved another man after Levi was taken. The Jewish-American community shunned her for it, but she never changed her mind. Levi wasn't murdered in cold blood. The prisoners were tasked with stuffing asbestos into the wings of the airplanes, which made them essential. There was a phrase made popular around the prison camps...Work will set you free!" Ruben paused and inhaled a deep breath. "There was an outbreak of dysentery in the camp, and scores of Jews wound up dying from malnourishment. At least that's what my research leads me to believe. Malnourishment is a terrible way to die. I'd almost rather believe he was shot to death and died instantly."

Yasmine waited until he was done talking. "How far do we still need to go to find the train cars?"

He frowned, and she felt her cheeks flush as she realized he'd wanted her to ask more questions about his ancestry. It wasn't her fault. It wasn't like he'd handed her a script or a prepared set of questions. She pressed the *stop* button on the camera, brushed the swarm of mosquitoes away from her face, and said, "Look, I'm doing this because I love you and I know how important this is to you, but at this point it feels like you're keeping secrets. So, if you have something you want to share, now is the time to tell me."

"I'm not keeping anything from you. I swear it." He unslung his backpack and pulled out a bottle of water. The water was lukewarm, but Yasmine didn't care. She swiped the bottle from his hand.

"We've been making pretty good progress today. We're going to find the graveyard before sunset. I'll get the tent set up and you can crash for the night. I won't disturb you until you wake up tomorrow."

Yasmine drank half the bottle in a few enormous gulps, and handed it back. She closed her eyes and massaged her temples for a moment, and then pressed the *record* button on the camera.

"We're traveling southeast on the G&D Railroad line, only there *are* no rails to follow. Just worn-out chunks of wood that look buried and probably want to stay that way, just like Germany's past. We're looking for five abandoned cattle cars out in the heart of Nazi country, one of which delivered your grandfather..."

"*Great* grandfather."

"Whatever! It delivered Levi Haim to Dachau, along with hundreds of other Jews. If Germany wanted to erase its history, why didn't it just burn the cattle cars, or take them apart and repurpose the materials? Why would they just leave them abandoned in the woods?"

"I don't know. All I know is..."

"What?"

"All I know is that when I saw the footage, there were people inside the cattle cars. People caught on film back in 1979, thirty years after Dachau was liberated. One of them looked exactly like me. I think it was Josef."

***

Five hours later Yasmine stopped the interview, stopped filming her fiancé altogether. The sun was sinking into the west, and it would be completely dark within an hour. Yasmine was already consumed with dread, feeling plagued by obscene shadows as they traversed the woods, and certain that she'd heard feint whispers and sniggering all around them. The paranoia of feeling watched grew deeper with every step she took. Pit stops so that she could relieve herself were filled with dread and shame, leaving her feeling more vulnerable than she'd ever felt in her life. Yasmine had to fight the impulse to either pick up stones and hurl them at Ruben—the man she'd considered the love of her life—or break down and cry. There were peanut butter and jelly sandwiches, crackers, and a handful of old granola bars in her backpack, but she was afraid to carelessly gobble up the last of the food. Ruben promised ranger stations every ten miles, but they'd yet to see one.

How many miles have we covered so far?

"Are you still filming?" Ruben called from ahead. He turned around, noticed that his fiancé was no longer holding the video camera, and stopped. "*Really*, hon?"

"What? The camera will be dead soon if all I'm doing is shooting your ass!"

"I *have* extra batteries. But this means you haven't been taping a goddamn thing I've said over the last...when did you turn the camera off?"

She smiled a bitter, contentious grin unlike anything he'd seen before. It made his arms and neck prickle with goosebumps. His fiancé was somewhere between seething hatred and panic, and that was not a good frame of mind.

"Where's the graveyard, Ruben?"

"Yasmine, calm down."

"Fuck you, calm down. I'm tired! I'm hungry! I'm still pissed at you for withholding information that would have probably dissuaded me from coming with you. I'm not even sure how I'm going to react when I see those abandoned freight cars but right now I'm dreading it. The sun will be setting soon and you have fuck-all information about how to find them."

Ruben threw his arms around her and held her as tight as he could.

"I'm scared, too. I'm terrified about what we'll find when we get there. I'm hoping those goddamn train cars are abandoned. If they are, I swear on my life that I will dowse them with oil and burn them. If the whole forest goes up with them, so be it. But I *need* to see them! I need to know that whatever footage was shot on my grandfather's camera was a hoax and that my grandfather isn't being held against his will."

"The Nazis are dead now," Yasmine retorted. "Nuremberg ended the German Nationalist Party over half a century ago. The Third Reich has been hunted down and punished. I don't know what happened to your grandfather, but the probability that he's still alive..."

"*Something* happened!"

He was going to ask her to take the Sony out and start shooting again, but the look of absolute hatred now spreading across her face insisted he stay quiet. He turned and lumbered forward, stomping down on the wooden ties with the heels of his hiking boots. The wood was soft, decayed, and sank under his weight. Yasmine stayed rooted to where she was, afraid and vulnerable, and needing him by her side if they were going to make this trek together. She waited, and panic grew to despair when he'd traveled nearly fifty yards ahead without looking back.

It was when he froze in his tracks that the real terror filled her heart.

Ruben began walking around in circles. He spun through the overgrown brush and weeds, the color draining from his face. Yasmine pulled out the video camera and pressed *record*. She held the camera up to her eye as she hustled to catch up to him.

"What is it?"

He froze, and the look of terror on his face was unmistakable. He let out a long, defeated sigh.

"The ties have disappeared. It's like the earth just swallowed them whole." Ruben looked directly into the camera. "The G&D railroad line ends here." Ruben threw his hands up in defeat, went to undo his backpack, and then gasped out loud.

"What?"

He pointed at the space of burned up wood and dead thickets about twenty feet away from where he was standing. There were charred remains of some kind of structure, obviously burned away to almost nothing.

An abandoned ranger station, with its beams and joists burned and weathered down to nothing more than a decimated carcass of black, ashy timber now overgrown with fresh weeds and scrub.

The sun was beginning to set.

***

They set up camp where the railroad ties ended. Ruben pitched the tent on the flattened weeds where the railroad line once ran, once carried his great grandfather in a freight car meant for livestock. He promised he'd show her the footage from the Minolta, but she was no longer speaking to him, and no longer cared. He didn't blame her. He'd had nightmares for days after seeing the footage. All the sleepless nights where his mind had drifted to the face of Josef Haim peering through the slats of the cattle car. Zaydi had come here to Germany to retrace the path *his* father had taken and had unwittingly spiraled into a living nightmare. Someone had found his grandfather's camera and found a way to ship it to him, drawing him into this continuing horror. Yasmine was right; it was very unlikely that Josef was still alive, but in his dreams, he always saw that same moment where his grandfather stepped up to the slats, gazed out with a look of absolute insanity, and screamed.

When she asked if he wanted a sandwich, he nearly jumped out of his skin.

"I'm not hungry, thanks."

"You need to eat. I've eaten already, and it really helped. At least eat half a sandwich and drink some water. After, you can build a fire. It's gonna get cold tonight. I don't think it will fall below freezing, but I'd rather stay warm tonight all the same. If we can't sleep, we can at least stay by the fire and look up at the stars." She thought of those awful shadows, and the voices she was now certain she'd heard as they hiked through this godforsaken forest. "Just please don't leave me alone because if you do, there will be no wedding in our future. If you really love me, you won't make me a prisoner to all *this*. When we leave, we leave all of *this* behind. Can you promise me that?"

She held out a peanut butter and jelly sandwich. He looked up at her suspiciously and took it. Once he'd taken a bite, his inhibitions lowered, and he devoured the meal in a few quick chomps. When it was gone, he took the bottle of water and guzzled it down. She was right; having his belly full helped a lot. Ruben went out into the darkening woods and gathered some branches and had a fire going in no time. The flames sent a flurry of shadows dancing across their tent. To her, the shadows looked very much like phantoms dancing in the deepest pit of hell.

Yasmine replaced the batteries in the Sony and returned to the fireside. She pressed *record* and pointed the camera at him.

"Where are we?" she said.

"We're somewhere between Freiburg and Dachau," he answered. "The trail of railroad ties ended, but that won't deter us. Somewhere ahead is the cluster of abandoned cattle cars we're looking for. There's no sense in denying, so the reality is that we've lost our trail once the ties disappeared. But we also have GPS, and we're perfectly capable of finding our way out of the woods."

"What if we don't find the cattle cars?"

Ruben was suddenly lost for words. He looked at the campfire and thought of Dachau, and of his great grandfather stuffing asbestos into the metal wings of airplanes that dropped bombs on London and France. He thought of Levi, kidnapped at gunpoint outside the clock shop where he worked, hauled away in broad daylight before he could even unlock the door. He looked up at her camera, trying to mouth some sentence that would add gravitas to this pilgrimage he'd forced her into, but before he could say anything, the night filled with the sound of a low, wailing steam whistle from behind them.

***

Yasmine turned the camera toward the abandoned ties. The Sony's flash lit up the abyss of forest darkness, its LED spilling waves of brilliance against the trees. When she breathed, a cloud of vapor floated into the light, causing eerie ripples.

"What the hell is going on?" she whispered.

Ruben stood beside her. "I don't get it! Maybe there's another railroad line somewhere nearby."

She turned on him. "Are we following the wrong line?" Tears formed in the corner of her eyes. "I want to go home. I don't want to see your cattle cars. I *don't* want to be here anymore."

"We're on the right line," he insisted. "I've been tracking our movement with my GPS. We're *exactly* where the G&D railroad used to be!"

She turned the camera on him, the bright LED blinding him momentarily. "If that's true, then how many more miles do we have to go to reach Dachau? Where's the next village, Ruben? How far? Because if it's less than five miles, we're leaving here right now."

"We're about two miles away from the Danube River. There's a town there, with a bridge we'll need to cross. But if we leave now, in the dark, there's a chance we get lost. We're safe here, so let's just go back inside the tent and try to sleep. We'll be up at first light and move on. When we get to the river tomorrow, if you want to just check into a hotel and wait for me, I'll make the rest of the journey by myself."

Yasmine's jaw dropped. She lowered the camera. "We could have been sleeping in beds tonight? Jesus, you're an asshole. Why did you want us to camp out here?"

He sighed. "I don't know what I was thinking. Honestly, I think we've already passed the graveyard. We should have seen it miles ago. Everything we've passed so far was on the film from my Zaydi's camera. I..."

The steam whistle shrieked like a dying monster. Yasmine rushed into his arms. He could feel her trembling against his body, could feel her heart pounding. There was no logical explanation to be had, but the whistle was coming from the direction of the abandoned railroad ties they'd been following. It was still a ways off; a mile, maybe two. If they stayed here, it wouldn't take long for this invisible monster to reach them. He gently pushed her away, took the Sony from her, and shined the flash back on the ties.

"We're going," he said, taking her hand. "I'll come back tomorrow and get our stuff, but we have to leave *now*."

***

The forest was so dark now, as if the stars decided to cower in fear. Yasmine had to struggle to keep up with Ruben. His tall legs parted the weeds and thickets like Moses had parted the Red Sea. The Sony was recording, its LED flash careening around the trees, making her dizzy if she tried to focus her eyes on it too long. The steam whistle blasted behind them, closer still and gaining ground. They could hear the low thrum of a locomotive coming up behind them, and the turning of giant metal wheels, guided by pistons that hissed and spat with each rotation.

That, and the whispers and maniacal laughter floating in the night air around them.

At some point, Ruben had grabbed her by the wrist and pulled her along, causing her to nearly lose balance and tumble into the brush and weeds of the forest floor, and she had to fight to stay upright. Yasmine could feel the tears as they began to slip down over her hot cheeks.

Without warning, Ruben froze, and she nearly knocked him over as her body collided into his. Ruben held up the camera, shining its flash along the massive iron skeleton that stretched out through the trees.

The missing iron tracks had been forged into a blasphemous sculpture that resembled a jungle gym, or a monstrous animal carcass. The rails were bent and crooked, both haphazardly welded together and connected with rusted rivets that looked like bloodied scabs in the light of the Sony's flash. *This* wasn't *on the Super 8 footage*, Ruben thought. *None of this was on the footage. How long has this been here?*

Yasmine saw lights ahead of them, just beyond the rails of this hideous metal sculpture; halogen bulbs shining from within a vacant ring of trees somewhere in the distance. Fog swirled around the floor of the woods, rising like a veil that hid whatever thing was throwing off those lights. Yasmine counted the lights as they passed beneath the arch of the sculpture and hurried toward them; *one, two, three, four, five...*

She froze, her eyes wide with terror. She'd stopped so abruptly that Ruben nearly toppled when her hand yanked out of his. He lifted the camera and aimed it at her face. Yasmine was crying.

"Those are your cattle cars," she whispered.

He turned to where her finger pointed, and could see the silhouettes of five freight cars, scattered inside the vacant field ahead. And then they heard footsteps all around them, and whispers passing through the darkness. The voices were barely audible, but Ruben could tell the language was German. From behind them, another blast from the steam whistle. It was almost upon them.

He grabbed her hand and pulled her into motion. They sprinted toward the cattle cars, running as fast as their legs could carry them. When they were less than thirty yards away, figures started jumping down from the opened doors of the cars; a few at first, but then more and more followed, forming a line in front of the freighters. The figures were diminutive, and as the two approached, they realized that they were surrounded by children. They looked pale, unnatural, as if sentenced by inbreeding to lives of misshapen faces and gangly parts. They were clothed in black, each with a band around their left arm with a Swastika stitched upon it. There were too many to count in the darkness. The tallest of them, the one in the middle, stepped forward into the light and raised his hand in a *Sieg Heil* salute. In his hand was something ancient and leathery, which he tossed at Ruben's feet.

It was the face of Josef Haim, its skin parched and wrinkled, and frayed where it had been severed off a once-living human being. There were patches of scalp still attached, with Zaydi's black hair now grayed and mottled with dried blood; a grisly mask that looked very much like an older version of Ruben Haim. From behind them, the steam engine ground to a halt just behind the massive iron skeleton that separated the woods from the clearing, blowing one final blast from its whistle. It shrieked into the darkness, and Yasmine felt her bladder release as the children moved toward her.

Ruben Haim dropped the video camera, and waited for these inbred Hitler Youth to come for them. In the darkness, two separate fires were lit, and he could see the children working together to prepare two spits as the others fell upon them. He could hear the words, "Work will set you free," as they gathered as one to cook and eat their next meal.

The German sky once again filled with smoke.

Peripheral Vision

"Mr. Danvers, I'm surprised to see you again."

Sister Margaret Willis slid out from behind her desk and closed the distance between herself and the man entering her office. It had been nearly five years since Theodore Danvers had last set foot in this room, had last called on her for her official duty as the church's "bereavement counselor" after his son Timothy passed away. Danvers was only twenty-seven at the time of the car accident. Now, here he was at thirty-one going on seventy. Danvers looked as if he hadn't slept in weeks; his hair prematurely graying and disheveled, the unkempt growth of whiskers on his cheeks, and the bags under his eyes suggested that he'd all but given up on living. And sadly, this wasn't atypical for a man who'd lost his child in an accident, and then was abandoned by his wife, who tried to drown him in a sea of blame and resentment before divorcing him directly afterward.

Sister Margaret extended her arms to embrace him, but instead caught him as he collapsed into her arms. She thought at first that she might drop him, and was surprised at just how light he felt in her grasp. Danvers had lost weight; another sign of giving up hope. She gave his breath a cursory sniff and was relieved when she detected no trace of alcohol.

"Mr. Danvers? Ted, are you okay?"

The man trembled and wept in her arms. His body shook and convulsed as he sobbed and gasped for breath. Sister Margaret held him tight, let him ride out the storm that raged inside until it ebbed to a quiet rainfall. Eventually even that subsided, and Danvers allowed himself to be led to the chair that sat directly across from her desk.

"I'm sorry," he stammered as he withdrew a handkerchief from his pocket. He blew his nose and wiped the tears off the puffed-out skin of his cheeks. "I didn't know anybody else I could talk to, anyone I could trust. I have nobody left."

Sister Margaret sat down behind her desk. She reached across and gently grasped his hands, enveloping his shaking digits and easing them down until they rested on the desktop. For the moment, Danvers couldn't raise his eyes to meet her own, but that would come in time. As a grief counselor, and one that had been practicing probably since before Danvers was even born, she knew what to look for, and how to get him to eventually open up.

After all, the two of them had gone through this dance before, just after the accident took his son's life.

Danvers sniffed again, and then took a deep breath. He exhaled, and then finally looked up at her.

"I didn't know where else to go," he repeated.

"It's okay, my son. I've seen many parents over the years that have had trouble coping after losing a child. It's the most awful thing for a parent to outlive their children. It goes against the nature of life that God has intended for us as humans. And after Trish decided to move on, you must be feeling terribly lonely as well."

Ted Danvers withdrew his hands from her grasp, covered his eyes, and began to weep again.

"That's the thing," he sputtered as his body convulsed with sobs. "I'm *never* alone! Timmy's come home, and I can't stop seeing him!" After a moment, he pulled his hands from his face, and his tired, bloodshot eyes gazed into hers in a cold, dead stare that passed into forever.

"Timmy's changing," he whispered in a cold, confidential tone. "He's becoming terrible."

***

The five-year-old version of Timothy Danvers was pronounced dead at the scene of the accident, out on the stretch of Route 196 where the exit ramp off Route 295 merged into the westbound lane heading into Topsham. Ted Danvers had been driving the boy home from a playdate that Saturday afternoon, and made the snap decision of swinging by the grocery store to grab some snacks and a six-pack for the football game the following evening rather than stopping at the light and turning left toward home. The other vehicle, an industrial-sized logging truck, had decided to put the pedal down and blow through the yellow light rather than try to bring the rig to a complete stop on such short notice. Danvers gave a cursory glance before likewise stomping on the pedal and making his turn and sending his only child into the afterlife.

***

Somebody had put together a roadside memorial where Danvers's sky-blue Toyota got creamed by the tons of 18-wheeler that collided with it before pushing it into the guard rails at the side of the road. The memorial went up overnight, neither of Timothy's parents knowing who'd put together the little wooden cross adorned with red roses and placed it where Timothy Danvers drew his final breaths before succumbing to internal injuries. By the time Timmy's body was lowered into the ground and covered with dirt, the memorial had grown into a shrine. People had visited and left flowers and photographs and mementos honoring a little boy that loved to smile and play and make people laugh.

The more the shrine grew, the more Trish Danvers hated her husband for having the accident. On the one-year anniversary of Timothy's death, Trish finally found the nerve to tell Ted Danvers that she wished *he* had died instead. She left him the very next day, which was good because Ted already hated himself enough for two, and hated her reminding him with her accusatory silence that everything was his fault.

"I decided to take down the roadside memorial," Ted started. "I just showed up one day to where I had the accident and took it all down. I didn't know what else to do. Every time I drove by it, it made me sick to my stomach. It was killing me. Seeing it was a hint of accusation from the world at what I'd done."

"How did that make you feel?" Sister Margaret sat across from him, never taking her eyes off him, even though she'd pulled out a legal-pad and began jotting down notes.

"I felt angry," he replied. "I didn't just take it down, I destroyed it. I'd been building up all this anger inside, and it finally had to come out of me. I kicked down the cross with Timmy's name on it and stomped on it until it splintered into a million little pieces. I ripped up old photos that had been stapled onto the wood...shredded them and tossed them into the wind. Trish's folks had collected his stuffed teddy bear, somehow snuck it out of our house after the funeral and left it there at his memorial. Can you believe that? I picked up the bear and started punching it. Just freakin' wailed on it right there at the side of the road, with other cars passing me by. After a while, people began to rubberneck and watch me, and traffic backed up. I didn't care. I beat on that goddamn bear until its stuffing began to ooze out."

"And then what happened?"

"A police car was dispatched to see what was creating the traffic jam. The line of cars on Route 196 parted like the Red Sea, and a pair of cops from the Topsham police department paid me a visit. They were pretty understanding, all things considered. The one guy, the senior of the two, politely told me that if I'd worked out all my frustration, I was free to clean up the mess and move on. Otherwise, they'd have to cuff me and I'd be appearing before the judge before the afternoon was over."

"Are you sorry you did it?"

Ted looked down at his lap, where his folded hands had come to rest.

"Yes, but only because that was when Timmy first came home."

***

Ted Danvers came home after the memorial-smashing incident feeling better than he had in a long time. Once the cops showed up, he'd managed to compose himself, and discovered that a great deal of the guilt and rage that had eclipsed his life had now given way to some sunshine and light. He picked up all the remnants of the memorial, everything he'd trashed and torn to shreds, and dropped them in the trunk of his new vehicle. Afterward, he drove to the town landfill and threw everything away. Everything except for the teddy bear. He clutched the bear in his hands, tried to let it go and drop it into the giant metal hopper, but couldn't. The damn thing *still* held the scent of his dead son. He held the toy up to his face and sniffed long and hard, and could detect the odor of Timmy's body oils, and the faint scent of the shampoo that his mother used to clean his hair. Smelling these scents brought tears to Ted's eyes, and he began to weep openly.

"I can't keep doing this," he whispered. "I'm sorry, son, but I have to let you go."

Ted Danvers dropped the bear into the hopper. He watched as the toy bounced off the cold metal walls of the hopper, and then settled lifelessly against the pile of trash bags and debris. The bear sat looking up at him. Cold, white stuffing oozed out of the tears and rips in the bear's skin. It made Ted think of the last time he saw his son, strapped into his booster seat (the one Trish had picked out *because* it was supposed to be the safest in the event of an accident), slowly hemorrhaging both internally and externally. Thank God the boy had been unconscious as his life slipped away.

He saw his child out of the corner of his eye. A quick blur within his peripheral vision as Ted made his way through the kitchen door and dropped his car keys on the counter. It happened so fast that he stopped in his tracks and craned his head toward the door to the living room where the blur had fled. When his gaze found nothing, Ted followed the blur into the living room.

***

"So what happened next?" Sister Margaret had been hanging on his every word. She could tell by the clarity of his voice and the way his eyes kept trying to meet hers that he believed every word he was saying. And why not? Why would Ted Danvers make the effort to drive way out here to St. Joseph's Cathedral and call on her, just to regale her with some crazy ghost story about his late son? Maybe he was slowly going crazy. Maybe the wall of isolation he'd built around himself was finally getting to him, and he was ready to tear it down.

Maybe.

What made all the difference in the world (and she noted this on her legal pad) was that he wanted the ghostly appearance of his child to stop. While most parents of departed children would be thrilled at having the spirit of their child nearby, where they might perhaps be in contact with it, be able to communicate with it, Danvers *didn't*. Ted was finally ready to let go and move on, but according to his story, something from beyond was trying to hold him back.

"I walked into the living room and was met by the coldest chill I'd ever felt. It felt invasive, kind of like something was trying to penetrate my skin and freeze up everything inside me. I walked into the room and scanned all around, but I saw nothing. No sign of life at all. I found myself walking through the whole house, feeling certain that something was in there with me...some other presence that I just couldn't see. I knew it was Timmy. I could feel it with the same certainty that I knew my own name, or that one plus one equals two. I went through that whole goddamn house, feeling that same blast of cold chill in every room. Finally, when I got to his old bedroom, I saw it."

"You saw your son?"

"I saw the teddy bear. The one that I had just gotten rid of at the dump. It was sitting on Timmy's bed, with its blank stare gazing back at me. Beside it was two pieces of wood, fastened together to form a little wooden cross, just like the one at Timmy's roadside memorial."

***

Ted Danvers rushed into the room and picked up the bear. He grasped it tight, brought it up to his face, and began to cry. He sobbed until his body hitched and gasped for breath. After a few minutes, he pulled his face away and looked back at the bear. His pupils fixed upon it as he tried to decipher how it had gotten here. It was as he stared at the toy that the shape in his peripheral vision reappeared.

Timmy was in the room with him.

He wanted to turn and look at the boy, wanted to see the phantom of his late son, but he couldn't. For starters, he knew that if he tried to look directly at him, his son would disappear, just evaporate like steam from a teakettle into the cold ethereal of the beyond. Ted wasn't ready for that. Instead, he continued to stare at the teddy bear and watched his child's ghost out of the corner of his eye.

"I'm so sorry, Timmy," he whispered.

The ghost merely sat there, watching. Because he couldn't turn his head, Ted's eyes couldn't focus on the face his son made, couldn't detect any kind of emotion from it. It hovered in the corner of the bedroom, waiting.

"It was an accident," Ted continued. "It should have been *me* that died. I would do anything to take your place, but I can't."

The ghost waited.

"I can't go on like this! I have to let you go. I want you to move on. I want you to move on and be at peace..."

The ghost screamed, and he could hear his son's voice, like a needle piercing his eardrums and trying to stab into his brain. Ted dropped the toy bear onto the ground and raised his hands up to his ears to cover them. He swung his head around to face his son, and just like he knew it would, the ghost vanished before Ted Danvers could look upon his dead child.

***

"I started using the bear as my conduit to communicate with my son," he said. "I could always tell when Timmy was there with me. The room would go ice-cold. The curtains would ruffle and sway when he passed by. Timmy would have been turning ten this September, but he still whispers to me in the voice of a five-year-old. I suppose ghosts don't age or celebrate birthdays. They just stay where they are, like prisoners or something. When he was there with me, all I had to do was lift up the bear and stare into its eyes, and I could see my son's shape in my peripheral vision. At first, he was docile, as if maybe he was sad and confused. I guess I can't blame him for that. But after a while, it was like he was growing restless or angry, like he wanted something from me and just couldn't communicate what it was."

Sister Margaret stopped scribbling on her pad for a moment and looked at him.

"What do *you* think he wanted?"

"I have no idea. I'd apologized to him for the accident. I told him I wanted him to be at peace, told him I wanted to move on. But now that I'd found this way to communicate with him, it was like he wanted it all the time. It was like he wouldn't let me be. I was beginning to lose sleep at night. He'd enter my bedroom when I was asleep and find ways to wake me up. One night he knocked over a glass of water I'd left on my nightstand. It shattered against the wall and the floor, and I bolted upright. Timmy had brought the bear into my bedroom and had left it on my pillow right beside me. I turned on the bedroom light and stared into the bear's eyes, and saw my son in my peripheral vision as he began to tear my bedroom apart, throwing my clothes on the floor and knocking pictures off the bedroom walls in this fit of rage that continued to grow inside him."

"Ted, you said this all began right after you destroyed the roadside memorial. Have you, perhaps, thought of putting up a new memorial? Maybe your son is angry with you because you destroyed his shrine. Maybe he's angry because you're trying to destroy your memories of him."

Ted sighed and sat back in his seat.

"I did think of that. That was one of the first things I did. I drove back out to the site of the accident and put up a new shrine. Timmy was there when I went downstairs to my workshop and built a new cross to put up for him. I painted the new one white and stenciled his name in gold letters across the horizontal bar. I went back and found some old photographs of him and placed them in a new photo album, which I also left at the shrine. I put up flowers and everything. By the time I was done, the shrine was bigger and better than before."

"Did you return the teddy bear?"

"No, I didn't."

"Why not?"

"I was using it to communicate with him. I wanted to see if maybe he was pleased with what I'd done. I was waiting to find out if this all would bring him peace."

"Was he pleased?"

"No. Things got much, much worse. He wasn't pleased at all."

"What happened next?"

"I got angry with him. I was so pissed that he still wouldn't leave me alone that I destroyed the teddy bear."

Sister Margaret gasped. "You destroyed it?"

"I was angry! I lit the bear on fire and dropped it in the bathtub. Timmy was with me as the damn thing burned down to ashes. The whole time he shrieked and beat his hands against the bathroom walls. It was absolute agony for me. I'd almost preferred watching my son die again rather than going through that awful tantrum."

"What happened after that?"

"After that, I didn't need the teddy bear to see my son anymore. After that, I began seeing him all the time. I could see him as plainly as I'm looking at you right now. After that, he began to change..."

***

The little boy that was Ted Danvers's son began to turn sour and rot. Somewhere in Hillside Cemetery was a child-sized coffin with the real remains of Timothy Danvers. And inside that coffin was a tiny body, still well-preserved with chemicals, and yet still decaying. Perhaps the coffin had ruptured, had allowed in air and dirt and moisture and insects. Perhaps one or more of those elements combined to make his corpse begin to fester.

It was as if Timmy's ghost was decaying along with it.

The first time Ted had witnessed the ghost (not in his peripheral vision, but right in plain sight) was the morning after the bear-burning incident. Ted had raided the liquor cabinet and drank until his body could no longer tolerate it, and he simply slumped down on the kitchen floor and passed out.

When he awoke, Timmy was there waiting for him.

The phantom sat before him on the kitchen floor. Its skin was almost translucent, allowing beams of sunlight from the kitchen window to pass right through it. Only, as the sunbeams passed through, they seemed to collect the ice-cold chill that radiated from the boy, forcing droplets of condensation to form on Ted's skin. Ted wiped the droplets away, and was repulsed to feel how sticky they were, as if he was somehow coated in ectoplasm while he slept.

"Please, please go away. I don't want to see you anymore."

The ghost scowled and pushed an object toward him on the cold tiles of the kitchen floor. It was a butcher's knife.

"No...no, I'm not going to kill myself!"

The ghost's scowl turned to rage. Its hand shot down and tried to pick up the knife. As it did, Ted's hands shot out and tried to grab his son's throat. He'd meant to strangle his son, choke the life out of him, but his hands, instead, passed right through his son's neck. They pushed out through the back side, and the ectoplasm residue coated Ted's skin and turned to ice. The ghost lurched backward in fear, and then raced off through the house, shrieking and wailing in its dead five-year-old voice.

***

"It's been this way for weeks," Ted confessed. "My son wants me to die too. That's what he wanted all along. I should have died in the accident along with him. Now he won't leave me alone."

Sister Margaret listened quietly. She'd tried not to be judgmental, but it seemed as if perhaps Ted Danvers *had* gone off the deep end. Her job here at the church was as a bereavement therapist, but she was not a doctor of psychology, not clinically licensed to prescribe medication or make psychiatric assessments.

"Mr. Danvers...Ted," she began. "I think perhaps you should consider an evaluation."

"You think I'm crazy, don't you?" Ted sighed. "I'm not crazy, Sister. I can prove it."

"You've been through an awful lot since the accident."

Ted stood up. He pulled his shirt out from where it had been tucked inside his jeans and fished out an object. It wasn't clear at first what it was, so she waited.

"Timmy is here with us. Right now! All you have to do to see him is hold this up and stare at it. You'll see him out of the corner of your eye."

Ted handed over the remains of the teddy bear. It was now a charred lump of fuzz and material that had somehow melded together under the heat of the flames. Ted tried to pass the bear along to her, and as he did, she felt the ice-cold chill of something else in the room with them. Sister Margaret took the toy from Ted's hands. Her own hands trembled as she held the bear out in front of her face.

She began to cry as the ghost stared her down. It no longer looked human.

Sister Margaret Willis never saw Ted Danvers pull the pistol from his pocket, hold the weapon to his head, and pull the trigger. She only saw the bear, and the blinding flash of light behind it as the gun went off. There was a deafening POP, making her jump in her chair, and the immediate burn of gunpowder as Ted's lifeless body fell to the floor. Her gaze never left the bear, nor the phantom child in the corner of her eye. She wept as the second ghost came into focus and joined him.

Trailertrash Annie

Mama had always warned us to keep away from Mrs. Winslow. That was how we were to refer to her whenever my brother and I saw her: Mrs. Winslow, instead of the more appropriate nickname, Trailertrash Annie, which the other residents of the Lisbon Gardens Trailer Park called her. It wasn't a rare thing to see her, either. On the way to our own home, we would have to pass by her unkempt, crooked little box of a trailer, and most days, when weather permitted, she would be out sitting in that rickety old rocking chair on the patch of dirt just outside her door. She would usually be out there knitting or cross-stitching some damn thing or other to keep those bony, liver-spotted hands of hers busy. Surrounding her would be her six or seven cats, each one's shiny little eyes fixed on what her hands were working on, as if they were hypnotized by the palsied movements they made. When she would stop working, they would begin to move about, mewling and pacing frantically.

We would have to pass by her place both to and from our bus stop on Route 196. This meant that sometimes we would see her twice a day, depending on how early she got out of bed and made her way outside. Toward the end of the school year, when the weather was warm and sunny, she would be out there bright and early. Rocking away in that damned chair, her hands flailing away at whatever she would be working on. She rarely bathed, and most mornings when we saw her, she would stink to high hell; bad enough for us to smell her all the way to the bus stop.

But worst of all, her grin. Her malignant, awful grin, with those dry, crusty slits of flesh that were her lips stretched out over those dirty cheeks. Her swollen, purple gums barely holding captive what was left of her decayed, crooked teeth. Her tongue, a long, pointed mound of serpentine flesh, would loll about like a wounded animal whenever she laughed.

And Trailertrash Annie loved to laugh, especially at me and my brother George.

Whenever we passed by, the old crone would stop knitting and sit up straight in her chair. Immediately, the trance that held over her cats would break and they would line up in front of her, yowling and hissing at us as we passed by. And she would laugh the whole time. That terrible laugh that sounded half-screech, half-cackle, as if a thousand fingernails were being raked down a chalkboard. We would pass by silently during those terrible moments, those hideous fits of laughter. Most times I would have to grit my teeth and clench my hands into fists to keep myself from going crazy. George, my elder by two years, would grab me by my arm and yank me along faster until we were safely past her lot.

Mama warned us to stay away from her.

I wish to God we'd listened.

***

"She's a witch, you know," George had told me in the spring before he disappeared. "Not just because she's like she is and all. But a real witch! Just like in the movies."

I was old enough to know that whatever George had told me was the god's honest truth. He had been right about Santa Claus being make believe. I had doubted him at the time when he told me. But after our father died and Santa hadn't come to our house that Christmas, I knew he was telling the truth. Mama couldn't afford to buy us toys that year and she was too proud to take gifts from her sister's family. So instead of us opening Christmas presents, Mama told us that we were old enough to know that Santa wasn't real. That was the year before Mama had to sell our house and move us into that damn trailer park.

"How do you know?" I asked him.

"Bennie Long told me," he answered. Bennie Long and George were best friends since forever. The two of them had started their freshman year of high school the autumn before. I was still in seventh grade. "Bennie said that she is the great, great, great granddaughter of Mabel Holmwood, who was burned at the stake for being a witch. He said that Trailertrash Annie has what's left of her bones somewhere inside her trailer." George turned to me and smiled. "Pretty cool, huh?"

"Yeah," I responded, my mind filled with the terrible pictures of what might actually be inside her trailer. I imagined the place filled with spider webs and animal bones amidst its dirty, dimly lit confines. I could see books of magic and witchcraft on the shelves, and miscellaneous jars filled with eye-of-newt and toads' feet, and all of those creepy, unnatural ingredients witches use to cast their spells. But mostly, I could picture her eyes peering through the darkness and that terrible grin of hers as her bony little hands mixed away at something dreadful brewing in a deep, black cauldron. "Yeah, I'd believe it," I said aloud. "I bet that is exactly what she is."

"When we pass her place," George said as he grabbed his knapsack and slung it across his shoulders, "we have to fork the sign of the evil eye. That will protect us from whatever spells she may try to cast on us. Let me see you do it, so I know if you're doing it right."

I forked the sign at him.

"Is this right?"

"Perfect. Now grab your bag and c'mon. Mom will have a cow if we miss the bus."

Trailertrash Annie was out in her chair that morning, surrounded by her cats. They watched in fascination as those hands stitched at whatever project she was working on. She saw us coming and stopped immediately. As usual, the cats jumped to their feet and paraded around her, forming a line in front of her chair. With their backs hunched up and their fur standing on end, they began to hiss and wail at us. I remember that it struck me funny that her cats looked so clean compared to that rotten old woman. Her terrible eyes glared at us, and she fell into a fit of that horrible chalkboard laughter.

"Why, good morning, George and Eric Paige!" she called out between gales of laughter and snorts of breath. "How are you fine young gentlemen today?"

"We're fine, Mrs. Winslow," George responded, grabbing my arm and rushing me past her yard. My legs were shorter than his and I stumbled a little trying to keep up his pace.

The old witch continued to laugh. "I know what you are thinking, young George!" Her bony old hand dropped the stitch work into her lap and an accusing finger pointed directly at my brother. George stopped walking suddenly and stared at her. His immediate halt stopped me as well. I looked up at him, and I could see the fear in his face. He'd gone pale white, as if someone had knocked the wind out of him.

"You'd like to see me burn at the stake like my sweet old relative had. You'd like to see my bones burned all black because I frighten you." Another gale of that terrible laughter, sending goosebumps all over my skin. "Come inside my house, Georgie. You want to see those bones of hers, don't you? I know you do!" Her cats shrieked louder now, and rows of tiny paws were now waving claws into the air.

And then she pointed at me.

"And you, young Eric. I scare you even worse, don't I?" Her wicked old eyes caught mine and I felt my head grow dizzy, as if she were trying to hypnotize me. "You think I want to eat you for dinner," she yelled at me, her accusing finger pointing in my direction. "Why, I wouldn't even feed you to my cats!" Her hand pulled up to her forehead as she howled with laughter.

I was paralyzed with fear. She was actually reading my mind.

It was George who broke my trance.

"You don't scare us, Trailertrash Annie!" he screamed at her, and immediately forked the sign of the evil eye in her direction. Following his lead, I did the same, but fear was washing over me like a tidal wave. The moment I made the sign, however, the hypnotized feeling fell away from me and I could feel my legs begin to move again. George was moving as well, and when we were past her lot, our legs moved a lot faster as we broke into a sprint that carried us all the way to the bus stop.

***

"We should tell Mama," I remember saying that night. "She can call the police or something."

We were sitting in our bedroom: he at his desk doing homework, myself laying in bed reading a comic book.

"What are the police going to do?" he offered dubiously. George closed the book he was reading and looked over at me.

"She read my thoughts," he started, and then a fit of trembling overcame him. "She knew exactly what I was thinking. And she read yours too, didn't she?"

I nodded silently.

"So what are the police going to do? If she knows they're coming she could probably read their minds and escape before they even made it to her door. And I really don't want Mom going over to her place to confront her. Do you?"

I remember the knot in my throat as I tried to say, "No."

"Me either." He turned the lamp off at his desk and climbed into his bed. "Mom will be home from work pretty soon. She'll be in to say goodnight. Don't you say a word to her about what happened this morning." He folded his arms behind his head and stared up at the ceiling. I put away my comic book and did the same.

It was a long time after Mama came in to say goodnight that we finally fell asleep.

Both of us had nightmares that night.

***

Trailertrash Annie wasn't sitting outside the next morning, and for that we were thankful as we hurried by. Nor was she waiting for us as we went by on our way home. In fact, days began to pass without the old witch outside to torment us as we made our way to and from the bus stop. And soon days became weeks. It was when a whole month had passed by without us seeing her that my brother began to grow suspicious.

"Where do you think she went?" I asked him one night. "Do you think she's still in her trailer?"

"I don't know," George answered. "Maybe she died in there or something." The look on his face said he believed otherwise. George looked at me, and I could see the fear in his eyes. "I hope she is dead!" he said, almost in a whisper. "If I knew she was for sure, I'd go over there right now and burn her ratty little trailer to the ground."

"Don't even say that!" I said in terror. "What if she can still read our minds?"

"I don't care," he responded indignantly. "So what if she knows? It's the truth. I'm sick of being afraid of that old witch." George was pacing the room. "What's the worst that she could do?"

"She could cast a spell on you or something!"

"The evil eye protected us. You felt it, didn't you? When she was reading your mind. She was trying to put you into a trance, and we broke it with the evil eye."

"Maybe she wasn't trying that hard."

"Maybe she was!"

George continued to pace, and in the small confines of our bedroom he resembled a giant wind-up toy. After a few minutes of pacing, he stopped and looked at me.

"I have to know," he said. He walked over to the closet and opened the door. After a moment of scanning the shelf above the clothes bar, he pulled down a flashlight and was walking toward the door.

"Where are you going?" I asked, dreading the response.

"To knock on her door. If she answers, then she's still alive. If she doesn't, then either she *is* dead or she's not home. Are you coming with me?"

I didn't want to but I couldn't say no. I followed him through the trailer into the kitchen, where he grabbed a book of matches from the counter drawer. He meant what he'd said about burning her trailer. He walked with deliberation as he exited our home and marched toward the witch's house.

I was never more terrified in my life as I followed him. It was the last night I would ever see him again.

Or so I thought.

***

Her door was open when we reached her trailer. Open wide and inviting, like the mouth of a Venus flytrap. He stopped us by the tree at the corner of her lot and pulled me close.

"I want you to stand guard," he said, his eyes meeting mine, trying to look brave and failing miserably. "If she comes back while I'm inside, start screaming your ass off. Anything to distract her so I can get out safely. Got it?"

"Please don't go in there." It was all I could say. I was horrified at the thought of Trailertrash Annie catching my brother inside her house. I think I was crying when I said it.

"I'll be okay. I just want to see what's in there."

"What if she's dead? What if you find her dead body?"

He didn't respond. Instead, he pulled out the matchbook and held it up for me to see.

"I'll be quick, I promise." He put his hands around me and hugged me one last time.

"If anything does happen, you run straight home and call the police. Then call Mom at work and tell her to come home." And then he was running toward her door, the flashlight out in front of him, cutting through the darkness like a fiery sword. I stood behind the tree and watched him pass over the dirt lot and by her filthy old rocking chair. All the lights were off inside her trailer, and through the windows I could see the beam of the flashlight as it penetrated the doorway and bounced off the walls.

And then George disappeared inside.

It felt like an eternity was passing from the moment he went in. I kept one watchful eye on the road and around the house to see if she might be sneaking back home. Time and again I would see the beam of the flashlight as it moved about inside the trailer. I could feel my heart pounding in my chest and the sweat beading under my armpits. He was in there for so long. Looking back, I can only imagine what he found inside that wretched trailer house.

And then my brother George was standing in the doorway, a horrified look on his face. He was holding the flashlight in his right hand. In his left was a big burlap bag, which he proceeded to dump down the doorway of her home.

Bones. Old, brittle, charred remains of the great, great, great grandmother of Trailertrash Annie. George let them spill noisily to the ground, watching the clouds of dust, soot, and ash billow into the air. I put a hand up to my mouth as I tried to repress the gag in my throat. George shined the flashlight down over the charred remains, then glanced at me.

And then those terrible, bony old hands sprung out from behind him, one wrapping around his mouth, the other around his chest. It happened in a split second; so quickly that I would have missed it if I blinked. And then my brother was gone. Pulled back into her house, the door slamming shut behind him.

***

There was no trace of my brother by the time the police arrived. Nor was there any trace of Trailertrash Annie. There was nothing left but a broken, run-down trailer and a handful of those cats, wailing and hissing into the night as the police conducted their investigation.

The worst part was having to explain to poor Mama, who listened with tears in her eyes as I told her everything from beginning to end. There was so much anger in her by the time I finished and, as difficult as it must have been, she managed not to lose her temper with me. Instead, she just wrapped her arms around me and cried.

The search party for my brother lasted weeks. People from all over the state had come to our small town to try and help locate my brother, but to no avail.

But worst of all, wanted posters with a police sketch of the face of Trailertrash Annie Winslow were posted everywhere around the state. I had to see that wretched face of hers in store windows, at the post office, the bank, everywhere. And every time I saw it, I wanted to cry. For my poor brother, for my mother, for my own sanity. I knew it hadn't been my fault, but somehow a part of me felt responsible. And when enough time had passed for my brother to switch from being missing to presumed dead, enough time for Mama to give up hope, they found Trailertrash Annie. At least it looked like her. The woman who may or may not have been that old witch was found dead just outside of Salem. It gave Mama a little relief, but not much.

Two years had passed since I last saw my brother alive. But tonight, I got to see him again.

I was awakened tonight by the sound of a cat shrieking, and for a brief, disorienting moment, I thought I was having a nightmare. I sprang upright in my bed, the sweat pouring off my body, my blurry eyes glancing about the room. The cat continued to shriek just outside my window. When I glanced out at it, the cat stopped shrieking and glared at me. It began to purr, walking around in circles, swishing its long, black tail at me. And then it nodded, as if making some sort of gesture that it wanted me to follow it.

I threw on a pair of jeans and a t-shirt and left the room that once belonged to my brother George and I. I walked out to the front door where I slipped on my sneakers and then I left the trailer. The cat was waiting for me out front.

I followed the cat on down the street and stopped dead once I realized where I was being led to. It was the trailer that I had last seen my brother in. The home of that rotten old witch, Trailertrash Annie. I gasped in horror.

The front door was open.

I was about to turn around and run back home but the sound of the cat stopped me. It was purring again, brushing up against my legs as if trying to stop me. I knelt down and started to pet the cat, but when I did, the cat lit off into the darkness and entered the open door of the trailer. After a few seconds, it returned with something in its mouth. I reached down and removed the object and burst into tears. The cat had given me a book of matches. The same book of matches that George had taken on that terrible night, as he meant to burn down this awful place. And as I held the book of matches in my hand, a terrible realization came to me. The cat was my brother, George! The witch had cast a spell on him and turned my brother into one of her terrible pets. And then I noticed all the other cats lined up in front of the rocking chair that the old witch used to sit in. Could they have once been children too? They watched me silently, waiting to see if I would continue the task my brother had set out to do.

I burned that horrible old place to the ground. The fire spread quickly, consuming the tiny box as if it were made of nothing more than paper. And as it burned, I felt a burden being removed off my shoulders. I felt the anger and the fear and the sadness all melt away from me. As one final gesture of contempt for that old crone, I snatched up that crooked old rocking chair and threw it into the fire. The line of cats had scattered away as I did this. They tore off into the woods, each finally free of the witch. Only one remained. I stood there, watching the fire burn into the night, and didn't leave until I heard the screaming sirens of fire trucks approaching. The cat that had once been my brother followed, swishing his tail contentedly.

I never had the heart to tell my mother that the cat we were adopting was actually my brother. I simply asked if it would bother her if I named him George. She was hesitant at first, but the way that cat would purr so beautifully when she held him, she could hardly say no.

Rest in Peace

Robert walked into the main gallery of the Portland Museum of Art and stared at the empty room, knowing that his heartrate should be skyrocketing but feeling decidedly calm. By the end of the day the room would be filled with his works: close to one hundred black and white photographs, paintings in oil, acrylic, and watercolor, charcoal sketches, and of course, the headstone rubbings. His subject matter always remained the same; he'd spent the last fourteen years capturing the artistry of American cemeteries. The title of his gruesome little traveling display was "Robert Pierce, *R.I.P.*," and in the grandest of irony, it was his life's work. At least until this moment. With his book contract already in place and his plane ticket waiting on the nightstand in his hotel room, this would be his final exhibit.

Most of the original pieces in his collection were for sale, although most people opted for the cheaper reprints or the postcards—his obvious bestsellers. People seemed to love viewing his work, but the subject matter always seemed a bit too dark and unsettling for average folks to want to hang on their walls. Robert didn't care. This was how he subsidized his lifestyle after the stipend from the National Endowment for the Arts and the paltry gallery appearance fees ran out. At his last show in Boston, he'd amassed a small fortune for two of his headstone rubbings. The first had been a rubbing of Edgar Allan Poe's headstone; not the memorial marker out in front of Westminster Church in Baltimore, but the grave itself behind the church. The second had been that of Elvis Aaron Presley (which was usually a good seller. Robert made frequent trips to Graceland in the winter, and usually took at least a dozen rubbings of the King's stone during each visit. Long live the King!). As it were, the money from the sale would be enough to last him through the remainder of the month. Any money coming in from this exhibit was strictly bonus. But that book deal...

He strolled leisurely around the empty room, his hands stuffed inside the pockets of his sport jacket, taking mental notes of where he would strategically place his strongest works. Generally, the exhibit would begin on the east wall, where his "sunrise" works would be placed, followed by the south and north walls respectively, then the west wall (the sunset wall) would end the journey. This was the formula he'd stuck with after it brought him rave reviews in Washington, DC, and New York. It had been Melissa's idea, of course. That bitch always had the best ideas. Melissa Fagan had been his agent before his artwork and his career took off. Then she became his lover. She had mentioned one time that his exhibit needed a sense of balance, a definite beginning and ending, so that the viewer felt as if they were being taken on a journey.

"Otherwise it's just a collection of pictures and sketches," she had said over dinner. He could picture her in his mind; the way she had twirled her long, curly blonde hair with her fingers as she waited for her chicken Florentine to be served. "You want the viewer to walk away feeling like they've had an experience." She picked up her glass of chardonnay and took a sip. "Use your works to tell a story, Robbie dear. Make 'em feel moved when they leave the gallery."

Christ, he hated when that bitch was right.

Footsteps echoing off the walls of the empty hallway alerted him that someone was coming. Robert turned and watched the figure enter the room. An elderly gentleman, slightly short and slightly balding, approached him with his hand outstretched.

"You must be Robert Pierce," the man announced, a pleasant smile plastered across his face. "I'm Sidney Graham, the assistant curator."

Robert extended his own and shook Sidney's hand, his eyes examining the man's navy-blue suit and the necktie with da Vinci's *Mona Lisa* printed on it. Typical to the point of stereotypical.

"Pleased to meet you," Robert said politely.

"Likewise. I'm quite anxious to see your exhibit. I've heard terrific things about it." Sidney reached out and put a hand on Robert's shoulder. "Tell me, young man. How did you choose such a morbid subject for your work?"

"Both my parents died when I was young," Robert recited for probably the thousandth time. It was the standard answer he gave every time an art critic or newspaper columnist approached the subject. "I ended up doing the charcoal rubbings of their headstones. I usually have them displayed at the beginning of the exhibit. That way

I feel like they're still with me. From there, I found a sense of completion in the beauty of mortality, and I just wanted to share it with the whole world." Robert let out a calculated sigh, one that begged the older man to perhaps share one or two of his own losses, but the assistant curator appeared too busy for it.

"Smashing," the old man chuckled. "Well, feel free to start setting up your display whenever you're ready. And remember, our staff is at your disposal. I'll send in some free hands to help you get started."

"Thank you, but I think I can handle most of the legwork." Robert smiled in relief and turned back toward the bare walls. The truth was he didn't really want to be bored with another unwanted sob story, but at least he offered the opportunity; the high price of singing for his supper. The past fourteen years had been filled with people viewing his exhibit, but really looking to be comforted for their own losses. It was maddening, but at least this time around he wouldn't have to deal with any of it. By tomorrow night, he would be on a tropical island, drinking rum cocktails and preparing to live off book royalties if everything went perfectly. In the meantime, he was considering which pieces would be displayed and which would have to remain in the van. This was definitely one of the smallest galleries he'd been stuck with. He would have to pick and choose a few pieces to not be displayed, just to make the exhibit fit without cramping everything together. Behind him, he heard the old man's footsteps stop, and his voice call out to him.

"I almost forgot... Are you planning on doing your own PR? If you'd like, I'd be more than happy to contact the local newspaper and have them send someone over to do an interview."

Robert smiled.

"That won't be necessary, but thank you. I usually do some publicity stunt or other. I just need time to come up with something fresh."

"Fabulous. One can never have too much publicity. Self-promotion is one of the cornerstones of art." Sidney offered one last smile and left Robert to his work.

***

It was late afternoon by the time Robert had his exhibit properly displayed. For the most part he only needed the museum's staff to help him move a few partition boards around, so that the display formed the obvious path Melissa had suggested. He made all the trips to his van by himself. Everything he brought to Portland made it inside, except for the footlocker and a few cardboard boxes filled with his less-desirable pieces. Robert had stolen an old bellhop's trolly from a hotel in South Carolina, and he managed to wheel everything inside in three trips. It would have been helpful to have an extra pair of hands, but he found that when people helped him set up, they often asked a million questions. It grew tiresome, answering the same questions over and over again. A few months back, when Melissa was still part of the equation, he didn't have to worry about it that much. She had a natural gift of gab, and kept people occupied so that he could work in peace. Melissa answered all the questions for him. All he had to do was concentrate on his work, either the creative end or the business end as he was now, in finishing the display. She had handled all his publicity as well. Now that she was gone, it had become his problem.

At first, he had been really good at it. Not the typical interview or run of the mill poster-canvasing and handbills in the local papers, but down-and-out guerilla warfare; front page-grabbing publicity stunts. It had become another form of art to him.

He remembered the first solo publicity stunt, the first after that bitch Melissa finally left him. He had hired a bunch of college girls to strip naked, paint their bodies white like ghosts, and dance about in the Tarrytown cemetery—Sleepy Hollow, to fans of literature—as he photographed them. The pictures had come out spectacular, and he sent a bunch of them out to local newspapers with a fabricated testimony about seeing real ghosts while doing his artwork. Of course, his hoax was exposed for what it was, but people had flocked to his exhibit in record numbers.

Another stunt he had done had been the *Celebrity Deaths* bit. He had chosen a dozen or so famous people, had mock tombstones made with their names on them, and did his rubbings of them for display. One of the celebrities, a shock-rocker named Mick Munroe, had been so pleased with the stunt that he actually flew out from Los Angeles during a break in his concert tour to see the exhibit. Five of the other celebrities (whom Robert's lawyer insisted remain nameless) were mortified and threatened him with lawsuits if their names weren't withdrawn from the exhibit. The rest of the celebrities laughed it off and dismissed the event publicly, even though Robert had a good suspicion that they liked the free publicity. It had been a crying shame, overall. Robert had put in as much effort in designing the mock tombstones as he would in any of his artwork. And again, people flocked in to see the exhibit, but after all the legal fees, he'd barely broke even.

There had been other stunts. Some amazingly clever, some downright tasteless (these latter, the "sacrilege" stunts, had been the best crowd drawers). *Always a full house!* That had been his credo. It helped to build his reputation and promote his artwork. And his big break finally came right before this trip to Portland, when Weston House offered his first book deal, with a considerable advance and a fair percentage of royalties. The offer had been a career high for him, and with Melissa gone and his situation approaching dire, he couldn't refuse.

Now things were finally looking up. Except, of course, that his publicity stunts were losing their freshness. As it were, he had no idea of what he would do to promote this Portland gig. He needed to brainstorm. Come up with something different. Robert only had one evening ahead of him to figure it out. The flight out of Portland's jetport would leave by noon on Sunday, with or without him, and there were loose ends to be tied and that one last publicity stunt to ensure the book's success. He needed a cemetery to help him think. The fresh air would do him good, and perhaps being in a graveyard might get the promotional juices flowing.

Robert was putting the final touches on the west wall when Sidney came back in to check up on him.

"I see you are almost finished in here," the old man offered politely. "Quite an impressive collection, if I may say so."

"That's very kind of you," Robert replied as he straightened a crooked picture frame. "You aren't waiting for me to finish up in here so you can call it a day, are you?"

"Not at all," Sidney responded. "But if you are finished in here, we may end up leaving early after all."

"Yeah, everything's all set." Robert stood back and admired his work. The two were surrounded by pictures of tombstones: old white slates, charcoal-gray granites, marbles, crooked, straight, small, large, clean, and dirty. It had the overall effect of standing in a real graveyard. It felt almost serene, if you could get past the macabre sensation.

"Then, if everything is all set, we'll see you Tuesday morning for the grand unveiling. I took the liberty of contacting the newspaper after all, along with some of the more charitable members of Portland's art community. I think your exhibit should be a rousing success." Sidney offered his hand again, which Robert obligingly shook. The assistant curator was on his way to the door when Robert called out to him.

"Say, can you tell me if there are any really good cemeteries nearby?" Robert blushed. "I mean, anything historic or noteworthy?"

"Of course. Are you looking for anything specific?"

Robert thought for a moment. "Yeah. Perhaps something a little spooky. You know...like with ghostly hauntings or infamous murderers. Stuff like that."

"Oh." The old man laughed nervously. He waddled back over to where Robert was standing, rubbing his chin in deep thought as he closed the distance between them, his *Mona Lisa* necktie now loosened and flapping as he moved.

"Well, yes...there are 'supposed' hauntings in the Scarborough Cemetery. I can't think of any murderers buried around here offhand—dreadful topic and not my cup of tea. But there *is* this one you might be interested in."

Robert's face perked up with excitement. "Yeah, I'm listening."

Sidney offered a mischievous smile. "There is a legend that out in Windham, there is a vampire buried in the Smith-Anderson Cemetery. I don't know how true it is though. You'd have to do your own research, if you take my meaning."

Robert's eyes lit up. *Thank you, Gods of Publicity!*

"Really? What was his name? What does his headstone look like?"

"I'm afraid I don't know. Like I said, it is just a legend. It's maybe a half hour's drive west of here, and I'm sure if you ask around..."

Robert thrust his hand out and shook Sidney's again, this time much more heartily, and then he was rushing toward the exit. "Don't worry about it," he called out over his shoulder. "I'll figure it out! I'll see you Tuesday morning. You have a great night!" Robert sprinted to his van, knowing he would never speak to the man again.

***

Finding the town of Windham hadn't been that difficult. The GPS on the van's dashboard had him passing through the small town in less than an hour. Unfortunately, the town had no motels to stay in, and Robert was forced to spend the night in Westbrook. He found a cheap motel just outside the town line—a roadside hole with pink neon lights and a parking lot probably filled with townies renting rooms for trysts without their spouses knowing—and checked in. Melissa would have scowled in disgust if he'd tried to bring her there, but that no longer mattered. That bitch was ancient history now. The room was small but accommodating, and Robert spent his evening drinking cheap beer and eating bad Chinese takeout while Googling Windham's vampire legend. He went to sleep with a bad case of indigestion and nothing to show for his efforts. When he finally fell asleep, he dreamed of his dead parents, and of Melissa chiding him for his follies.

On Saturday morning, Robert was up bright and early. He drove back into Windham and stopped at the town hall on Route 302. Although the staff had tried to be as helpful as possible, he was unable to get any information out of them. They suggested that he try the town library or the Windham Historical Society.

Those two venues held no helpful information for him, but he couldn't shake the feeling that he was being purposely lied to or misled; both times he climbed back inside his van with his cheeks burning with embarrassment for even asking. In the back of his mind he thought of Melissa, with her gentle teasing and his *hating* her being amused at his expense. But after hours of researching to no avail, he stumbled on a genuine piece of luck. He'd overheard a bunch of kids discussing the legend of the vampire while waiting in line for ice cream cones at the Dairy Maid. A crisp new twenty-dollar bill had gotten him all the information he needed. They even offered to go with him and point out the exact place where the vampire was supposedly buried, but Robert politely declined. For the rest of his day, he needed to be alone.

***

He drove his van down the hidden dirt road and through the tall, black iron gates of the Smith-Anderson Cemetery just after two p.m. It had been one of those ancient-looking graveyards, the oldest, most weathered stones toward the front of the lawns, and getting progressively more recent the farther in he drove. From the entrance it had been one of the best-looking cemeteries he'd ever seen, although it had been rather bothersome that the borders of the yard were surrounded by acres of Maine woods, filled with mosquitoes and mayflies that swarmed incessantly.

There was something about cemeteries that Robert really loved, not that he could put his finger on it. Sidney had been right when he called it a morbid fascination. He just loved old tombstones. Especially the yellow-white slate ones that somehow resembled bone fragments lodged in the ground, looking like crooked teeth on a lower jawbone.

He admired the primitive craftsmanship in how the names were hand-chiseled into the stone, and the sculpted faces of angels—cherubic, with delicate wings gracefully spread, watching over the mounds of dirt that contained once-living souls. Each with a lifetime of stories buried with them, their headstone serving as a table of contents: Date of Birth, Date of Death, Husband/Wife to, Father/Mother of. Some with favorite bible references, some with personal quotes, some with words of remembrance: An angel on loan from heaven; A blessing from God; The way life should be; Rest in Peace.

"It's fucking weird, if you ask me!" Melissa had told him one time. He'd taken her on a picnic one spring afternoon. She had assumed they were going to a park or a nearby lake, or at least *someplace* romantic. Instead, he'd taken her to Willis Grove Cemetery, where his parents were buried. She followed him silently to his parents' plot and watched in horror as he spread the blanket out over the area of earth that was their final resting place. She watched, hypnotized, as he opened the picnic basket, pulled out the bottle of wine, and popped the cork.

"You've *got* to be kidding me," she said, a trace of anger in her voice.

"What's wrong with it?" he asked. To him, this was the perfect place for a picnic.

She retorted with the *fucking weird* statement.

"This is my life," he said as he first poured her, then himself, a glass of wine.

"No, it is your *job!*" she answered, throwing her hands up into the air. "Life is for the living. What kind of relationship are we going to have if all you want to do is hang out in cemeteries? What if we have kids, Robbie? I don't want them playing around graveyards like they're ghouls or something. It's not healthy."

Robert stood up, a glass of wine in each hand.

"Who said anything about kids?" He tried to hand her a glass, but she wouldn't take it from him. "Listen, you already knew all this about me. Why are you trying to change me?"

"I'm not trying to change you." The tears flowed down her face. "I'm trying to have an 'us,' okay? I want 'us' to work." She brushed the tears away with the sleeve of her cashmere sweater. So attractive she was that even though they were arguing, he wanted to paint her picture, weeping in the cemetery. It felt like she belonged in his exhibit, and he knew that at some point, she somehow probably would be featured, in one way or another.

"How can there be an 'us' when you want everything *your* way?" He hadn't noticed, but his hands were shaking enough to splash wine out from the glass and onto the blanket. "Christ, I feel like you're only happy when you're right and I'm wrong!"

"Maybe if you grew up a little, you'd be right once in a while too." With that, she stood, dusted the dirt and grass off her pants, and stormed off. In a fit of anger, Robert threw first his glass of wine, then hers, against his mother's headstone. In his heart, he knew their romance had died right there in the cemetery where his dead parents silently watched. To Robert Pierce, that felt right.

***

The name of the alleged vampire was Adolphus Stone. From the information Robert had purchased from the teenagers at the Dairy Maid, Stone had feasted on the blood of nearly twenty people before he was discovered and put to death. It was not known exactly how he came to be a vampire, but while he was still mortal, he had been a local farmer and had served as a volunteer in the town's fire company. Legend had it that toward the end he had been responsible for setting several night blazes in town, and when the inhabitants of the burning houses had tried to escape, he would be waiting for them. To drink their blood and then throw their dying bodies back into the conflagrations.

By the time the other citizens had caught on to what was happening, Stone had been responsible for burning almost a dozen houses to the ground. Legend had it that they had gathered one Sunday morning with rifles, pitchforks, and a long wooden stake to destroy the fiend. The townspeople paraded quietly up to his house, where they found him in his basement, resting peacefully in an old pine coffin. His mind filled in the blanks—some angry father who'd lost his whole family hoisting the stake and driving it deep into the fiend's heart, destroying him forever as the crowd cheered...

The murder they committed was never reported to the authorities. Nor was his death recorded in any of the local records or history books. Stone had disappeared off the face of the planet, his whereabouts marked only by a small slate tombstone that bore no name. Only a tiny, weathered cross carved into the cold, white slate served as a table of contents to his personal history. Everything about his life before the change was completely stripped away. The grave itself was toward the back of the cemetery, where the newer plots resided, and it occurred to Robert that Stone's existence and his crimes were far more recent than he'd have guessed. Even, quite possibly, within the turn of the new millennium, where the whole thing could have been captured on smartphone videos and posted for the world to see on the internet.

Not that anyone wanted to see or hear or remember. How a town could keep something *that* horrific a secret spoke volumes of the citizens themselves. The people only wanted to forget, and to *not* draw attention. And he had every intention of bringing the horror back into the spotlight, dragging them all kicking and screaming if he had to, if he were to make both the exhibit and his new book a success. In his mind, *Rest in Peace* was already a bestseller.

Robert Pierce had little difficulty in finding the stone. It was in a secluded corner of the cemetery, under the shade of leafy oak limbs, the tips of its leaves already turning orange and red with the coming autumn and its cache of acorns already spilt for the squirrels to gather. He began to ponder exactly what kind of stunt to pull with this gem of a find as he began his first charcoal rubbing of the headstone, but in his heart he knew that his stunt was already pulled. He knew that whatever he dug up no longer really mattered.

***

"You must be out of your mind." Robert could hear Melissa's voice in his head as he drove to the local hardware store. "This is a terrible idea. People get arrested for stuff like this. They're going to catch you, and I hope they do!"

"This is a *great* idea," he answered aloud. "This will pack 'em in. You're just being a jealous bitch. You hate it that I can do your job better than you." Robert drove into the parking lot and went inside the shop. He returned a few minutes later with a pickax, a shovel, and a Coleman gas lantern. He placed these items in the back of the van, then climbed into the driver's seat. He paused momentarily to pull out his digital camera and check how much charge was left in the battery.

Just enough.

It would be murder having to wait until sunset to get started on his project. He wanted to be sure no one was around when he started to unearth the vampire's coffin. And finally emptied the footlocker in the back of the van.

***

The boys had told him such a wonderful tale that he almost wished he'd written it down to accompany the snapshots he planned to take.

Priceless! Christ, he could have hired them to just stand around during his exhibit and have discussions about it while the real audience (the rubes paying his commission fees) made their way through the exhibit.

"He started by eating bugs," one of the boys told him. A slim kid in a white t-shirt and flat-top haircut, who looked as if he believed every word he was reciting. "Y'know...spiders, flies, even worms," he said between licks of the mint chocolate chip cone that Robert's twenty had purchased.

"Frogs and rats too," added another boy in husky-sized jean shorts and a Red Sox jersey.

"People just thought he was going crazy after his wife died," added a third boy, wearing only khaki cargo shorts and a pair of flip-flops. "But most people think she was actually his first victim."

"And then the fires started," interrupted the first boy again. "He'd show up with the fire company, but he'd only be pretendin' to be fighting the fire. He'd really be looking for people trapped inside so he could drink their blood." The boy made a sour face as if grossed out. The other two boys laughed at this. Robert laughed as well.

He thought of this as he began to shovel away the dirt from the vampire's resting place just after sunset.

It was very close to midnight when he felt the shovel smack down into the hard wood of the coffin. His back throbbed with pain, and he cursed himself for not buying a pair of work gloves while he was back at the hardware store. His hands rippled with blisters that shifted around painfully when he gripped the shovel. Occasionally one would burst, leaving a sticky mess of pus and blood on the wooden handle. After reaching the coffin's lid, he climbed out of the hole and sat with his feet dangling in.

"You should just listen to me," Melissa's voice chided him. "The man from the museum knows you are here. Even if you quit now, you still have to cover the hole up again. You can't just leave it as it is. And look how tired you already are!"

"I'm just catching my breath," he said icily into the darkness. "I know what I'm doing. And I have plenty of time to recover once I reach the Bahamas. Nobody will know a thing until they see the pictures in Monday's edition. By the time the exhibit opens on Tuesday, the gallery will be packed. By Friday, when my book goes national with its release, nobody will know where I am."

He took a moment to turn the flame of the lamp up a notch. It was considerably dark, despite the starlight that kept him company.

Surrounding him had been the noisy chorus of chirping late-summer crickets serving as his lookout. When they grew silent, he would stop digging and dim the lantern, his heart pounding in his chest like a frightened child's. These moments had been few and far between, thankfully. The work had gone smooth and quick.

When he caught his breath, he jumped back down into the hole and finished uncovering the wooden box.

***

He couldn't believe that he found himself afraid to open the lid. All the work he had done to unearth the coffin and now here he was, actually shivering in fear at the prospect of having to look at the dead body inside. The body of a vampire, no less. He didn't know what to expect, and that was the part that frightened him.

No, that wasn't true. The body in the box meant absolutely nothing to him. The body in the footlocker, however...

Robert had seen his share of dead people. His own parents, for instance. He'd only been thirteen when they had their accident. They had been coming home from a parent-teacher conference one winter evening when his father had lost control of the Chevy Tahoe on a patch of black ice. Robert had been doing poorly in his math and science classes, and the later the time got as he waited, the more afraid he had grown that they would yell at him when they came home. Perhaps a grounding, or a loss of privileges, or maybe even Dad removing the belt from his jeans and teaching one of his "lessons."

It was very late by the time the police arrived to break the news that he was now orphaned and would have to figure everything out on his own.

He remembered seeing them one last time at the memorial service. The tears of pain he had cried when he looked upon their waxy-whitened faces, believing deep down that none of it would have happened if he'd studied harder. If he'd been a better son. If...

"If you'd just listen to me..." Melissa had said before their breakup. "You *never* listen. It's like talking to a brick wall. Why are you so fucking selfish?"

"Fuck you!" he whispered aloud. He wedged the shovel under the moldy wooden lid and popped it open.

And there lay the body: no wooden stake buried into his chest over the area where his heart would be, just hands folded gently over the torso, a strand of rosary beads wrapped around his fingers. The man's face looked waxy and serene; the look of a kind old grandfather who was more apt to help you find your lost puppy rather than burn your house down. Robert wasn't surprised. He knew a thing or two about folklore and superstition. It was meant to caution the living.

He climbed out of the hole and snatched up his camera. He opened the shudder and zoomed the lens out to fit the cadaver's entire form into the picture. He pushed the button, and the camera's flash filled the crypt with an eerie explosion of light. Robert zoomed in and flashed a second shot of the face. The fear had subsided, and the excitement of pursuing his best publicity stunt to date had taken control. In his mind he was recreating the story the teens at the Dairy Maid had shared with him. He would write it all down back at the hotel while preparing the file to send to the *Portland Press Herald* before hitting the road Sunday morning for the jetport. The story would make Monday's early edition; plenty of time before the exhibit's grand opening on Tuesday, and long after his plane touched down on the island of Nassau.

Still, he'd hoped for a vampire! A fucking real-life, flesh and fang, blood-sucking demon of the night. He wanted to find it lying inside the coffin like a statue, frozen in its final moment among the living, in the moment of terrible truth that it was not immortal, that it, too, could be sent to hell. A look of terror in its wide-opened eyes, the way one of his own victims might have looked at him before he drove his razor-sharp fangs into their flesh and drank their life away.

The way Melissa looked when Robert wrapped his hands around her throat and squeezed the life right out of her in her Manhattan apartment. She'd called him over to come collect his belongings after she'd ended their relationship, even though Robert wasn't ready to let her go. For Robert Pierce, everything he loved ended in death, and he loved Melissa Fagan more than his own life. Had he been braver, he would have buried her remains along with his parents, but *this* was business, and the business at hand was creating the perfect publicity stunt—one that would surely bring in both the art critics and the curious public, who could never resist something so ghoulish and titillating.

Robert went back to his van and opened the rear doors. It took some effort to drag the footlocker from the vehicle to the gravesite, but he was already catching his second wind. The blisters on his hands no longer bothered him. He dragged the luggage over to the hole, opened it, and dumped Melissa's body into the grave, spilling her on top of the corpse. Robert had stuffed her inside the locker before rigor mortis had set in, and now she was enveloped in an eternal fetal position, her lovely face still blue from strangulation and her perfect, dead eyes still wide open in surprise. Her flesh was now beginning to rot, but not overpowering just yet. He took a few steps backward.

When he caught his breath, he approached the tomb and shined his flashlight down on top of the two bodies. Melissa's naked form filled most of the plot, and she was so fucking beautiful. He could even see the bruises from where his hands had squeezed around her throat until those beautiful blue eyes went wide and her windpipe collapsed like a snapped twig. Now, here she was, finally silent and decaying from within. *Erosion begins with "Eros,"* he thought with wicked satisfaction. *How can I not be enamored with her as her body comes undone?* With that, he unbuckled his belt, undid his jeans, and slid them down. His manhood stood out hard against the cool evening air. He climbed down on top of her and pried her legs apart.

"One last time, my love, and then I'll let you rest in peace."

After he finished, Robert readied his camera, leaned over the hole, and with trembling hands snapped pictures of his deceased lover on top of the corpse. When he was satisfied, he picked up the shovel and filled in the grave. When the grave was once again covered, Robert Pierce climbed into his van and drove away.

***

The *Portland Press Herald* received an overnight email from an anonymous account, showing the photographs and detailing the strange case of the Vampire of Windham. It made local headlines over the weekend, of course, but by Tuesday morning, the A.P. and the cable news networks were all covering the bizarre murder of Melissa Fagan and the strange disappearance of her former lover, Robert Pierce, who was supposed to be premiering his exhibit that day. His own disappearance only added to the hype, and that was okay by him. In his own mind, he wasn't quite ready to join his parents and his beloved girlfriend in the final act of his traveling cemetery show. He only needed to figure out the perfect ending to his exhibit. In the end, island life suited him much better than what he considered reality.

And, of course, Robert's publicity stunt had been a *smashing* success. In the entire length of his career at the museum, Sidney Graham had never seen a larger turnout.

Publication History

About the Author

Peter N. Dudar has been writing and publishing fiction for over two decades. Born in New York, Peter is a graduate of Christian Brothers Academy and an alumnus of the University at Albany, where he studied English literature.

After graduation, Peter moved to Maine and launched his writing career. He served a true writer's apprenticeship during his first two years; occupying a studio flat in Portland's Old Port district and working third shift at the United States Postal Service, and spending every free moment writing on an old Panasonic word processor.

Peter's debut novel, A REQUIEM FOR DEAD FLIES, was released in 2012, and was a finalist for the Bram Stoker Award in 2013. His body of fiction continues to receive critical acclaim and the adoration of fans of the horror genre. He is a proud member of the Horror Writers Association, the New England Horror Writers, and the Horror Writers of Maine. Peter lives with his wife, Amy, two daughters, and a dog named Princess Cupcake Zippety Dudar. He swears he had nothing to do with naming the dog.

(Photo by Sea Mist Photography)